Where The

Bellbird Sings

by

Elaine Blick

Strategic Book Group

Strategic Book Group

P. O. Box 333
Durham, CT
www.StrategicBookClub.com

ISBN: 978-1-61204-604-4

DEDICATION

This book is dedicated to my father, Harold Blick, 1909-1990, who loved Nelson and the old family home, which he looked upon as a "pearl of great price."

To Cathy, Debbie & Emma
Happy reading & best wishes
From Elaine Blick
29/11/11

PREFACE

I felt impelled to write this book when I heard that our old house in Nelson, New Zealand, and the land on which it stood, were for sale and would be going out of the family. We had owned the property since 1842. I have drawn on my memories of the house as I knew it in the nineteen sixties when Aunt Ethel, the last of her family, was living there alone following the deaths of her brother Martin and sister Lylie.

'Brookfield House' is based on Blick House, which was built in 1860 by James Blick, for himself and his new bride, Sarah. The land had been purchased from the New Zealand Company by his father Thomas Blick , a weaver by trade, who set sail from England for Nelson, New Zealand in 1842 with his wife Hannah and seven children.

When he arrived in the new settlement he saw there was a need for woollen cloth to be produced locally so he set about building a loom and employed German women to spin the wool. In this way began the first woollen mill in NZ. Blick Tweed, as it was known, won an award at the Great Exhibition in London in 1851, but unfortunately Thomas was not alive to receive it. The medal is now in the Nelson Museum. Thomas's son James did not continue with the production of woollen cloth but became a tanner. The tanning pits mentioned in the book are still in evidence today although they are now on council land.

The references to the Dun Mountain railway are entirely factual and today there is a track following the route of the old railway which is popular with walkers and mountain cyclists.

Thomas and Hannah Blick were foundation members of the Baptist Church in Nelson and several of their children, including James and Sarah, continued to be staunch members. Two of their nine children, Jessie and Walter Blick (my grand-father) left Nelson to go to China as missionaries.

Katey's journal is fictional but I have drawn on factual material gleaned from a newspaper of the 1890s, the Nelson Examiner, which was very informative about the Hardy School for Girls and the Nelson College for Girls. Miss Kate Edgar, the first woman to graduate as a BA in the British Empire, was principal of the college and she was followed by Miss Gibson. As this is a work of fiction the descriptions of the characters and incidents are all imaginary.

I have also drawn on my own experiences as a young teacher in the 1960s to provide authentic detail, although the characters and incidents are fictional.

I based the incident of the prayer for Mrs. Bulloch on an actual event which took place when my father was prayed for by proxy during a prayer meeting conducted by Mr Subritzky of Auckland, NZ. My father was at home at the time and knew nothing about it, yet simultaneously while prayer was being made for him my father experienced a sensation of release and was miraculously healed.

The bellbird is found in certain parts of the South Island of NZ, but the only place where I have ever heard one was at Blick House and it came to symbolise to me peace and continuity, hence the title, Where the Bellbird Sings.

ACKNOWLEDGEMENTS

I am grateful for the use of the internet in researching the historical background to my book. Being able to use Google as a browsing tool has been of inestimable value. Several websites were particularly helpful: - theprow.org.nz - provided me with information on the Dun Mountain Railway and also the background of Miss Kate Edgar, first Principal of Nelson College for Girls.

I am particularly indebted to Papers Past, which provides digitized pages of The Nelson Examiner and the Nelson Evening Mail, dating from the early days of the colony. I was able to read reports of school committee meetings and inspectors' comments on schools that were visited in the region, which threw light on many aspects of the educational system, but also brought to life this period in Nelson's history. Much of the background for Katey's journal is derived from this source. (When scanning through one paper of 1890 I was thrilled to discover that Ethel Blick, the original for Miss Rose Brookfield, had won second prize for sewing when she was in Standard Four.)For information on my ancestor, Thomas Blick, I am grateful to The Nelson Historical Society.

I would also like to thank several kind friends from Clarks Beach:- Rebecca, Ann and Dorothy, who read the early chapters of my manuscript while I was writing it. Their enthusiasm encouraged me to continue. Thanks also to Dr. Mary Tucker who advised me on medical details, especially in regard to the attempted suicide of Mrs. Bulloch. My good friend, Pauline Stansfield, who was nursing during the 1960s in New Zealand,gave me valuable information on the hospital system of the time. I am also grateful for her enthusiastic response after she had read my completed manuscript.

I would like to thank Ray and Joan Markley who read my manuscript with close attention and gave me helpful advice. Ray, in particular, brought to my attention several points regarding historical authenticity that I had overlooked.

Last but not least, I am grateful for the companionship of my little cat Katey, who sat patiently with me each morning as I typed that day's portion of my book.

CHAPTER ONE

The agent chattered brightly, her long blonde hair swinging over her shoulders, as she led Elizabeth along the uneven path leading to the front door of the house. She turned the key and the door swung heavily on its hinges.

"Of course, the house is very old, built in 1860 I believe," she said confidentially, "so don't expect many mod cons. It's a period piece."

Elizabeth smiled to herself. *She could tell this young woman all about the house, but no, she would say nothing.*

As they entered the dark old kitchen and her eyes grew accustomed to the dimness after the glare of the midday sun she looked around searching for any reminders of the past. Yes, there was the old oak dresser against the wall, denuded of any crockery but just as solid as she remembered it. The timbered walls with the slatted boards painted a bright green were just the same. A calendar hung from a hook and Elizabeth noted that it was open at May 2010 and here it was August. No doubt the owners had moved out about that time.

"And this is the parlour, so called," said the agent. "Mind the step, it could be a bit slippery," she added, glancing at Elizabeth's legs.

I suppose she sees me as an old lady a bit shaky on her pins,

1

thought Elizabeth glancing down at the step which was quite worn, even more than she remembered it.

The room had been papered with a modern design that looked out of place against the old fashioned windows with their square panes and the tiled fireplace. Elizabeth remembered the pattern of roses and twining vines that used to cover the uneven walls. Amazingly, on one wall there was a painting of the house and garden, a rather faded watercolour that seemed somehow familiar. Apart from that, the room was quite empty and yet instead of looking larger it seemed smaller and somehow diminished. This little room had always been the heart of the house and Elizabeth thought with a pang of the many winter evenings she had sat here reading in front of a leaping fire, enjoying the sense of being enclosed by warmth.

The agent turned to her curiously. "I suppose you would plan to make all sorts of changes if you bought this place. You'd probably install a gas heater as we are no longer allowed open fires in Nelson, or perhaps you'd have a heat pump. That seems to be the most efficient method of heating these days. Rather spoil the old world ambiance, though," she added.

"Just what I was thinking," said Elizabeth.

"Now let me show you the bathroom. That is the one room in the house where you need modern conveniences, don't you agree?" She opened the door directly in front of them. Yes, it was a shining example of modern plumbing:- glassed-in shower in one corner and large vanity with a huge mirror over it. The agent glanced into it, automatically putting up her hand to pat her hair.

I look so old, thought Elizabeth glimpsing her image behind the young woman's. *Well, I suppose when you are nearly seventy that is inevitable. Odd, when she was last in this house she was still in her early twenties.* She had a sudden flashback to this bathroom as it once was, the old iron bath with its claw legs and yellowed stain where the taps had dripped. In the corner under the window had been a deep porcelain basin

2

with tiny cracks, where she used to wash her hair and carefully pick out hairs from the basin before flicking them out of the window. That old window was gone, replaced by a large pane of frosted glass.

"The lavatory is separate, through that door," said the agent.

It always was, thought Elizabeth, *and there was a door leading to the verandah so you could use it from outside.* The indoor toilet was a vast improvement on the outside 'lav' at the end of the path, with its wooden seat over a long dark hole and the spiders that lurked in corners.

"I suppose your husband will come and have a look at the property too, Mrs. Stephens. Is he a handyman? It would certainly help. As you can see there's plenty to do here."

"Mm," Elizabeth murmured. *She certainly wasn't going to tell this smart young woman that her husband had died only four months ago, suddenly of an aneurism one Saturday morning.* What she couldn't bear were the polite expressions of sympathy from strangers, for a grief that that they could not understand and that was still so raw.

As though determined to harp on family matters the girl said as she led Elizabeth down a narrow passage leading to the verandah.

"They sure did have large families in those days. There are actually five bedrooms in this house, three enormous ones upstairs and two downstairs." She opened a door on the left. "I think the previous owners must have set this up as a flatlet. You see where they installed a sink unit and there would have been a cooker in the corner. Of course, there is the usual fireplace. They must have had a full time job in the past keeping all the fires going. Still, it would have been cosy."

Elizabeth looked with interest around the room. It had certainly been altered from the last time she had seen it. Then it had been Aunt Gertrude's room, cluttered with Victorian furniture and smelling of lavender talcum powder. She remembered it well.

"The other bedroom is across the passage," said the agent briefly. "Nothing very different there." She opened the door quickly and true, the room did look bare. This had been Aunt Rose's bedroom and again there was nothing left of the past. The words flitted through Elizabeth's mind, "and the place shall remember them no more."

She hasn't shown me the living room yet, and that is surely the most important room in the house. As though tuning into Elizabeth's thoughts, the agent glanced over her shoulder and said casually, "Sorry, I can't show you the living room. The owners keep it locked. They have left all their private possessions here rather than put them into store."

The locked room, always the locked room, thought Elizabeth. She felt a sudden wave of dizziness. "Do you mind if we go outside. I feel a little faint," she murmured.

"Here, let me take your arm. We can go and sit outside on the verandah." The girl's voice was concerned. Gently she led Elizabeth outside and drew up one of the two plastic chairs that were placed at a table. "Look, I'll go and get you a glass of water," and she hurried off.

Elizabeth breathed in the crisp air, which had a whiff of something sweet. Of course, it was jasmine. The old vine was still growing at the corner of the verandah. With the scent memories came rushing back. That unforgettable day in early September:

- ⊙ ⁂ ⊙ -

It had all begun like any other school day:- the order of lessons laid out in her workbook open on her desk, the children seated in their groups busy with their reading activities, then moving on to arithmetic and finally copying the writing exercise from the blackboard. In the corner of the room waited the milk crate, filled with the quarter pint bottles, probably rather warm now after sitting outside in the sun where they had been unloaded from the milk truck.

4

Promptly at 10.25 Elizabeth stopped the class, telling the group leaders to collect the books and the milk monitors to give out the straws. There was the usual rustle of anticipation as the children waited for their turn to go to the crate and collect their milk and a straw. Once this daily ceremony was over Elizabeth dismissed the class and like a flock of chattering sparrows the children swarmed towards the glass door leading into the playground.

Elizabeth picked up her handbag and opened the door into the corridor. She could see her friend Mary just coming out of her classroom next door and waited for her to catch up. There was something different about her face, a look of suppressed excitement. With her nondescript features and frizzy brown hair, Mary was not the sort of girl you would notice in a group, yet today with a flush in her cheeks she looked almost pretty.

"What's up with you?" said Elizabeth curiously. "You look all lit up."

"Oh, I suppose it's because I'll soon be out of here."

"You make it sound like a prison. It's not that bad in this school, could be worse."

"No, it's not the school particularly. I'm just excited because I've booked to go to England in December on the Northern Star."

"Oh, Mary, I thought we were going together next year."

"Sorry, Elizabeth, my cousin Margaret wanted to go this year. You know, she's a nurse and already she's been promised a job in one of the London hospitals. My parents and hers think it's a good idea if we go together. She's two years older than me and my parents think she'll keep an eye on me. You know what they are, always fussing over me."

Walking along the corridor to the staffroom Elizabeth found she had a bitter taste in her mouth. It was hard to speak, not that she needed to say much as Mary prattled on happily. Elizabeth was more disappointed than she would have believed possible. The thought of going to England in a year's time had buoyed

5

her up at this difficult time. She needed something definite to look forward to, something to fill the void in her life.

Her mother had warned her when Elizabeth had applied for the job. "It's a sleepy place, Nelson. You'll find it quite different from Auckland and it won't be easy to come home, Elizabeth. If you want to have a change, why not take a job nearer so that you can come home at weekends. That way you can keep up with your friends and your life here."

Her eyes, which usually sparkled, looked dull. At that moment Elizabeth knew that Mum would feel her going away sharply. They had always been more like sisters than mother and daughter, able to laugh at the same things and speak openly of their feelings to one another and they had never been separated before.

She wavered. "I suppose I could apply for another job. There's one in Hamilton here. That's not so far away."

Then her father spoke up. "I think it would be a great experience for you to go to Nelson. You would be going back to your roots." He ran his hand through his hair in a way he had when he was enthused. "I spent my happiest times as a child there, up in the old house with the aunts and Uncle Mal. We used to fish for cockabullies in the brook and the aunts made delicious scones that they spread with butter they had churned themselves." He added reflectively, "They were much younger then. All the same it is a large house. I wonder if they would be prepared to board you."

His enthusiasm was contagious. Elizabeth found herself being swept along as her father recalled his boyhood memories. Suddenly the prospect of teaching in Nelson took on a kind of glamour.

"Well, Dad, I haven't got the job yet," she said at last.

"I can still write to the aunts and sound them out," her father replied.

And that is how it all came about. Aunt Rose had replied immediately saying that Elizabeth would be very welcome to

6

stay with them. They would like to have some youth around the place and there were several empty bedrooms for her to choose from. Then Elizabeth's application was accepted and one Saturday at the beginning of February she travelled down to Nelson to begin her new life.

As soon as she saw the old house she knew she would feel at home here. It stood overlooking the valley, framed by trees, its red roof and white verandah outlined against a gently rounded hill.

The house looks so right in this setting, Elizabeth thought, *as though an artist had stood back and decided to place it there, to create the right effect for his landscape.* She stood gazing up at it for a few moments before pushing open the small iron gate. Carefully she closed it behind her then put down her suitcase. She was glad to rest after the hot and exhausting walk from the bus stop in the glare of the afternoon sun and it was pleasant under the shade of the large tree growing by the gate.

As she rested Elizabeth took in the scene before her:-a winding path led up a grassy slope to the house, bordered on each side by old fashioned rose bushes that gave a glorious and extravagant display of rich colour. Directly ahead of her was a row of shrubs and through the gaps between them was a glimpse of what appeared to be an orchard, judging by the large number of fruit trees laden with apples and plums and figs. Yet this was no ordinary orchard with trees laid out in neat rows. These trees seemed planted at random and had no uniformity as though at various times someone had thrown a stone or pip from fruit they had been eating and from it a tree had sprung up.

As she gazed around her Elizabeth felt that this was an enchanted place. There was a peace in this garden; the only sound being mingled birdsong which somehow emphasized the silence. It was a noisy world today, people playing their transistors on the beach or in their back gardens, boys 'souping'

7

up their cars so that they would make a hideous racket as they drove along quiet streets, canned music blaring through loudspeakers in department stores. In here that world seemed very far away.

Feeling as if she were in a kind of dream Elizabeth picked up her suitcase and began to climb the narrow path, catching the scent of roses as she went. At the top of the rise there were some shallow steps which joined the path leading to the porch. She walked up to the door and hesitated. *Was this the front or the back of the house? Perhaps she should follow the path that continued to the right. It might lead to the front door then again she couldn't be sure. Well, she would try knocking and see what happened.* Coming to this decision she put down her suitcase and knocked. Nothing happened. She tried again, more loudly this time. Still nobody answered. Perhaps she would go round the side path after all.

Turning the corner of the house she had to walk past a large bow window before mounting steps on to the verandah. In front of her was an elaborately carved door with a stained glass window, the front entrance obviously. Her hand was poised to knock, when around the corner of the verandah appeared an old man with shaggy white hair and an unkempt moustache. His trousers, which were too large for him, were held up by a belt tied in a knot around his waist. He peered at Elizabeth from under his heavy brows.

"Who are you, Miss, might I ask?" He glanced at her suitcase. "Do you want directions to somewhere?"

"Well, no. I'm actually expected here. I'm Elizabeth Brookfield. Miss Rose Brookfield wrote to my father and said that I could board here."

"She did, did she? She never said anything to me about it. I suppose she never thought to mention it. Well, now you're here you'd better come inside."

He opened the door, motioning Elizabeth to follow him. As she bent to pick up her suitcase he waved her impatiently away and lifted it as though it weighed nothing. *He seems to have surprising strength for an old man* thought Elizabeth as she followed him into the passage.

"Gertrude! Rose!" he called at the foot of a narrow staircase leading off from the passage. There was a movement above them and the sound of footsteps coming slowly down the stairs.

"What is it Malcolm?" said a quiet voice.

He did not reply but set Elizabeth's suitcase down, gave her a nod and shambled off down the passage. Elizabeth waited for the owner of the voice to appear. A little old lady, scarcely higher than her shoulder, stepped carefully down the last step. She looked directly into Elizabeth's face from eyes that were astonishingly clear and blue for one so old. She was wearing a blue twinset over a grey skirt and her hair which was fine and white was drawn neatly back from her face. *She would make a perfect Miss Marple,* thought Elizabeth, who was currently going through an Agatha Christie phase.

"So you're Elizabeth. I'm your father's Aunt Rose which makes me your great-aunt doesn't it? You must call me Aunt Rose too. All the young people around here do, as it is. I suppose when you get to my age you become everyone's aunt. Anyway, enough chat, my dear. I daresay you're very thirsty after your journey. Would you like a cup of tea or a glass of lemonade? Of course you can have both if you prefer." She gave Elizabeth a kindly smile and Elizabeth felt as though she had at last come home.

Ten minutes later she and Aunt Rose were seated companionably at a solid wooden table outside in the porch. The table looked as though it really belonged in a dining room but had been demoted to do duty out of doors. In front of them was an oilcloth and on it a plate piled high with freshly made scones, a jug of lemonade and a couple of plastic beakers. Aunt Rose poured the lemonade into the beakers and handed one to Elizabeth.

"Our own brew," she said.

Elizabeth took a sip. "It tastes like nectar," she murmured. Mingled scents of lavender and stock drifted from the flowerbed behind them while bees busy among the flowers kept up a steady hum and butterflies hovered over the lavender. Surely any moment now she would wake up and find this was a dream. Aunt Rose's voice broke into her thoughts. It was a low husky voice rather at odds with her appearance. "My sister will be here any minute. Earlier today we both attended a little ceremony for the unveiling of a plaque commemorating the Dun Mountain Railway. My sister called in on a friend in town. Oh, here she is now."

Swivelling round on her stool Elizabeth was just in time to see a red Morris Minor turning into the drive from the road. A few minutes later a gate clicked and Elizabeth jumped up watching the tall woman who strode purposefully towards them. She wore a smart woollen skirt of fashionable length, topped by a short box jacket in the latest mustard yellow. On her head was a pillbox hat tilted to one side. Elizabeth had seen a similar outfit in a Simplicity pattern book recently.

Her hair was short but slightly bouffant. As she came closer Elizabeth was amazed to see that her skin was unlined under her discreetly applied makeup. *Surely this couldn't be Aunt Gertrude. She must be seventy if she was a day, yet this woman could pass for any age between forty and sixty.*

"So this is Elizabeth," she said, running her eyes over her, as though noting her homemade blouse and skirt. "I had expected someone older and more teacher-like, from your father's letter."

"This is only my second year of teaching. I was a PA last year," faltered Elizabeth.

"What is that?"

"It stands for Probationary Assistant. We do not get our teaching certificate until the end of the year, if we are considered competent."

"So this is your first job as a fully-fledged teacher then. You still look very young to me. I suppose if you had been the prim and proper type we would always be watching our Ps and Qs. Isn't that right, Rose?"

"You do speak nonsense sometimes, Gertie."

"I see you have been having some afternoon tea but where is the teapot? I'm dying for a cuppa. Muriel can't make a decent cup of tea, always so weak. Don't get up, Rose, I'll put the kettle on."

A few minutes later she emerged with a tray on which were a teapot, cups, milk and sugar. She laid it down on the table. "Milk for you, Elizabeth?"

"Yes thank you." Elizabeth noted the deft and confident way she poured the tea. Gertrude handed her a cup, not raising her eyes.

"Have you shown Elizabeth her room, Rose?"

"There hasn't been time. She only arrived half an hour ago and I thought she needed some refreshment first."

"Good idea, first things first." Turning to Elizabeth she said, "I made up your bed in one of the upstairs rooms, the one overlooking the valley. We both sleep downstairs, because of our advanced age but we always put visitors upstairs. You will have it all to yourself up there. There are three rooms, all enormous, so you'll be able to spread yourself."

"Dad told me that this house was built in 1860."

Gertrude looked up sharply. "What else did he tell you?"

"Oh, not much, he said that your father's name was Enoch and your mother's was Hannah and that they had nine children."

"Well, those are basically the facts. Now, if you've finished your tea, Elizabeth, I'll show you your room."

They all stood up and Aunt Rose began packing away the tea things. Elizabeth followed Gertrude as she strode ahead through the kitchen, up a step into the parlour and down into the narrow passage which led to the front door. Her suitcase was sitting where it had been left, at the foot of the stairs.

"Can you manage that, Elizabeth? It's a tight fit on these stairs. I could get Malcolm to carry it up for you."

"No, I'll manage. Thanks all the same."

Gertrude was at the top of the stairs while Elizabeth was still trying to manoeuvre the suitcase round the first bend. Then she discovered that there was not room for herself and it. Gertrude saw her predicament. "Get yourself and the dratted thing back down into the passage and I'll go and fetch Malcolm," she called.

Elizabeth dragged the suitcase down the last two steps and into the passage while Gertrude waited on the stairs until the way was clear. She swept past Elizabeth and disappeared through the front door. Minutes later she returned with Malcolm in tow. Without a word he up-ended the suitcase, heaved it over his shoulder and mounted the stairs. Elizabeth waited until she heard his footsteps crossing the floor above their heads.

"You go on up," said Gertrude. "I'll follow."

Elizabeth began climbing the steep staircase. *How on earth did a whole family manage with only one flight of stairs to the top storey, which was so narrow only one person could go up or down at a time* she wondered?

Like a rabbit popping out of a burrow Elizabeth stepped out onto a wide landing. In front of her were double glass doors that opened onto a verandah. *What a marvellous view you would get from there,* she thought fleetingly.

"Are you there, Missy?" It was Malcolm calling from the room to the right of the landing.

"Yes, coming."

The door was open so Elizabeth walked through then stopped. Her mouth fell open. Why, this was like something from a novel. Two large sash window rose from floor to ceiling, the one directly in front looking right across the valley with a glimpse of the sea in the distance; the other, with a view of hills beyond. Elizabeth stood transfixed, taking it all in. Then slowly she gazed around the room. A double bed with a white coverlet stood with the head against the back wall, positioned so that it faced the window. Beside it was a small table with a brass lamp on the polished surface. In one corner was a beautifully carved dressing table in light wood with a swing mirror. In the opposite corner was a chest of drawers of the same light wood. Just inside the door was a wardrobe which must have been part of the bedroom suite as it too matched the other furniture. The only colour in the room came from a large Persian rug next to the bed. Instead of looking stark the whole effect was simple and uncluttered. *Utterly beautiful*, thought Elizabeth. *Oh, I will be so happy here.*

"You like the room?" Malcolm's voice broke into her thoughts.

"Yes, it's lovely. It will be just wonderful to wake up in the morning to that marvellous view."

"Hm, not so good in winter when we have hard frosts. These rooms upstairs are difficult to heat. I've known a hot water bottle freeze to the floor up here."

"Did you ever sleep in this room?"

"No, this was for my parents. We children slept in the other two rooms, the boys in the one across the landing and the girls next door to this."

"What about the rooms downstairs?"

"One was for visitors and the other was a study for father."

"It seems rather a pity that such lovely large rooms are empty now."

"No good for us in our old age, Missy. That staircase is a deathtrap, much better for us to be downstairs."

Elizabeth longed to ask where he slept but surely that would sound impertinent. He looked at her from under his shaggy brows.

"I suppose you're wondering where my place of abode might be." Elizabeth did not dare meet his eyes. "I have my own den outside. I call it the "whare". That is where I have my meals and sleep. It suits me and it keeps me from getting under the feet of the two downstairs. Now you know, Missy."

Elizabeth felt strangely drawn to this old man. She sensed

there was a lot more behind his words and she hoped that one day he would confide in her and that they would become friends. Elizabeth did not notice footsteps approaching and jumped when Gertrude appeared in the doorway. "What do you think of your room, Elizabeth? It's roomy enough for you, I imagine." She glanced down at the suitcase. "You don't seem to be overloaded with stuff."

"No, the room is perfect and I just love the view."

"Yes, I always considered this was the choicest bedroom upstairs. Well, I suppose we should leave you to do your unpacking. Come along, Malcolm."

She talks to him as though he were a child, thought Elizabeth.

Gertrude turned on her heel and walked briskly towards the door, where she paused for a moment. "Oh, I nearly forgot to mention. We have tea at six. Come down any time before that if you'd like to, though I suppose you may want a rest after your journey, but then again you are young and probably don't feel the need to lie down." This was said with a laugh as she left the room.

Malcolm had already gone so Elizabeth was alone at last. She went across to the window that overlooked the valley and stood gazing down at what lay below. To one side of the orchard was a fence and beyond that, a paddock with a cow and a few sheep. Fenced off in one corner appeared to be a vegetable garden with neat rows of runner beans or peas and tomato plants. On the far side of the paddock a stream meandered slowly between banks of yellow gorse, widening as it approached a rough wooden bridge below the orchard. A red brick shed stood on the bank of the stream above the bridge. It had a solidity to it that was unusual for today.

Most sheds are corrugated iron structures and rather ugly, thought Elizabeth. She wondered what this one had been used for originally. She must ask Uncle Malcolm. There was a lot she wanted to ask him. She wondered if he would take her on a guided tour of the grounds. That way she might to get to know something of the history of the house. Instinctively Elizabeth felt that neither of the aunts really wanted to discuss the family nor the past. It would probably be best not to ask them questions.

Reluctantly she turned from the window and bent down to open her suitcase. Her clothes looked oddly forlorn as she lifted them out one by one and laid them on the bed. Elizabeth viewed them with distaste. Her dresses and skirts were so home-made looking, compared to Aunt Gertrude's smartly cut suit. Well, she would have to make the best of them for now and perhaps after her next salary she would be able to afford to go and buy some fashionable new clothes.

At least I am a standard size, she thought with some satisfaction, *and not bad-looking. Mum once said she didn't know why Elizabeth fussed about her clothes so much, she had youth on her side and looked nice in anything she wore. That was all very well, but it would be lovely to have some really smart clothes, like those she saw in English women's magazines. One of these days...*

At last all her clothes were put away and her toiletries laid out on the dressing table. Her little travelling clock was on the bedside table with her Bible and her most recent Agatha Christie:- "They Came to Baghdad". What an adventure that girl had got herself involved in. Though the plot was improbable Elizabeth enjoyed following the fortunes of Victoria. She seemed like a girl who would be ready for anything.

Elizabeth thought that perhaps she would take Aunt Gertrude's advice and lie down for half an hour and have a little read. She kicked off her sandals and turned back the coverlet, then lay down with a sigh of relief. It was just so peaceful here. Picking up the book she read a couple of pages and was not aware of it slipping from her hand.

When Elizabeth awoke three hours later the clock by the bedside showed five thirty.

Was it morning already? No, it couldn't be, the sun was too bright. Slowly it came back to her. This was her room in the old house in Nelson and it was still Saturday afternoon, which gave her less than half an hour to wash and change for dinner. Aunt Gertrude had specifically said that tea was at six o'clock and in this house they were bound to be sticklers for time.

Hastily Elizabeth caught up her toilet bag and the towel laid so carefully at the foot of the bed and went to find the bathroom. It was to the right of the stairs. Elizabeth pushed open the door and was immediately struck by the smallness of the room with its sloping ceiling. Surely this must once have been a storeroom as there was scarcely enough space for the toilet and hand basin. Directly above the basin a small window overlooked the back of the house showing a large expanse of red roof, with a huge walnut tree successfully blocking any view of what lay beyond.

Elizabeth gave herself what her mother would call "a lick and a promise" and hurried back to her room to change. She decided on a sleeveless white cotton top and a gathered skirt. The general effect was fresh and crisp. Then she crossed over to the dressing table and bent to the swing mirror to study her reflection. *My hair looks terrible*, she thought. *Even though I washed it yesterday it's gone flat.*

She gave it a few impatient flicks with her comb then took up her lipstick and hastily applied it to her lower lip first. She was careful not to outline too definitely the curve of her upper lip as she could not bear to emphasize its fullness, seeing nothing attractive about it. She was quite unaware that in her piquant little face, her mouth with its generous curves made a delicious contrast. Hastily she dabbed powder over her nose and mouth. Then she checked the time. There were five minutes to get downstairs.

Aunt Rose was working at the sink when Elizabeth entered the kitchen. "Go into the living room, dear," she said, pointing to a door leading off the kitchen. "We always have tea in there."

Elizabeth went in. Aunt Gertrude was already seated at one end of the table with a large silver teapot in front of her. She

16

looked up and smiled, sweeping her eyes appraisingly over Elizabeth's outfit.

"You look fresh and rested, my dear, rather different from when you first arrived. Did you manage to have a little sleep after all?"

"Well, yes, I did. I started to read but then I nodded off."

"Now, how do you like your tea? " She had the teapot poised over a cup. Elizabeth noticed there were only three cups and three places laid at the table.

"Isn't Uncle Malcolm going to join us?"

"Oh no," said Aunt Gertrude lightly, "he takes all his meals in his whare, as he calls it, has done for years. He prefers not to be with 'chattering females', he says." She looked at Elizabeth quizzically. "You may find our ways a little strange at first, until you get used to us."

"I was just wondering if Uncle Malcolm comes and gets his own meals or do you take them to him?"

"Since you ask, Rose usually carries them to him on a tray. That is where she is at the moment. I'll wait till she comes before pouring her tea."

"Here she is now," she added as Aunt Rose entered the room and took her seat at the other end of the table.

"First of all, we'll give thanks," Aunt Rose said quietly and both sisters bent their heads while Rose gave a short grace. "Now do help yourself, Elizabeth. In front of you is ham and lettuce, tomato, and spring onions, all fresh from the garden," said Aunt Rose. It all looked so colourful and inviting Elizabeth felt suddenly very hungry. As she ate she thought she had never tasted salad vegetables so crisp and delicious.

Halfway through the meal Aunt Rose looked up and said, "Have you given any thought to tomorrow, Elizabeth? We leave for chapel at 10 o'clock and our service is at 10.30. You can accompany us if you wish."

Elizabeth thought quickly. *If she agreed to go to church with the aunts tomorrow she might feel obliged to continue each Sunday. She wanted to be free down here. At home in Auckland she had attended the same church since she was a child. Now was her chance to break away and try out things for herself.*

"That's very kind of you," she said slowly, "but I think I'll take it quietly tomorrow and sort myself out." She was aware of a silence. Looking up she was just in time to catch the look of disapproval that passed between the two sisters.

"Very well," said Aunt Rose, her tone distant. "You are free to do as you want, but if you change your mind, let us know."

The atmosphere at the table was now constrained and Elizabeth was relieved when the meal was over. She helped clear the table and carried dishes into the kitchen where Aunt Rose had already begun washing up. Aunt Gertrude had disappeared. Elizabeth picked up a tea towel and carefully lifted a plate from the rack. She searched for something to say.

"Aunt Rose, do you grow all your own vegetables?"

"We always have done. My brothers used to have a fine garden and we had enough to give away or exchange for other things. Now Mal looks after the garden and it is considerably smaller."

"I would love to go and have a look at it this evening and have a little wander around. It's so lovely and quiet after Auckland."

"Your father loved it here when he was a boy. I remember the way he and his cousin Charlie used to roam around for hours and come in just for meals. They were always ravenous." Aunt Rose looked searchingly at Elizabeth. "You remind me of Charlie's mother. Strange these family likenesses."

"What was her name, Aunt Rose?"

"It was Katherine, but that was all a long time ago." She stopped abruptly and turned to the sink. "No, you go and have a look around this evening. Put on a cardigan, it might be chilly out there. Once the sun goes down the temperature drops."

As Elizabeth went upstairs she thought about their

18

conversation. It was tantalizing to have just a scrap of information about Katherine. *Why did Aunt Rose clam up so suddenly?* Elizabeth found herself becoming more and more curious about this family.

She took a cardigan out of a drawer and slowly made her way downstairs, through the parlour and into the kitchen. There was no sign of either of the aunts so she went through the door and turned left along the path that led past the verandah. As she came round the corner she saw Uncle Malcolm's whare for the first time, a wooden structure like a miniature cottage, the front door flanked by windows. A platform went across the front of the building. A bucket stood by the door with a few garden tools propped up in it. Otherwise there was no clutter anywhere and the place gave an impression of orderliness.

Elizabeth took all this in at a glance as she followed the path which angled off from the verandah past the whare. She came to a gate with a chain loosely hanging over the gatepost and paused before lifting the chain. She looked across to the paddock beyond it. On the far side she could see the banks of the stream overgrown with gorse and broom.

To her left a few sheep were grazing. *This must be the top half of the paddock I saw from my window,* Elizabeth thought. She began walking towards the stream and as she went she looked up at the hill on her left which now seemed to tower above her. A fence ran across the base of the hill dividing the paddock from the open area beyond it. Outcrops of gorse made splashes of yellow on the hillside and in the setting sun the shadows outlined the undulations of the land. Elizabeth felt a sudden desire to cross over into this wilderness and explore. She would climb this hill as soon as she could, she promised herself.

The sun was sinking rapidly now and reluctantly she retraced her steps across the paddock to the fence behind the whare. At first she did not notice the figure of a man but as she drew closer she saw it was Uncle Malcolm leaning over the

19

gate smoking a pipe. Suddenly she felt awkward and a little shy.

"Hello, Uncle Malcolm," she said. "I was just wishing there was enough time to have a really good look around, but it will be dark soon."

"Aye, there is a lot to see around here but you would not understand or appreciate half of it. For instance, do you notice anything over there, amongst the gorse?" and he jerked his pipe in the direction of the stream.

"It could be the edge of a wall," said Elizabeth slowly, noticing something grey amidst the growth.

"No, that's one of the tannery pits. There are eight of them altogether. They're overgrown now but in my father's time they were in use, the same as the brick shed there."

"Was your father a tanner, Uncle Mal?"

'That's right, Missy, the best in Nelson and probably the best in the South Island. His leather would outlast any on the West Coast and that's saying something, it's so wet across there. Father's leather was used for saddles and harness that were shipped off to the Boer War," he added. He drew on his pipe and gazed into the distance as though lost in memories of the past. Elizabeth wished he would go on, but he seemed to have forgotten her.

"Well, I'd better go in now," she said moving towards the gate.

"Goodnight, then," he said and stepped aside to let her pass.

As Elizabeth entered the kitchen she saw that the light was on in the living room. She glanced through the door. Both aunts were seated beside the fireplace though there was no fire in the grate. Aunt Gertrude was reading a book by the light of a lamp on a side table at her elbow.

Aunt Rose was embroidering something that could have been a table cloth. It looked a cosy domestic scene.

"I think I'll go on up to bed now," Elizabeth said.

"Won't you have a drink first, a cup of cocoa perhaps," said Aunt Rose looking over the top of her spectacles.

"No thank you."

Aunt Gertrude lifted her eyes from her book. "Good night, Elizabeth. I hope you sleep well, your first night in Nelson."

"Oh, I nearly forgot to mention," said Aunt Rose. "You'll probably have your breakfast after us, so I'll leave everything out for you in the kitchen."

"Thank you, Aunt Rose. Goodnight Aunt Gertrude."

Elizabeth withdrew feeling relieved at the way the two aunts had spoken to her. Their chilliness at the tea table seemed to have disappeared.

Once she was in bed Elizabeth turned over the events of the day. In the space of twenty-four hours her life had completely changed. She was now living with three people who belonged to the generation before her parents. She started reckoning up. Now, if Aunt Rose was eighty-two, then it would mean she was born in 1880, in the reign of Queen Victoria. When she was twenty-one, Elizabeth's age, it would have been 1901. What would life have been like then? Motor cars would have been invented but there were probably only a few in New Zealand at that date; and as for aeroplanes, the Wright Brothers might have just started flying, either in 1901 or 1903. Elizabeth was a bit hazy about dates. Even so, the idea of crossing the world by aeroplane would have seemed impossible to people then.

All three of them:- Uncle Malcolm, Aunt Rose and Aunt Gertrude, had lived through two world wars. The more Elizabeth thought about it the more she felt intrigued. *What changes had taken place in the world during the lifetime of these old people? If only she could get them to talk, but none of them seemed willing to discuss the past, or at least their own past. Why was it that the moment some mention was made of the family they clammed up or changed the subject? And what was the real reason that Uncle Malcolm kept himself apart from his sisters? Perhaps he was a recluse,* thought Elizabeth *yet it must be something more than that.* In some strange way she felt a sense of kinship with him. That brief conversation by the gate had been a start. *Perhaps if she could get him to show her around the property he might open up more about the family. Yes, that was what she would do tomorrow. She would suggest that he take her on a tour, that is, if it were permissible on a Sunday to go out walking.*

Her mind turned to Monday. It would be her introduction to the new school. She had to meet the staff for the first time and become familiar with a different routine. Then she would be preparing her classroom ready for the children on Tuesday. *It was all rather daunting but she would survive somehow,* thought Elizabeth, in her usual optimistic fashion. *Besides, there might be someone on the staff that she could make a friend of, like Pat in her last school.* They used to sit and chat in the staffroom after school over a cup of tea and laugh about incidents of the day.

Elizabeth had a sudden stab of homesickness. The family seemed a long way from here. Her mother would be putting her feet up after a busy Saturday while Dad would be in his armchair poring over the paper, occasionally reading out loud some paragraph or other. Her brothers, Mathew ten and John eleven, would be in bed by now while her sister Joan would probably be finishing a homework project. Elizabeth would have given anything to be back with them all. She turned over and tried to sleep but it was hopeless, she was wide awake. She switched on the light and picked up her book. Propping the pillows more comfortably behind her head she started to read. It was hard to concentrate at first but gradually she became immersed in the plot.

She had been reading for a good three quarters of an hour when suddenly she became aware of a noise, a kind of busy sound which was coming from the room directly below her. *That would be the living room* she thought. She listened carefully but then it all went quiet. *Perhaps the aunts were sitting up late tonight and were getting themselves a cup of tea. Oh, well, it was time she put the book to one side and tried to get to sleep.* This time her eyelids felt heavy and she knew nothing more.

CHAPTER TWO

When Elizabeth woke next morning the sun was already high and slanting across the room from the side window. She turned to look at the clock. It was ten already. The aunts must have left for church and she had heard nothing. Well, at least she was now on her own and could take her time and have a leisurely morning. She stretched luxuriously and looked across to the window. The sky was a deep blue and in the distance the strip of sea sparkled in the morning sunshine. *What a waste to linger in bed. She must get outside as soon as possible.*

She pulled open the wardrobe door and glanced along the row of clothes hanging limply from the hangers. She needed something bright and sunshiny to match the day. Quickly she made up her mind and pulled out a yellow cotton dress.

Downstairs everything was very quiet. As she entered the kitchen she noticed how neat and orderly it was. At one end of the table a cloth had been laid with breakfast things. There was a bowl and a packet of cornflakes, cut bread covered by a plate, butter, sugar and marmalade. Elizabeth went to the fridge to look for milk. Instead of a bottle she found a jug of milk covered with a small muslin cloth with beads sewn at the edges. As she poured the milk over her cornflakes she noticed its thick creamy texture; it tasted different too, richer than bottled milk but not unpleasant. Now she wanted a cup of tea. She looked around for an electric kettle but there was none to be seen. Then she noticed that to one side of the kitchen range was a large old fashioned kettle. She lifted it carefully onto one of the metal plates in the middle of the range and waited for it to boil. A few minutes later she was sipping a cup of steaming tea and feeling quite pleased with herself. She then began planning what she would do after breakfast, perhaps have a good look around the house and then take a walk in the orchard.

Elizabeth was on the point of leaving the kitchen when a thought occurred to her. The night before she had really only formed a brief impression of the living room. Why not begin her tour of the house by having a good look at it? She walked across to the closed door and took hold of the handle expecting it to turn easily. It would not give. She tried again but with the same result. The door was definitely locked.

Why on earth would the aunts do that? Surely they were not afraid of thieves. Perhaps they kept all their valuables there and were in the habit of locking the room whenever they went out, as double security. Then Elizabeth had another thought. *Perhaps they didn't trust her and wanted to prevent her from snooping around.* Elizabeth felt a chill go through her. She recalled the look of disapproval that had passed between Aunt Rose and Aunt Gertrude the night before when she said she would not accompany them to church. Suddenly the day seemed no longer bright and cheerful. Heavily Elizabeth walked towards the open back door. Outside the air smelt sweet with the mingled perfume of lavender, stock and roses, which grew in profusion beside the path, and the sun poured down out of a cloudless sky. The clear bell-like notes of a bellbird rang out in the stillness and as she listened Elizabeth felt peace returning to her.

She followed the winding path down the bank into the orchard which she had only glimpsed the day before. Now she saw that round the base of each tree were flowers of every

24

variety:- pansies, begonias and large daisies. Somebody lovingly tended these, somebody who loved colour, for the apple and plum trees were laden with fruit, ranging from rich purple to bright red. It looked like a scene from a child's picture book depicting the Garden of Eden. All it needed was a sly serpent coiled in the branches of one of the apple trees. Elizabeth reached up and picked herself a large red apple. She bit into it savouring the cool piquant sweetness. It was different from any apple she had ever tasted.

As she wandered around the orchard she lost all sense of time and it came as a shock to hear a car slowing down outside. She glanced at her watch. It was 12 o'clock so that would be the aunts returning from their service. It was probably best to let some time pass before going indoors. Elizabeth guessed that they would have a set routine on a Sunday and she would be in the way if she appeared too soon. She sat down on a wooden seat under one of the trees and absorbed the stillness, watching a blackbird near her as it hopped a short way then cocked its head, as though listening intently for movement in the earth below. A quarter of an hour passed very pleasantly in this way and with some regret Elizabeth stood up and started towards the house.

As she entered the kitchen Aunt Rose looked up from where she was working at the sink. She smiled warmly at Elizabeth. "It's good to see you, dear. I was wondering where you could be as you were not in the house when we came in."

"No, I went for a walk around the garden, Aunt Rose. Well, in the orchard actually. It's so lovely there, like a park, with all the flowers growing around the trees. It must be a lot of work keeping it all so beautiful."

"We all have a hand in that. Mal mows the grass and Gertrude and myself look after the flower beds. Once upon a day we used to have afternoon teas out there on tables under the trees. Sometimes as many as twenty sat down to tea and cakes, but that was a long time ago. Now there are only three of us left." She lifted a lettuce out of a colander and began stripping off the outside leaves.

"Is there anything I can do to help?" asked Elizabeth.

"Well, you could take those things into the dining room." Aunt Rose pointed to the table, on which were various dishes to accompany a cold lunch:- several types of chutney, cut bread and butter, mint sauce, mustard etc. "You can lay four places today, Elizabeth. Malcolm always has Sunday lunch with us."

Elizabeth carried as many items as she could through the open door into the living room. *Should she mention the fact that she had found the room locked while they were out? No, that would show that she had tried the door.*

As she went into the room she looked around curiously. On the mantelpiece were several china ornaments, a small silver box, some little ivory elephants and a vase of dried flowers, but no photographs. In one corner was a glass -fronted bookcase with more ornaments on the ledge but again no photographs. The picture over the mantelpiece was of cattle grazing beside a lake with large mountains in the background, evidently a Scottish scene. On the wall opposite was a similar painting, both Victorian she guessed. In other old houses there were framed photographs of family groups standing stiff and unsmiling, but here there was nothing.

Going back into the kitchen to collect more dishes she glanced at Aunt Rose, standing with her back towards her, her hair in a neat bun and a snow white apron tied around her waist. She was the epitome of a gentle old lady, yet behind that respectable front could there be a different person?

"Is there anything more I can do to help?" Elizabeth asked.

"No thank you. You're free until lunch time."

Elizabeth went upstairs to her room and sat down on the edge of the bed. She found herself wondering again about the locked room and the absence of photographs. This family seemed to have secrets. How she would like to find them out.

At lunch Uncle Malcolm sat at the head of the table and Aunt

Rose opposite him. Elizabeth and Aunt Gertrude faced each other. While Uncle Malcolm carved the joint of cold lamb little was said. He was very quick and deft with the knife Elizabeth noticed.

"Would you give thanks, Mal?" said Aunt Rose when he had finished carving and they all bowed their heads as he prayed. It was only after the dishes had been passed around and everyone had helped themselves that any conversation took place.

"It was a pity you weren't at the service this morning," began Aunt Gertrude. "The minister preached on new beginnings, taking as his text, 'Behold I make all things new.' Since you are starting at a new school tomorrow you might have found it helpful." Elizabeth felt uncomfortable.

"I shall probably go next week or at least I will go to a service somewhere."

"The Brookfield family has always worshipped in the Baptist Chapel in Nelson. Our grandparents were founding members in 1850 and our father and mother were married there," said Aunt Gertrude.

"No need for Elizabeth to follow family tradition. She must go where her conscience directs her," said Malcolm gruffly.

"I suppose young people today have greater freedom than we ever did," said Aunt Rose gently. "It's a different world today." Elizabeth glanced at her and noted the thoughtful look in her eyes. "I'm sure Elizabeth needed a quiet morning."

"Yes, I did enjoy walking around the orchard. It was so beautiful and peaceful."

"Well, that is what a garden is for," said Aunt Rose. "I like that little poem that says, 'One is nearer God's heart in a garden, than anywhere else on earth.' I suppose that is why God created the Garden of Eden at the beginning," she added.

"It was soon invaded by the enemy," said Aunt Gertrude with a dry laugh.

"By the way, I ate one of the apples from the tree nearest the fence at the bottom of the orchard," said Elizabeth, anxious to steer the conversation off theological matters. "It was delicious, like no other apple I've ever tasted."

"That would be one of the oldest apple trees here. Seeds were brought over by our grandparents from Gloucester when they came here in 1842," said Uncle Malcolm.

Elizabeth said hesitantly, "I would really like to know more about the early days, what it was like for the first settlers when they came to Nelson, for instance. They must have had great courage and initiative. You said yesterday that your father was a tanner, Uncle Malcolm. I would love to see the tanning pits."

"So you shall, Missy. I will show them to you this afternoon."

"I thought your habit was to have a quiet nap on a Sunday afternoon," said Aunt Gertrude, her tone slightly mocking.

"I don't usually have the company of someone who is interested in the old place. In fact, it will be a change to have company at all." His sister glanced at him sharply but made no reply to this pointed remark.

Aunt Rose coughed and stood up. It was the signal for the end of the meal. She began gathering up plates while Gertrude and Malcolm slowly folded their napkins. Aunt Gertrude left the room but Malcolm remained sitting. Elizabeth thought she should assist Aunt Rose so she picked up a couple of dishes and moved towards the kitchen. As she passed Uncle Malcolm's chair he said quietly, "I'll expect you this afternoon, at say, two o'clock. If I'm not around just knock on the door of the whare."

Elizabeth smiled at him. "I'm looking forward to it," she said.

When she went out to the kitchen she saw the two aunts were busy with the washing up. "We can manage here," said Aunt Rose. "You go and get ready for your walk. You'll need some good walking shoes, especially if you climb Sugarloaf. The ground can be quite rough in places and the gorse will scratch your feet if you only wear sandals," and she glanced at Elizabeth's feet.

28

"Thanks, I'll find something suitable," replied Elizabeth quickly.

Back in her room Elizabeth looked at the row of shoes at the bottom of her wardrobe. There was really nothing that would pass as walking shoes, only a pair of low heeled slip-ons. *Hardly the best footwear for climbing hills and walking around farms,* she thought. Perhaps she should wear her jeans as well to prevent being scratched by gorse. As she changed Elizabeth felt a surge of excitement at the thought of exploring unfamiliar territory and maybe learning something about the background of this intriguing family that she was now a part of.

At five to two she left her room and made her way downstairs. She let herself out through the front door, closing it quietly behind her. As she stepped onto the verandah she noticed that the blind was down in Aunt Gertrude's room. So as not to disturb her if she was sleeping, Elizabeth stepped off the verandah and onto the path in front of the house. Around the corner was Uncle Mal's whare but there was no sign of him. Elizabeth wondered whether to knock on the door. As she stood hesitating a voice boomed out behind her, "There you are, Missy. Right on time too."

"Oh, I didn't hear you coming, Uncle Malcolm. I thought you were inside."

"I came up from the orchard, along that path behind you there," and he jerked his thumb over his shoulder. Elizabeth had not particularly noticed this path before as there was a large rhododendron bush on the corner that partly obscured it from view.

"If you're ready we'll start the grand tour. I see you are dressed for it, very sensible too, if I may say so," as he glanced approvingly at her jeans. "Now, first we will go through the gate which you used last night as that will take us across the paddock to the tanning pits."

Elizabeth followed him through the gate and had to trot to keep up with him. He had a fast stride which was surprising in a man who seemed so slow and deliberate in every other way. When they reached the clumps of gorse growing thickly on the bank of the stream she saw that what she had mistaken for a wall was actually the side of a brick-lined pit. Uncle Malcolm pointed down into it. "This is one of the tanning pits. There are eight altogether but gorse has grown over them. One of these days I may get around to clearing it away. Not that anyone is much interested in the pits these days," he added.

"I'm sure they would be if they knew they were here," said Elizabeth enthusiastically. "Why were there eight tanning pits, Uncle Mal?"

"Well," he said slowly, "the tanning process is lengthy. For a start, the pits have to be built near running water that is soft, not hard. When Grandfather Brookfield arrived here he saw this place was ideal for setting up a tannery because a stream ran through his property. He also realized that leather was something that the new settlement would need, so he set about building a tannery."

"That was enterprising of him," commented Elizabeth.

"Aye, but it all took time. I suppose his sons helped him with the building of the pits and the sheds that were needed for drying out the leather. There were three of them along here," and he swept his arm to the right of where they were standing. "When my father died he directed in his will that the tannery was to be closed down, so gradually the sheds fell into disuse."

"Why did he want to close it?" asked Elizabeth curiously. "Surely he had enough sons to carry on the family business."

Uncle Malcolm cleared his throat and Elizabeth noticed he seemed embarrassed. "He had sons enough but none of them was interested in tanning leather. Your grandfather, Walter, carried on for a while though his heart wasn't in it. He was never a very practical chap, more interested in spiritual things rather than earthly."

"He became a missionary, didn't he?"

"Yes, he went to China in 1897."

"So who helped your father with the tanning business after that?"

"Arthur and Samuel worked in the tannery for a couple of years but they wanted to go in for farming and left Nelson for Blenheim in 1900. After that Father closed down the business."

"What a pity," said Elizabeth thoughtfully. "Didn't you say yesterday that the leather produced here was used for saddles that were sent to the Boer War?"

"And regarded as the best leather produced in the dominions," added Uncle Malcolm.

"What was the reason for that?"

"It could be due to the quality of the hides. They were imported from Belgium. Then it could also be because of the bark he used." Seeing Elizabeth's puzzled expression he enlarged. "You see, there are a number of steps in the tanning process, Elizabeth. First the hides have to be washed and softened so they are put into a soak pit. Then they are placed into a lime pit to remove the hair. When the skins come out they have to be scraped and soaked in fresh water. Finally they are ready for tanning which means they have to go into the tanning pits where they are soaked in liquor made from bark. In England this bark is from the oak tree but out here the bark is from a native tree. My father never let it be known where he got his bark from but he used to go into the bush for it. He kept this a secret all his life."

"That must have been why his leather was the best."

"Yes, it was said that leather from here was the most durable on the West Coast, and that it could last for seven years."

"Did you never want to go into the tannery business, Uncle Malcolm?"

There was a bitter note in his voice as he said, "No, I thought I was cut out for better things. I went in for the law."

Elizabeth waited for him to add something further but he said no more. She felt instinctively that she had touched a raw spot, so she said brightly, "Now that you have told me all about the tanning process could you take me on the next stage of the tour?"

"We'll look at the woolshed next," he said briefly.

As they walked towards it Elizabeth glanced sideways at Uncle Malcolm. He seemed to have lost some of his jauntiness and there was a set look about his face. She must try to restore the light-heartedness with which they had set out. Up close, the woolshed, built of red brick, was obviously old and weathered but it looked solidly constructed. At the side were steps leading into a kind of loft with a sloping roof and heavy beams. Uncle Malcolm went first and Elizabeth followed. The timber floor was swept clean and all along the sides were stacked garden tools:- sacks of manure, a couple of ladders, a lawnmower, pots of paint and several tin trunks. Everything had the same neat and orderly appearance of the outside of the whare. *Uncle Malcolm must have a tidy mind,* thought Elizabeth. *That would be of a piece with his being a lawyer.*

She became aware that he was speaking to her. "You've heard that expression, 'being on tenterhooks.' Well, those large hooks in the wall are the tenterhooks, where the skins were hung out to dry. They had to be in a dry place with plenty of air and no direct sunlight. That's why there are only a couple of windows up here."

"You called it a woolshed. Why is that, when you said this was part of the tannery?" asked Elizabeth curiously.

"Oh, didn't I explain? My grandfather set up a woollen mill here, after the tannery. He was a weaver by trade but he didn't bring out his looms from England. When he saw that the settlers needed cloth, as well as leather, he constructed a loom and began making tweed cloth which was popular. It was even worn by the constabulary. He sent a sample away to the Great Exhibition in London and won a medal for his tweed. Unfortunately, he died before the medal was awarded so he never knew about it."

"What happened to the business then? Did his sons carry it on after him?"

"No, his wife sold it to another weaver in Nelson and the name was changed."

"What a shame!" exclaimed Elizabeth, "Thomas went to all the trouble to start a business and then there was no-one to carry it on after him."

He looked down at her from under his shaggy eyebrows. "That's the way of it, Missy. Each generation has to make its way. You're young yet but you will find out," he added in a kindly tone. "Now I will take you to the ground floor. There are no indoor stairs here, as you see, so we have to go outside again."

Elizabeth followed him down the steps and along a bank at the side of the woolshed. The grassy slope led down to a drive at the back of the building. The closed double doors gave it a blank look. Uncle Malcolm continued around the side of the shed to the front. This was completely open and evidently a milking shed as there were two wooden partitions for bails. Elizabeth noticed a couple of metal buckets and a three-legged stool standing in a corner. Uncle Mal saw the direction of her eyes. "Yes, this is where I milk Bessie morning and evening. We've always had our own cow and made our own butter."

"What time do you milk, Uncle Mal?"

"Always at four o'clock, every day the same, cows don't make any distinction for Sundays."

"I would love to come down and see you milking, Uncle Malcolm. Perhaps you would let me have a go."

"Bessie might have her own thoughts about that," he said and glanced at his watch. "I'll be fetching her in an hour's time. You could go back to the house and have some afternoon tea while I sit here and have a smoke." This was clearly a hint so Elizabeth thanked him and walked back the way they had come.

As she approached the house she pondered what Uncle Malcolm had told her about the tannery and the woollen mill.

She reflected that in this place present and past were closely interwoven, but more interesting than the tannery pits or the woolshed were the people themselves who were living links with the past.

There was nobody in the kitchen when Elizabeth got back so she quickly poured herself a glass of water and went outside to sit and drink it in the porch. Once more the peace of the place lapped her around. The lazy hum of bees and the mingled scents of stock, lavender and roses combined to make her feel drowsy as she sat enjoying the warmth of the sun against her legs. She did not know how long she was in this half somnolent state but when she glanced at her watch she saw it was ten to four. She stood up immediately and went into the kitchen where she washed and dried the glass before replacing it on the dresser.

As she left the house she looked around to see if there was any sign of the aunts but all was as quiet as before. A few minutes later she was half way across the paddock when she saw Bessie ambling towards the brick shed, her tail flicking off the flies and her full udder swinging as she walked. Elizabeth followed the cow slowly as she rounded the side of the building and entered the first bail where she stood patiently.

Uncle Malcolm was bending over a box in the corner and had his back to Elizabeth. He did not seem to hear her approach so she gave a little cough. At this he turned around as though startled. "Oh it's you, Missy. I wondered whether you would bother to come."

"Oh yes, Uncle Malcolm, I have never seen a cow milked by hand, though I have been in a milking shed where they used machines. I followed Bessie as she was coming across the paddock. She certainly knew where she was heading."

"Aye and she knew what time it was. If you check your watch you'll see it's four o'clock. Regular as clockwork she is."

He lifted the three-legged stool and placed it close to the back legs of the cow as she stood in the stall slowly munching the cud, her large soft eyes with their long lashes watching him as he placed a bucket under her. Elizabeth gazed fascinated as Uncle Mal, leaning into the body of the cow, rested his head against her flank and began to milk her, his hands moving rhythmically in time to the splash of milk into the bucket.

"How much milk does Bessie give?" Elizabeth asked.

"Usually at this time of year, about three quarters of a bucket."

"That sounds a lot."

"It's quite enough for our needs. Of course, from that we make our own butter. Gertrude takes charge of it."

"Have you always had a cow, Uncle Malcolm?"

"Ever since I can remember. We had two when the whole family was at home and we used to share the milking. Even the girls took their turn. Katey was the best milker. She had good hands and the cows would always let down milk for her." Turning his head he studied Elizabeth for a few seconds. "It's a strange thing, Missy, but you're very like her, especially when she was your age. She was only a little thing too, but very determined and she had lots of spirit. She wanted to join in all our boys' games and was just as fast as any of us."

"Was she your favourite sister?" asked Elizabeth slyly.

He chuckled. "I suppose you could say she was. That made it all the harder when..." and he broke off, clearing his throat. Elizabeth longed to ask him what had happened to Katey but she dared not. There was silence except for the steady swish swish into the bucket.

At last Elizabeth spoke. "Uncle Malcolm, I was wondering if you had a bicycle you could lend me for a day or two, or until I get one for myself. I could walk to school from here but a bicycle would make it easier."

He said quickly, "Of course, Missy. We have a few in the garage, all old but none the worse for that. After we've finished here we'll go and look one out for you. By the way, didn't you say you wanted to try milking yourself?"

"Oh, that was before I saw you doing it. You make it look so easy but I don't think I could manage it."

"Come on," he said standing up. "You don't know what you can do until you try."

Elizabeth crouched on the stool as she had seen him do, moving close to the cow so that her cheek rested on Bessie's flank. It felt warm and a sweet smell emanated from her. She took the teats in her hands, squeezing and pulling them as she had seen Uncle Malcolm do, but not a drop of milk appeared. She tried again, conscious of the old man watching her.

"Not so hesitant, Missy, give them a good firm squeeze but don't drag on them,"

This time a spurt of milk shot into the bucket from one of the teats. "That's the way. Keep going. She'll let down her milk for you."

Amazed, Elizabeth watched as two streams of milk spurted into the bucket. She kept on squeezing and pulling on the teats and found she was establishing a rhythm.

"There, I knew you were a natural milker. You have the right touch and Bessie responds to you."

Elizabeth found she was enjoying this new experience. There was something soothing about the rhythmic action of her hands accompanied by the steady swish swish of the milk into the bucket.

"Keep going, Missy, I'll take over from you when you've had enough."

Elizabeth continued for another five minutes. Then she said, "I think you'd better carry on, Uncle Malcolm, the milk isn't coming so easily now."

She stood up and he took her place, expertly draining the last drops of milk. "Pass me that rag please, Elizabeth," he said pointing to another bucket full of water, with a wet cloth draped over the side. She handed it to him and he deftly wiped the teats with it. Then he pushed back the stool and gave Bessie's rump a firm pat. She backed out of the stall and ambled off in the direction she had come.

Uncle Malcolm picked up the bucket full of steaming milk. "Now we'll take this over to the house and find you a bicycle," he said briskly.

They retraced their steps but instead of going into the house they went through the porch, past the kitchen door and into a kind of outhouse that shared a roof with the main house. This seemed to be the dairy as there was a butter churn and various wooden implements on a ledge. Garden tools hung from hooks along one wall and a large mower stood in one corner, but what caught Elizabeth's attention were three bicycles leaning against the opposite wall. Two at least, were women's cycles and one had a basket in the front.

Uncle Malcolm went over to it and pulled it clear of the others. "This should suit you," he said. "I'll pump up the tyres and then you can take it for a test ride." After a few vigorous pumps the tyres were firm.

"There you are, all set to go," he said handing the bike to Elizabeth. "Take it through the side gate and onto the road. Mind how you go at the corner. You come on it rather suddenly."

Elizabeth wheeled the bicycle along the path to the side gate. Carefully she unlatched it and once she was in the drive she mounted the bicycle gingerly. Wobbling a little she set off along the drive until she came out onto the road. Then she turned left but found the gradient was steeper than she had thought, so keeping her foot on the brake pedal she coasted down to the corner. Here the road levelled out and widened as it went between rows of houses. Elizabeth began pedalling and as she felt the bicycle gather speed she felt a sense of freedom. She realized that for the past couple of days she had been under a certain constraint. *The old people had been very kind to her and tried to make her feel at home but they were well, old, and it was good to be once more on her own and away from the house.*

She was at the bridge and looking down into the water when she had a sudden urge to dismount and take a closer look. Her father had spoken so nostalgically about fishing for cockabullies here that Elizabeth wanted to enter imaginatively into his boyhood world and capture something of his simple delights. While she stood gazing down at the water as it tumbled over the stones in the shallow river bed she seemed to see boys of different generations playing in this very place.

Thoughtfully she remounted the bicycle and continued along the quiet road. At the corner she turned right to begin the steady climb that would take her back to the house. At last, the road became too steep so she got off and wheeled the bike all the way to the drive. Carefully she pushed it through the gate and along the path to the shed where she leaned it against the wall.

As she was about to leave she noticed the door was open that led to the back of the house. On an impulse she went through it. The large walnut tree she had seen from the bathroom window towered above her, the foliage so thick that it blocked out the light. Even the air felt dank and the rotted leaves lying on the path made dark smudges on the concrete surface.

She was walking along the path when she became aware of voices, the shrill tone of a woman's voice and the low murmur of a man's. She paused to listen. Unmistakably, the woman was Aunt Gertrude, but her voice was harsh and ugly.

"You had no business to offer my bicycle to Elizabeth without asking me. You take too much on yourself, Malcolm." The heat rose to Elizabeth's face at the mention of her name. "You're far too high-handed! You have been as far back as I remember. You may be my senior and a qualified lawyer but that doesn't give you the right to ride rough shod over me. Anyway, you left your office years ago now and you never gave us any reason for leaving. Poor Father was broken, especially after the money he had spent on your education."

Elizabeth did not wait to hear any more. She felt sick and miserable and could only creep back the way she had come. She had to compose her face before going through into the kitchen where Aunt Rose was bustling over preparations for tea. She looked up brightly. "Hello, Elizabeth, tea will soon be ready. Have you had a good afternoon?" With sudden concern she said, "You look rather pale, dear. Are you feeling quite well?"

"Yes, I'm fine thank you, Aunt. I'll just go on upstairs to my room and change for tea."

Thankfully Elizabeth escaped to her room. She flung herself on the bed. What a mess everything was. She must do something to set things right between Aunt Gertrude and Uncle Malcolm. Yet from what she had heard, bitterness and resentment must go back a long way.

A few minutes later, when they were seated at the tea table Elizabeth looked across at Aunt Gertrude. Her hair and makeup were impeccable as usual and her expression was bland. It seemed impossible that such a serene looking woman could be the owner of the harsh voice spitting out cruel things a short while since.

Elizabeth took a breath and began, "Aunt Gertrude, I hope you don't mind me borrowing your bicycle to take to school tomorrow. Uncle Mal let me try it out this afternoon. I should have asked you first but..."

Aunt Rose cut in unexpectedly. "I'm sure Gertrude wouldn't mind you borrowing the bike, would you, Gertie? You use it very rarely these days and if it helps Elizabeth that is all to the good." There was a pause and when Gertrude spoke her tone was even.

"Yes, you may use it Elizabeth."

"There, that is all settled then," said Aunt Rose. "Now let's get on with our tea. Elizabeth dear, eat up, you will need all your energy for tomorrow."

The meal went on smoothly and no further reference was made to the bicycle.

While she was helping Aunt Rose with the dishes Elizabeth asked if she could go and collect Uncle Malcolm's tray. "That is kind of you, dear, it will save my legs," responded her aunt.

The door of the whare was closed when she got there. Elizabeth gave a tentative knock and almost immediately Uncle Malcolm was standing in the doorway. He looked worn and the lines on his face seemed like deep cuts, but his smile was kindly as he beckoned Elizabeth to come inside.

"This is a nice surprise," he said, "Usually Rose brings my tray."

"I wanted to this evening, Uncle Mal. You see there is something I have to tell you, but pour yourself a cup of tea first or it will get cold."

"I think I will, Missy. I feel in need of a cuppa. Sit down, please. Just lift the books off that chair," and he indicated an easy chair in the corner, so old that it was frayed at the edges. Elizabeth removed the books and sat down while Uncle Mal sipped his tea. "Now what did you want to tell me?" he asked, looking at her shrewdly.

"It's just this, Uncle Mal. I couldn't help overhearing what Aunt Gertrude said to you this afternoon. I happened to be walking along the path at the back of the house. I didn't mean to eavesdrop but I heard enough to know that she blamed you for lending me the bicycle. I just want to say how sorry I am. At tea I asked her permission for the loan of the bike for school and she agreed."

Uncle Malcolm was listening to her intently and when Elizabeth had finished he said nothing for a moment or two. He appeared to be thinking deeply.

"I appreciate your telling me this, Elizabeth. As you probably realize there are certain issues between Gertrude and myself that go back a long way. I don't want to enter into them now. That would not be helpful. As far as you are able, please put out of your mind what you heard this afternoon. Don't let it spoil your feelings about us and I want you to know that we are all happy to have you here."

"Thank you, Uncle Mal."

"And one more thing, Elizabeth, you see the box standing

on the floor beside this table," and he pointed to a large tin box of the kind that used to be stowed in the hold of a ship. "That contains a lot of my personal memoranda. There is nothing intrinsically valuable there so it wouldn't concern any lawyer dealing with my affairs. If anything should happen to me I want you to have this. I will leave a codicil in my will to that effect. The key to the case is in the top drawer of my desk."

"I don't know what to say, Uncle Mal. I promise you that I will value everything of yours."

"I know you will, Missy. That is why I want you to have it. Now I will finish my tea and take the tray back to the kitchen later."

This was clearly a dismissal so Elizabeth stood up to go. At the door she turned and said, "Goodnight, Uncle Mal. Thank you for all your kindness to me."

She walked slowly away from the whare and lingered on the front verandah listening to the sleepy twittering of the birds. Suddenly in the silence a bellbird called, the notes rising and falling on the evening air. Elizabeth felt peace descend on her.

CHAPTER THREE

Elizabeth's first morning at school seemed unreal. Amazingly she was early, probably because in her nervousness she had prepared so carefully the night before. The bike ride took her only twenty minutes and she noted that there were no other bikes in the stand at the back of the school. She lifted her satchel out of the basket and went round to the entrance. A plump little woman with a cheery face came out of the office.

"Oh hello, are you Miss Brookfield, one of the new teachers?"

"Yes, but do call me Elizabeth."

"And you call me Tina," she said with a warm smile. "I'm secretary here. You're early for the first day aren't you? The others will probably drift in later this morning. The staff meeting isn't till 10 o'clock. Oh, there's the Head now." She broke off and went forward to greet the man coming up the steps.

Elizabeth stepped back, suddenly shy. He was a thick-set, middle-aged man with a smooth bland face. Coming up the step behind him was a woman of about his age. Tina said a few words to him then introduced Elizabeth. "This is the new teacher, Mr. Ray, Miss Brookfield."

Elizabeth was conscious of his shrewd appraising look as he said, "Welcome to Nelson, Miss Brookfield. I hope you'll feel at home with us very soon." Then half turning to the woman at his side he added, "This is my wife, Mrs. Ray. She's the Senior Teacher here."

Mrs. Ray smiled at Elizabeth, the skin of her face creasing into a network of lines, "Hello, my dear, I'm sure you'll be happy here. We are really one big family. Now let me show you where everything is." Elizabeth felt warmed by her manner.

As Mrs. Ray took her to the Ladies' toilet and then into the staffroom she kept up a flow of talk, obviously to put Elizabeth at her ease. "We each have our own mugs," she said waving a hand at the shelf behind the sink. "There is a spare one here that can be yours. Usually Tina makes a pot of tea before school and if anyone wants one, they can pour it themselves. This morning as I'm here first I'll make the tea."

She stopped as a woman came in through the door. "Oh, here's Jeanette, she'll soon show you the ropes. Hello, Jeanette, good to see you back. This is Elizabeth."

The woman coming towards them had a good-natured freckled face. She grinned. "Hi, you've come to join the happy crew have you? Where are you from, Elizabeth?"

"Auckland, though my family has links with Nelson."

"Well, that's a coincidence. I'm from Auckland too, been in Nelson seven years, but still regarded as a stranger here. Unless you're a Nelsonian you're always a foreigner." She chuckled. "But don't let it worry you. Have you been teaching long?"

"No, this is my first appointment. I was a PA last year."

"So this is your first proper class. I suppose you only had about twenty-six last year. You'll notice the difference when you have forty."

"Is that the average class size here?"

"Oh, last year I had forty-two," she said airily. "Mostly they're good kids and easy to handle. Don't worry, you'll manage. Just sing out if you have any problems. Anyone here will help you. Here's Mary, she was new last year." Elizabeth looked up at the short plain girl who had just entered the room. "Hi, Mary, meet Elizabeth, an ex- PA like you last year. You two should get on well."

Mary smiled. *Such a sweet smile,* Elizabeth thought. *It quite transforms her face, and she has perfect teeth.*

"Hello, Elizabeth, I expect you're feeling a bit nervous. I know I did when I started last year, but you will find everyone very nice and helpful." Elizabeth warmed to her immediately.

The room suddenly seemed full of people. They had all come in over the past few minutes. A quick glance at her watch showed Elizabeth it was five to ten. She saw Mr. Ray sit down at the head of the long table, with Mrs. Ray on his right and a quiet serious looking man on his left. Elizabeth guessed this was the Deputy Head. Everyone seemed to take their cue from the Head as they all sat down simultaneously. A few of them glanced across at Elizabeth in a friendly way then turned to look towards Mr. Ray as he shuffled a few papers in front of him.

"Well, first of all, welcome back, everyone," he began. "I hope you've had a good holiday. Judging by your tans you've had plenty of sea and sand and now you are all raring to go." Polite laughter greeted this. "Now, before we get down to business there is an introduction to make. We are very pleased to have Miss Elizabeth Brookfield join our staff. I'm sure she won't mind me telling you that this is her first appointment following her PA year and we all remember what that feels like, though it was a while back for some of us, wasn't it dear?" turning to Mrs. Ray. "Anyway, we want Elizabeth to feel at home amongst us and to feel free to ask for help if she needs it. Welcome, my dear, to the staff at Nelson Primary School." Elizabeth smiled shyly at him and glanced at the row of faces opposite her.

"Now we have other matters to discuss. Over the holidays we have had a few changes to some of the classrooms, improvements of course, and I'm sure you will be agreeably surprised. Most of you are returning to your old classrooms but I have had to make one or two changes. Miss Favill will be taking over Miss Fletcher's classroom of last year and Miss Brookfield will be going into hers. As you probably all know Miss Favill will have Standard Three this year."

44

He went on talking and Elizabeth tried to take in all the details of administration that he was outlining. She felt Jeanette moving impatiently beside her. She had probably heard it all before, if she had been here seven years.

At last the Head stopped, and looking around the table said, "Are there any questions at this point?" As there was no response he said, "Well, in that case I'll give out the new workbooks and registers and then you can go along to your classrooms and get sorted out." There was a general scraping of chairs and buzz of chatter as everyone stood up and moved towards the door. Mr. Ray looked towards Elizabeth, "Now if you come with me I'll show you to your room," he said.

She picked up her bag, register and workbook and prepared to follow him. He stood back courteously at the door to let her through, but she had the sense that he looked upon her as he would a new pupil. She felt very young and inexperienced walking beside him along the corridor. Odd, but Mrs. Ray had not made her feel that way, nor had Jeanette though they had been teaching for a long time. Behind Mr. Ray's smooth smile she was conscious of being summed up and judged as young and immature. She wondered if Mary had felt the same last year.

"Now this is your classroom, Room 5. You knew you were having Standard Two didn't you?"

"Yes, I was informed by letter."

"That's good, so you've been able to prepare yourself. What class did you have in your PA year?"

"It was Standard Three."

"In that case you have a good background for this year. Of course, it will be a bit different with forty in your class. It may impose some control problems for you, but you will have to be firm and set your standards high right from the outset. Don't take any nonsense from the children." He gave her a sharp look, *as though he doesn't trust me to keep control*, Elizabeth thought. *Well, he might be in for a surprise.*

45

"You are fortunate in having a walk- in cupboard," he said, opening the door at the side of the blackboard. "You'll find everything you need in there:- boxes of chalk, sets of arithmetic and English books, journals going back a number of years, art and craft materials. Anyway, you'll soon see for yourself. I'll be collecting your workbook each Monday morning," he added. "We do a half term plan. I'll get Jeanette Favill to show you hers to give you a guide. She's in Room 6 just next to you. I thought it might help you to have an experienced teacher to call on."

He did not need to say that, thought Elizabeth. *If he had set out to make her feel inadequate he had succeeded.*

"I'll leave you now," he said and left the room with heavy dignity.

Elizabeth sat down at her desk feeling deflated. She looked around the empty room with its rows of desks and the chairs stacked against the back wall. It was over to her to make this barren classroom look welcoming for the children coming in tomorrow morning. She pulled a piece of paper toward her. First, she would make a desk plan using the children's names from the register and then make a place mat for each one. She was so busily engaged on this she didn't hear the door open. She jumped at the sound of a loud cough behind her.

"Sorry to startle you. I should have knocked. I wanted to speak to you in the staffroom but the Head whipped you away. Let me introduce myself. I'm David, your next door neighbour."

He had an engaging smile but wasn't good looking Elizabeth decided, having eyes that were too close together over a rather large nose. He was surveying her appreciatively. "I'm glad you're young," he said. "Everybody, apart from you and Mary and perhaps Jeanette, seems to be married and getting on for forty. At my last school there was a good cache of young teachers. Anyway, welcome Elizabeth, and pop in anytime. Oh, and you will stop for a cuppa after three today, won't you?"

"Thanks, David, I'd like to."

"See you then," he said cheerfully and went off.

Elizabeth turned back to her work feeling cheered. David might not be a heartthrob but he was pleasant enough.

There was enough to keep her busy until after three o'clock. She had all her work chalked up for the next day on the board with the day's date. Now that the room was organized into groups it looked much more friendly, even without pictures on the wall. She would give the children an opportunity to paint places they had visited during the holiday and that would brighten up the walls. Before she left the room she had a quick look around trying to imagine what it would look like tomorrow once the children were there.

In the staffroom a few minutes later she found Jeanette, Mary and David already seated around the table drinking tea. Jeanette was leaning back in her chair drawing on a cigarette. "Come and join us, Elizabeth. David, be a gentleman and get the lady a cup of tea."

"Gladly," said David and hopped up from his chair. Elizabeth sat down by Mary.

"We were just discussing making up a group for the pictures this Friday night, Elizabeth, to mark the end of our first week back at school. Would you care to join us?"

"That sounds a great idea. I'd love to," replied Elizabeth eagerly.

David put a mug of steaming tea in front of her. "There you are, my lady," and he gave a little bow.

"Thanks, David." Elizabeth smiled at him, and noticed that he was gazing into her face a fraction longer than necessary. Elizabeth was used to boys admiring her but it never ceased to surprise her.

The next half hour passed very pleasantly and as they all got up to go Elizabeth felt as though she had known these people for much longer than one day. As they went through the door David came alongside her. "How far do you live from the school, Elizabeth?"

"Oh, about a mile away, up the Brook Valley. I came by bike."

"What a pity. I was going to offer you a lift. Well, another time." He added as an afterthought, "Perhaps on Friday I could come and pick you up for the pictures."

"Oh, that would be nice," said Elizabeth automatically. She had visions of the aunts not quite approving of a young man coming to take her out on her first week in Nelson. Well, she would think about that later.

"So long, till tomorrow, then," said David.

Elizabeth had a lot to think about as she cycled back to the house, so that she scarcely noticed the pretty front gardens that she was passing and was quite surprised when she reached the bridge that crossed the brook. She paused and looked down at the water as it gurgled and chattered over the stones. At the corner she dismounted and began pushing the bike up the slope. The house reared above her like a relic of another age, when life was quiet and slow. After the busyness of the morning and the welter of new impressions it seemed something of a refuge.

After she had put the bicycle away she went through into the kitchen. Nobody was there, but the kettle was boiling on the stove. Suddenly Aunt Rose came out of the living room. "Oh, you're home early, Elizabeth. I didn't expect you for another hour at least."

"It was a staff day today, Aunt, so everybody went off early. Tomorrow I'll probably not be home until about six."

"I have saved you a dinner. As you know we have our cooked meal at midday. We'll have to think how to arrange it so you don't have to have dinners reheated all the time."

"I'm quite happy with salad vegetables and cold meat, Aunt Rose. I can always boil myself a potato."

"Well, if you're happy with that... I know you girls today don't eat much. I suppose you want to keep your slim figures. Anyway, I'll make you a cup of tea for now and perhaps you'd like a slice of walnut cake with it."

"Sounds delicious."

48

When she had put the tea and cake in front of Elizabeth, Aunt Rose sat down opposite her. "Well, how did you find the new school? What were the other teachers like?" She looked at Elizabeth out of shrewd blue eyes.

"There are several younger ones that I think I will like. Mary is only a year ahead of me and she is very nice. Then there is Jeanette. She's been at the school seven years and seems very experienced. The Head has put me in a room next to hers so that she can help me if I need it."

"But you've already been teaching a year haven't you, and you are now a qualified teacher? Why should you need help?" *Aunt Rose was sharp,* thought Elizabeth.

"I think the Head has the impression I am young and perhaps too inexperienced to handle a class of forty."

"Nonsense! In my day there were often sixty or more in a class and our teachers kept order, and all the children learned. Don't let him undermine your confidence my dear. You are young and pretty and that's a start. I'm sure the children will like you, especially if you are kind and fair." Elizabeth laughed. Aunt Rose's formula was simple but there was some truth in it.

"Now once you've had your tea, you go up to your room and relax. You've had a big day."

"Thanks, Aunt Rose, but I think I'll go for a wander around the garden first."

She hoped to see Uncle Mal but he would have finished milking some time ago. Elizabeth wanted to keep up a daily contact with him. She had to wait until after the evening meal when once again she offered to take out his tray to the whare.

"Thank you, Elizabeth. He will be glad to see you," said Aunt Rose. Aunt Gertrude raised her eyebrows but made no comment.

Elizabeth picked up the tray and went outside. When she reached the whare the door was open and Uncle Mal came out to meet her. "Come in, Missy, I hoped I would see you. And how did you like your first day at school?"

49

"It was only a staff day. The children come tomorrow and then I'll be in at the deep end."

"I'm sure you won't find them any trouble. I remember my first teacher. She was young and pretty and all I wanted to do was please her."

"Have you been busy today, Uncle Mal?" she asked.

"I've been trying to clear the gorse around the tanning pits. After our talk the other day I thought you would like to get a proper look at them. I hope to have the job finished tomorrow."

"I'm looking forward to seeing them." A sudden thought occurred to her. "I've met some of the other teachers now and there are two in particular that might be interested in the tanning pits. In fact, they've invited me to go to the pictures with them on Friday. One of them has a car and has offered to pick me up. Perhaps they could come a little earlier and see the pits. That's if you don't mind," she added quickly.

He looked at her with a twinkle in his eyes. "The one who's picking you up wouldn't be a young man would he?"

Elizabeth blushed but met his eyes steadily. "Well, yes, Uncle Mal."

"He didn't waste any time, did he? Of course, my dear, you bring him here and I'll gladly show him the tanning pits."

Elizabeth left him then and made her way to the house, stopping on the verandah to breathe in the evening air and listen to the sleepy twittering of the birds. Suddenly the clear notes of the bellbird rang out through the stillness and Elizabeth felt at peace.

CHAPTER FOUR

Elizabeth woke with a start. One moment she was unconscious, the next her brain was fully alert. This was her first day of teaching, when she would meet the children. So much would depend on today. Her stomach turned a somersault but she quickly took a grip on herself. She was well prepared and so long as she kept calm all would go well. She would show Mr. Ray that she was quite competent to be in charge of a class. With this thought uppermost she dressed and went downstairs where her breakfast was laid out on the kitchen table as usual. There was no sign of the aunts, but just as she was leaving Aunt Rose appeared in her dressing gown and slippers, her hair neatly pinned back as usual.

"I just came to wish you a good first day, Elizabeth. Be confident, my dear. You have every advantage and I know the children will respond to you. I will be praying for you. Now don't forget to take your lunch today. I cut some sandwiches for you last night. They are in the safe wrapped up and in a paper bag."

"Thank you Aunt Rose, I really appreciate that," and Elizabeth went forward and gave her a quick kiss. She opened the door of the safe and drew out the brown bag, placing it in her satchel while Aunt Rose watched.

At the door Elizabeth turned and waved. Outside in the shed

she carefully clipped the satchel to the seat of the bicycle. She mounted it at the end of the drive and coasted down the hill. It seemed so familiar now, the route to the school and once she was on her way she enjoyed the smooth motion and the fresh air brushing her face. All too soon the school came into view and as she dismounted at the gate she was aware of several small boys watching her curiously.

"Are you a new teacher?" asked one, with a shaggy haircut and bare feet.

Elizabeth answered him politely. "Yes, I'm Miss Brookfield and what is your name?"

"Tommy."

"And what class are you in this year, Tommy?"

"I'm in Standard Two."

"Oh, that's interesting. You could be in my class."

He gaped at her as she pushed her cycle firmly through the gate and made her way towards the stand at the back of the staffroom. Well, she had met one of her pupils already. Judging by his ragged hair and bare feet he came from a home where his mother was too busy to care for him. *He might need my special help*, thought Elizabeth. She wondered if he had been given breakfast this morning. She propped up her bicycle in the stand and still thinking about Tommy made her way up the steps through the front entrance. There seemed to be no-one around this early so she went on down the corridor to her room.

Everything was as she had left it yesterday but the room had a waiting air. Elizabeth opened her new workbook and scanned the work planned for the day. As she sat at her desk she had the curious feeling that she was being watched. Involuntarily she glanced towards the window. There was a row of small boys, noses flattened against the glass, peering into the room. She recognized the shock- headed Tommy in the middle of them. Getting up she crossed over to the window and opened it.

"Hello, Tommy," she said with a friendly smile, "Are these

some friends of yours? Perhaps you would like to come in and help me?"

"Can we help too, Miss Brookfield?" piped up another ragamuffin.

"All right, come on in," and she opened the door for them. They tumbled over themselves with eagerness.

Elizabeth crossed to the cupboard and took out an armful of arithmetic books which she placed on the front group of desks. The children swooped on them. Very soon all were given out. She fetched an armful of English books and the same thing happened. The children clustered round her desk, eager for more.

"I don't think I have any more jobs for you just now, but thanks for what you have done. You might as well go and play outside before you have to come into school."

As they went through the door Elizabeth heard Tommy say proudly to the group, "What did I tell you? My teacher is really nice." Elizabeth smiled to herself. *Tommy was on her side and he could have been quite a handful*, she guessed.

Shortly after this Mary put her head round the door. She looked with interest round the room.

"Hi, Elizabeth, you've got everything looking nice in here."

"It will look better when there are some pictures to brighten up the walls."

"Did you know that the whole school has to assemble outside and then they will be sent off to their classes from there? Mr. Ray will read out the class lists." She glanced at her watch. "Goodness, that's in five minutes time. We'd better get moving. Oh, bring your register with you."

Elizabeth picked it up from the desk and hurried with Mary down the corridor to the main entrance. Already the other teachers were standing in clusters chatting round the door. Mr. Ray appeared from the office with a sheaf of papers in his hands, Mrs. Ray behind him. She smiled briefly at Elizabeth then followed her husband to the top of the steps. The bell rang loudly from behind them and like fowls running when wheat is scattered, children appeared from all directions and went to stand in lines before the steps. Mr. Ray raised his hand and there was instant silence as all eyes were fixed on him.

"Good morning, children," he said.

"Good morning, Sir," they chorused.

'Welcome to you all, this new school year of 1962. I know you are all going to work your hardest and make this your best year ever. Most of you know which class you are in but there have been some changes, so I am going to read out your names and you will go and stand quietly in line in front of your teacher. I will begin with Standard One. Your teacher is Miss Fletcher," and he gestured to where Mary was standing. Then followed a list of names and each child went to stand expectantly in a line facing her. When the last name was called Mary motioned the children to follow her and she set off in front of the building.

Allowing a couple of minutes for this Mr. Ray paused before continuing. "Standard Two is the next class. This year you have a new teacher, Miss Brookfield, and your classroom is number four. I know that you will all try and be as helpful as you can to Miss Brookfield and show her what a fine school this is. Now, go quietly and join the line in front of her when you hear your name called."

Elizabeth watched each child came forward and stand before her. They studied her with eager interest and she looked back at them steadily. At last the final name was called and she led them off in the same direction that Mary had taken, until she drew opposite her classroom door. Here she paused and motioned the children to wait in their line.

"I want you to go into the room very quietly and sensibly and stand behind a chair in one of the groups. Do not sit down until I tell you. Lead off now please."

The children did exactly as she had asked and remained waiting for the order to sit. The room seemed suddenly full of bodies.

"Now you may sit," said Elizabeth. There was a loud scraping of chairs and an outburst of chatter. "That will never do," said Elizabeth. "I know you can do better than that. Please stand again and this time when I give the signal to sit, try not to make the slightest noise." The second time round there was scarcely a sound.

"That was perfect," said Elizabeth. "Now each time you stand or sit down I want you to do it exactly like that." She seemed to have made her point because the children strained to do everything she asked. Elizabeth appointed monitors for distributing the milk and monitors for each of the groups. "We will have a change of monitor each week," she explained, "so that everyone has a turn. Today I have just taken names from the top of the register."

The children seemed to accept this happily and the milk distribution went smoothly.

When the bell went for morning break she dismissed the class group by group and they left the room without fuss. Elizabeth was surprised at how little effort it took to control a class of forty. This was clearly a well-run school and the children were used to orderliness.

David poked his head round the door. "Coming to get a cuppa, Elizabeth? How was the mob? I never heard a sound next door."

"Fine thanks. They seem well behaved children."

"Don't speak too soon," he said and grinned.

She joined him in the corridor and as he fell into step with her he asked, "Are you still on for Friday?"

"Yes, and I've had a word with my uncle. He would like to show you the tanning pits on his land. It was once a tannery."

"Gee, really historic."

"Oh yes, and it was once a woollen mill, the first in NZ actually."

David looked at her seriously, "I would very much like to see the place. I'm a bit of a history buff, especially NZ history."

By now they were at the staffroom door. Clouds of cigarette

smoke drifted from the room and the din of voices seemed extra loud to Elizabeth after her quiet classroom. Through the haze she saw Mrs. Ray coming towards her.

"How are you liking your new class, Elizabeth?" she asked in a kindly way.

"They are very good - so far. They seem to have been well trained by their previous teacher. Who did have them last year, Mrs. Ray?"

"Mrs. Jean Shaw. She left to have a baby. You are her replacement, Elizabeth. Yes, she was a good teacher and she established firm routines."

"Did she keep notes on the children that I could refer to? It would help to know a bit more about them, apart from what is in the Progress & Achievement Register?"

"Well, each teacher can keep notes for their own reference but it is not usual to pass these on to the next teacher. It could prejudice them against individual children." She looked at Elizabeth shrewdly. "Was there any particular child you were concerned about?"

"Not really, Mrs. Ray." Instinct warned her not to mention Tommy. As if on cue Mary came up to them and Mrs. Ray excused herself.

"Hi, Mary, about Friday," Elizabeth began.

"Yes, I was going to speak to you about that. Our party is getting smaller. Jeanette's boyfriend has just come back from a business trip and is taking her out to dinner, so that leaves just you, David and me."

"Well, I was wondering," said Elizabeth slowly, "if David would fetch you first and then you both came to my place. You see, my uncle is prepared to show us the old tanning pits on the property. David says he is interested."

"That's a good idea, Elizabeth. I would like to see where you are staying." She glanced across the room to where David was talking animatedly to a tall athletic Maori. Elizabeth followed her gaze.

56

"Who is that Maori chap, Mary?"

"John Tamati. Handsome, isn't he? He plays rugby and is hoping to join the All Blacks. If you look out of your window after school you'll see him training. He runs round the playing field every day after school. Don't get ideas, Elizabeth, he's married."

They both laughed and David looked over at them. He said something to John and detached himself, hurrying towards them.

"What's the joke, girls?"

"Nothing," said Mary and grinned at Elizabeth. "Actually, we were discussing Friday. Elizabeth has suggested we both go and look at her uncle's tanning pits before the pictures?"

"Oh, that's fine then. I'll pick you up first." He sounded a shade less enthusiastic than usual. *Had he been looking forward to a tete a tete with her first*, Elizabeth wondered. *Well, it would look better to the aunts if two of them arrived to pick her up.*

The bell rang out above the voices and there was a sudden scurry as people replaced their mugs on the bench. Elizabeth knew there would be another bell in five minutes which would be the signal for the start of lessons.

"You go on," said Mary. "I've just remembered something I need to pick up from the office."

Elizabeth hurried to where her class was waiting, lined up outside the classroom. When they saw her coming someone said, "Ssh!" loudly and they straightened up, falling silent. Elizabeth noticed Tommy was in front.

The morning's lessons went smoothly and the children were just in the middle of a writing lesson, copying laboriously the letters from the blackboard, when the door opened silently and Mr. Ray appeared. Elizabeth's stomach lurched but she smiled calmly at him. He returned her smile and then moved quietly around the rooms stopping behind some chairs as he looked down at the children's work. Elizabeth noticed that he spent some time behind Tommy then looked up at her shaking his head slightly. He left the room almost stealthily, closing the door quietly behind him.

Elizabeth let out her breath when he had gone. All the time he had been in the room she had felt as though she were being inspected. She knew this was only the first of several visits he would make to her classroom to keep a check on her.

At last morning school was over and she dismissed the children. They collected their lunches from satchels which hung in the corridor and then trooped out of doors to sit on benches outside the classroom. Elizabeth's duty was to supervise them during the ten minutes allocated for the eating of lunch and so she walked up and down trying not to appear as if she were watching them. The children munched busily and by the time the bell rang most had finished. They waited for Elizabeth to give the signal to put their rubbish in the bins then, like little animals full of pent-up energy, they scampered off.

With a sense of freedom Elizabeth went back inside and collected her own lunch. When she got to the staffroom she found it surprisingly empty except for a handful of teachers. Mary and David were missing but Jeanette was there, puffing a cigarette as usual and talking to Mac, the Deputy Head. She pointed to the seat beside her. As Elizabeth sat down Mac excused himself and moved off.

"Hi, Elizabeth, how's it going?" asked Jeanette, tapping ash into her saucer.

"Fine thanks. I am just a little curious about one of the children. I know you didn't have my class last year."

"No, Jean Shaw had yours."

"Did she ever mention Tommy to you?"

Jeanette raised her eyes to the ceiling. "Oh, so you've come up against him already, have you?"

"No, not really, he's been as good as gold."

"Well, watch out, is all I can say."

"What is his background, Jeanette? He doesn't seem very well cared for."

"That's not surprising. His Dad's in prison and his mother has a parcel of kids all younger than Tommy."

"Poor child, I suppose he has to take care of the younger ones," said Elizabeth with quick sympathy.

"Hmm," said Jeanette, looking at Elizabeth speculatively, "Just keep an eye on young Tommy."

Elizabeth thought it best to change the subject and so she asked Jeanette about her travels overseas. Soon Jeanette was launched on a fund of stories and time passed so quickly that when Elizabeth glanced at her watch she saw there was only quarter of an hour left to the lunch hour. She excused herself and hurried off to her room to prepare for the afternoon's lessons. Art was first and she had decided to let the children use crayons or pastels to draw their pictures. When it was time to bring the children in, she saw that Tommy was at the head of the line again.

Once the children were seated she explained to them that they could do some colourful pictures to brighten up the room and to choose one scene from their holiday that they had particularly enjoyed. They set about the task with a will and soon all the heads were down as they drew industriously. Elizabeth strolled around the room encouraging and praising their efforts. She suddenly became aware of a scuffling noise in the group furthest away from her. Turning around she saw Helen, a rather prim little girl, looking red and indignant, with her arm across her picture and facing Tommy who was leaning towards her.

"What is going on?" asked Elizabeth. By now all the children had stopped work and were staring at Helen and Tommy.

"It's Tommy, Miss Brookfield. He's copying my picture and keeps on leaning over me."

"Is that true, Tommy?" asked Elizabeth. He looked embarrassed and hung his head. "I think it would be a good idea if you changed places with someone else, Tommy, and I'll give you another piece of paper to start again. Are you happy with that arrangement, Helen?" The girl looked a bit sulky but nodded her head. "Tommy, there's a space in the group near my desk. Would you like to sit there?" He got up immediately and went to where Elizabeth indicated.

Once Tommy was seated with a clean sheet of paper in front of him, Elizabeth casually strolled over to him. He was gazing into space looking unhappy. "Tommy, you haven't started yet."

"I don't know what to draw. We didn't go anywhere during the holidays. I had to look after the kids." Elizabeth's heart went out to him.

"Then why don't you draw a picture of Nelson? I'm new here and I'd love a picture of Nelson. Draw one for me would you, Tommy?" His face brightened and immediately he picked up a crayon. After that the class settled down and Elizabeth was surprised at how quickly the afternoon passed. At three o'clock the bell went for the end of school. As the last children left the room Tommy lingered behind.

"Are there any jobs I can do for you, Miss Brookfield?"

"You can clean the blackboard if you would, Tommy." He scrubbed away with the duster until the surface was shining. "Thank you Tommy, you've been very helpful today. I think you had better go home now or you will be late."

"See you tomorrow, Miss Brookfield," he said happily and ran off.

Elizabeth sat down at her desk with a sigh. *What a day! First Mr. Ray and then the contretemps with Tommy. Life was not going to be all smooth with this class, but at least there had been no serious control problems, even with forty children.* She looked at the piles of books on her desk waiting to be marked. *Well, she had better make a start.* This time no David appeared at the door and Elizabeth worked on steadily. At five o'clock she began to pack up. Last of all, she went over to close the windows and caught sight of John Tamati in a pair of football shorts running around the playing field. He waved at her then slowed down and came over to the window.

60

"Hi, I haven't had the chance to meet you yet. I'm John. You're Elizabeth aren't you?" He smiled at her, his even teeth white against his brown skin. Elizabeth felt suddenly confused but she managed to smile back politely.

"I understand you train here every night after school."

"That's right; I have to keep fit for rugby, although the season hasn't started yet. How've you found your first day here?"

"Ups and downs, but mainly ups."

"You'll be fine. I'm sure you've made a hit with the kids. They like young pretty teachers." Elizabeth blushed at this indirect compliment.

"Well, I mustn't keep you from your training programme," she said quickly.

"No, it's time I was off home; see you tomorrow," and he turned back to the field.

Elizabeth closed the window thoughtfully. She felt annoyed with herself for feeling disturbed by this man. After all, he was married. Mentally she shrugged and picked up her satchel.

When she walked through the back door Aunt Rose was mixing something in a bowl. As soon as she saw Elizabeth she wiped her floury hands on her apron and came over to her. "Oh, Elizabeth, I'm so relieved to see you. I thought something must have happened to you. It's getting so late and school would have finished a few hours ago."

"I stayed on and did some marking and then put work up on the board for tomorrow. I don't like bringing work home, Aunt Rose. Last year I did that and it hung over me all evening. After a few months I came out in a nervous rash and the doctor said it was due to stress, so I decided that the best way was to do my work at school and then leave it for that day."

"Oh well, I can see the sense in that. You need to be fresh each day to cope with all those children. Now come and have your meal. Gertrude and I waited for you."

"Has Uncle Mal had his tea?" asked Elizabeth anxiously.

"Yes, and he asked where you were. He seems to enjoy your

company, Elizabeth. In fact," she said thoughtfully, "I haven't seen him take to anyone as he has to you, for a long time. He is quite a different person."

At that moment Aunt Gertrude walked into the kitchen from the living room.

"Not nearly so morose," she said dryly. "He's becoming almost human again."

"Gertrude!" said Aunt Rose warningly. Her sister shrugged and went back into the living room. Elizabeth looked around for something to carry in.

"You go on in," said Aunt Rose, "Everything is on the table."

Once more there was a delicious looking salad with various kinds of cold meats and a covered dish with hot potato for Elizabeth. She ate hungrily and Aunt Rose watched her with satisfaction.

"I'm glad to see you have an appetite, my dear. I suppose it is a long time since you ate."

"Oh yes, I meant to thank you for my sandwiches, Aunt Rose. I did enjoy them."

At the end of the meal Aunt Gertrude looked over to Elizabeth. "Well, how did you find your teaching today? What are your children like?" She seemed genuinely interested and both aunts leaned forward eagerly. Elizabeth told them about Tommy and how she had met him at the school gate and invited him in to help her set up the classroom.

"You might have to be careful there," said Aunt Gertrude thoughtfully. "You don't want the other children to get the idea he's your pet."

"I hadn't thought of that," said Elizabeth and proceeded to tell them about the incident with Helen.

"What is her surname?" asked Aunt Gertrude.

"Lockwood, Helen Lockwood. I remember thinking it reminded me of an English actress."

"Hmm, I wonder if that is the Lockwood who owns a big garage in Nelson. If so, her father is a very wealthy man and a councillor. I wonder what story his daughter has gone home and told him."

"Well, I think Elizabeth dealt with it very well," said Aunt Rose loyally. She got up from the table and began collecting dishes. Aunt Gertrude and Elizabeth stood up too.

"That's all right, Elizabeth, I'll help Rose. You'll probably want to collect Mal's tray." Her tone was kind and Elizabeth escaped from the room gratefully.

When she reached the whare the door was open but there was no sign of Uncle Mal. She looked along the path and there he was leaning over the fence smoking his pipe and gazing into the distance. He seemed not to hear her approach until she was right behind him.

"Oh there you are, Missy, I was beginning to think I wouldn't see you this evening." His voice was gruff but his eyes twinkled under the shaggy brows.

"I was later tonight and I'm afraid I kept everyone waiting."

"Was everything all right at school?"

"OK, though one or two things did happen. I was just telling the aunts." She explained about Tommy and Helen. He listened carefully.

"I think you did the right thing there, Elizabeth, but people are not always very fair-minded, especially where their children are concerned. I know that chap Lockwood and he is very powerful around here. If as you say, Tommy's father is in prison he is probably not very happy at his daughter associating with the boy. Just be watchful, Missy."

"I'm only just getting to know the children, Uncle Mal. It would help to know their backgrounds but the Senior Teacher, Mrs. Ray, seems reluctant to give information about them."

"She's probably not a Nelsonian, Missy. People here have histories that go back a long way and outsiders would not know the importance of relationships between families. Prejudice plays an important part here."

"So you think I should find out as much as I can about the children's backgrounds."

"Of course. Now," he said, breaking off, "come and see the tanning pits," and he pushed open the gate, ushering her through. They walked across the paddock, and Elizabeth drew in deep breaths of the cool evening air scented from the grass. As they came near to the pits she could see that the tangle of gorse and weeds had been cleared away so that the brick sides were now exposed.

"As you can see there are still four to go, but at least I've made a start," he said with modest pride. "By Friday I hope to be finished."

"That is wonderful, Uncle Mal. I suppose the pits haven't been seen like that for a number of years."

"Too many, I'm afraid."

Evening was closing in as they made their way back across the paddock. Elizabeth collected the tray from the whare and bade Uncle Mart goodnight. When she was in her room she sat on the bed for many minutes gazing through the window and down the valley. *What a day it had been and how thankful she was that it was over.* Later on, as she prepared for bed, she wondered what the next day had in store. *Thank goodness for sleep and oblivion before she had to get up and face a new day.*

CHAPTER FIVE

I f she had hoped for an uneventful day Elizabeth was going to be disappointed. Almost as soon as she entered the school gates she sensed trouble. Tommy was there with his little gang of henchmen just as yesterday, but the difference was that today there was another group of small boys standing in a semi-circle facing them. Elizabeth recognized the one in the middle as being from her class. He was a pale stolid boy with a bullet like head and a short blonde crew cut. *A real little thug,* thought Elizabeth to herself. She recalled that his name was Bruce. From the stance of both groups she recognized the beginning of a fight. She wheeled her bicycle between them, turning first to Tommy and then to Bruce.

"Hello, boys," she said brightly, "you are nice and early this morning. I was just thinking how I could do with a couple of helpers. Would you like to come and give me a hand, both of you?" Tommy looked up at her eagerly.

"Yes, Miss Brookfield."

Bruce said nothing but stared at the ground, his bottom lip thrust out.

"Well, what about you, Bruce?" Still he remained silent. "I'll take that as yes, then. Here, Bruce, you can take my satchel," and she lifted it out of her basket and thrust it into his hands.

Both boys followed her into the school keeping strictly one

on each side. As they passed the office Tina looked through the glass hatch and raised her eyebrows.

"I see you've got two willing helpers there, Miss Brookfield."

"Two helpers anyway," said Elizabeth winking at her.

Once they were in the classroom Elizabeth knew she had to get them busy right away. She could see that Bruce was simmering with resentment. On a side table were the pictures drawn by the children the day before.

"Would you like to pin these up on the back wall, Bruce? I'll give you some drawing pins but make sure you don't prick your fingers. If you stand on a chair take care." Elizabeth fetched a packet of drawing pins from the cupboard and handed them to Bruce. Already his expression had changed from stubborn indifference to interest. Tommy looked on a little enviously.

"Would you hand out all the marked books, Tommy? That will be a real help to me," and she gave him a beguiling smile.

For the next ten minutes both boys worked industriously. Elizabeth was relieved that they seemed to have forgotten each other. When Bruce had pinned up the last picture, ignoring the fact that most looked a little drunken, Elizabeth said to him, "You've made a really good job of that, Bruce. Now the classroom looks so much more colourful. Thank you for your help. Would you like to go and have a play before the bell goes?"

"Thanks, Miss Brookfield," he said and ran out of the room, leaving Tommy and Elizabeth together.

"What was going on this morning, Tommy?" she asked looking into his face. "There was going to be a fight wasn't there? You can tell me about it, Tommy. I won't be punishing you. I just want to know the truth."

Tommy looked at her and hesitated. "It's like this, Miss Brookfield. Bruce's dad owns a dairy and he sometimes pinches sweets to give to other kids so that they will join his gang."

He looked suddenly anxious. "You won't say anything to anyone about me telling you this, will you?"

"No, of course not, Tommy; I don't betray confidences."

"Well, because my Dad's in prison for embezzling the other kids say I'm a thief like my father, but I'm not, Miss Brookfield, really I'm not. My mum has told me never to steal anything or I'll end up in jail like Dad and she said she couldn't bear that. I love my mum, Miss Brookfield, and I'd do anything for her."

Elizabeth said gently, "I'm sure you do, Tommy."

"Anyway, whenever anything goes missing at school the other kids say I've taken it. Bruce said this morning that he's going to get me into trouble with his dad. That's because his dad knows that someone's been stealing lollies from the shop. When he said that, I said that me and my friends would beat him up."

"And that was when I came along was it, Tommy?"

"Yes, Miss Brookfield."

Elizabeth thought for a moment. "Thank you for being so open with me, Tommy. Now, this is what I want you to do. Promise me that you won't get into any fights with Bruce and even if he does report you to his dad, promise me you won't beat him up. After school today please go straight home to your mum and don't wait around for your friends. That way you'll avoid any trouble with Bruce. You don't have to worry about Bruce's father. He will find out the truth, have no fear, but don't, whatever you do, take the law into your own hands. Now will you promise me this?"

"Yes, Miss Brookfield," said Tommy fervently, his eyes shining from under his thatch of hair.

"Now you go outside into the playground and have a run around before school begins." As he went slowly outside Elizabeth sighed. The day had hardly started but she felt as though she had just been through round one of a boxing match.

The rest of the morning was uneventful. All the children worked happily at the routine tasks until morning break. Elizabeth made her way to the staffroom and through the haze of cigarette smoke saw that most of the seats round the table were filled. David was sitting next to Mary and when he saw Elizabeth he immediately sprang up, his eyes eager.

"Hello, stranger, what happened to you last night? We kept expecting you to show up but when you didn't we thought you'd gone home."

"I seemed to have a lot to do, books to mark, work to prepare." She tailed off feebly.

"Now, Elizabeth, that's simply not good enough. You come to the staffroom first for a cuppa then you go back to your work. It quite spoiled my day," he said, dropping his voice and glancing at Mary, who was watching them.

"Well where were you at lunchtime anyway?"

"Oh, I always go back to my digs for lunch. I have an arrangement with my landlady. She likes to cook in the middle of the day and so it suits her to have a meal ready for me then. Of course, on my duty days I stick around here."

"Talking of duties, where is the duty roster?"

"It's just gone up. Come with me and I'll show you." He took her arm, unnecessarily she thought, and led her to the notice board. There they were joined almost immediately by Mary. Elizabeth was aware of a watchful expression in her eyes. David seemed oblivious and carried on talking in his usual lively fashion, but Elizabeth had read the signals. Mary carried a candle for David but he seemed unaware of it or at least pretended to be. He also was paying Elizabeth too much attention. The situation was a potential minefield and Elizabeth knew she would have to step warily. She was glad when break was over and she was back in the classroom once more. Somehow teaching was so much more straightforward than adult relationships.

She kept an eye on Bruce and Tommy but both of them kept their heads down all morning and worked earnestly. It was the same at lunchtime. They sat well apart and took no notice of each other.

In the staffroom it was hot and stuffy and everyone seemed lethargic. Even Jeanette was unusually quiet. Elizabeth ate her lunch and then went back to her classroom where she opened all the windows before tackling a pile of marking. The temperature in the afternoon climbed and the children were hot and sleepy. Elizabeth decided to take them outside to read from their journals under the trees at the side of the playground.

They were all seated in the shade enjoying the gentle breeze that played on their bare arms and legs when Elizabeth looked up and saw Mr. Ray hurrying across the grass towards them.

He looked grim. He beckoned to Elizabeth to step to one side and in a low voice said, "This really will not do, Miss Brookfield. You cannot take the children outside unless you have made arrangements with me beforehand. Supposing other teachers decided to take their classes outside as well, we would have chaos. I'm afraid you will have to take the children back indoors right away."

Elizabeth flushed, cut by his words. *He had as good as said that she was thoughtless and irresponsible, when she had only been concerned for the children. Oh dear, she was getting off on the wrong foot with him.* She murmured an apology and told the children to stand up and prepare to go back into school. They looked at her puzzled but did as they were bidden and feeling like a scolded child herself she led them back to the classroom. At least, they seemed refreshed by their time in the open air and the rest of the afternoon passed pleasantly.

After school when all the children were preparing to leave Tommy came up to her.

"I'm going straight home, Miss Brookfield. I won't stop for anyone."

"Well done, Tommy. I'm sure your mum will be glad to see you home so early. You might be able to help her."

"Oh I will, Miss Brookfield," he replied happily.

Elizabeth watched him hurry off then she let herself out of the room and made her way to the staffroom. Several teachers were there already and there was a buzz of chatter. As she came in the room fell silent. Jeanette was the first to speak. "Well, you took the biscuit today, taking your class outside to sit under the trees. I watched the Head go out and call you back inside."

David then spoke up, "I think Elizabeth did what all of us would have liked to do; only she had the guts to do it. It was impossibly hot this afternoon and nobody should be expected to teach in temperatures like that. It was eighty-five degrees in my classroom, even with all the windows open."

Mac had been listening to this. "Elizabeth shouldn't have taken an action like that without consulting the Head first."

"Oh come on, Mac, Elizabeth showed common sense. It's not right to expect young children to work in heat like that. Why don't you bring the matter up at the next staff meeting? Surely there should be a policy on what we do when the temperature gets beyond a certain point. I don't like to think of my child having to sit in conditions like that. Couldn't school finish early, for instance?" This suggestion came from Rosa, an attractive married woman in her forties.

Just then Mrs. Ray walked into the room and there was silence as everyone looked at her. "I just caught the end of what you were saying, Rosa. I suppose you've all been discussing what happened this afternoon when it got so hot. I can understand why Elizabeth thought it best to take her class outside. The trouble is we can't all act independently of one another and we have to follow school protocol."

She turned to Elizabeth with a kindly smile. "At least, my dear, you have brought this matter to a head. February is a difficult month. It's usually the hottest time of the year and yet the children have to go back to school then. We certainly will discuss the matter at the staff meeting tomorrow."

The subject seemed to have exhausted itself and people broke up into twos and threes. David and Mary came over to Elizabeth.

"Goodness, you've only been here a couple of days and already you've set a cat among the pigeons," said Mary with a laugh.

"I never saw it that way," said Elizabeth. "It seemed the obvious thing to do at the time. I suppose it was thoughtless of me, but I felt so sorry for the children."

"Act first, think later, eh, Elizabeth. It's part of your charm." David said this airily but Mary gave him a sharp look that was not lost on Elizabeth.

"Well, I think I'll grab a cup of tea then get back to work," she said, leaving the two of them standing together.

Back in her room she tried to work but the heat in the room was oppressive and she could feel the sweat trickling down the back of her neck. It was no use; she simply had to give up for the day. She crossed over to the window and there was John Tamati, jogging wearily around the field. When he saw her he came across to the window smiling.

"Hi, Elizabeth, I just wanted to say, good on you, for having the courage to take your class outside today. It's time this school came into the 20th century. On hot days we should all be able to go and sit outside. Perhaps after this something will be done."

"Mrs. Ray said just now that it will be brought up at the staff meeting tomorrow."

"High time too, we needed someone like you, Elizabeth, to give us a jolt, in more ways than one," and he winked at her, making Elizabeth blush, *like a silly schoolgirl,* she told herself sharply.

"Well, I think I'm giving up for today," he said. "It's too hot to run. I think I'll go home and have a beer instead."

"Good idea. I'm going early too," she said, shutting the window.

It was really quite pleasant cycling alongside the brook. She created a little breeze that fanned her face and arms and she had the half guilty pleasure of leaving work early. After she had put the bicycle away she went into the kitchen looking forward to a nice cool drink. There was no sign of the aunts so she went to the refrigerator and took out a jug of homemade ginger beer and poured herself a glass. She sat at the table in the porch and took a long draught of the cool sweet liquid, leaning back and letting the tension of the day ebb out of her. Suddenly, Aunt Gertrude appeared at the door.

"You're home early, Elizabeth," she said with an abstracted air. Her hair, usually so sleek, looked in need of a brush.

"It was too hot in my room to work."

"Yes, it's been terribly hot here as well. In fact, we had a bit of a fright with Mal. He collapsed outside in the sun. He was trying to clear the gorse over at the tanning pits. So unnecessary, they've been choked up for years."

A shiver went down Elizabeth's spine. "Where is he now, Aunt Gertrude?"

"Oh he's back in the whare, lying down. We did call the doctor but he said it was heat exhaustion and Mal must rest and not go out in the midday sun. Common sense really, but it did give us a fright."

"Do you think I could go and see him, Aunt Gertrude?"

"Well, I wouldn't just yet, Elizabeth, he's probably sleeping. The doctor did give him some pills to reduce his temperature." She seemed genuinely upset and concerned, not her usual cool sardonic self.

Although the sun still shone from a hard blue sky Elizabeth felt chilled. Supposing Uncle Mal had died out there in the heat, it would indirectly be her fault. She must assure him that there was no need to bother about clearing all of the pits. It was sufficient that he had revealed four of them.

That evening at tea, both aunts were quiet and asked Elizabeth nothing about school. Nobody seemed to have much appetite although there were fresh boysenberries and cream for dessert. After helping with the dishes Elizabeth went up to her room and was glad to be on her own at last. She needed to think. If anything happened to Uncle Mal it would be unthinkable. She saw the Bible on the bedside table and reached over to pick it up. It fell open at the twenty-third Psalm. That was her mother's favourite. As Elizabeth read the familiar words she paused at, "though I walk through the valley of death I shall fear no evil." It seemed that today Uncle Mal might have passed through that valley. How important it was to have a faith at times like this. Elizabeth slid to her knees beside the bed and prayed earnestly for Uncle Mal. Her eyes were wet with tears and when she stood up she felt a new kind of peace.

CHAPTER SIX

T hursday promised to be as hot as the previous day although at nine o'clock it was still cool indoors. Elizabeth had just started the children on their first lesson of the day when Tina appeared at the door. She tiptoed across the room and handed Elizabeth a folded piece of paper, "Note from the Head," she whispered and went out. Elizabeth's heart began to thump as she opened the slip of paper.

Elizabeth,

Would you please come to my office at break. I need to discuss with you a matter concerning Tommy.

D. Ray.

Elizabeth glanced across at Tommy where he was writing, the tip of his tongue protruding in his effort to concentrate. She then looked at Bruce on the other side of the room and was in time to see him take something from his pocket and slip it into his mouth. Had he stolen more sweets from his father's shop? He had not noticed her eyes on him so Elizabeth decided to wait until lunch before speaking to him.

The time until break seemed interminable. As soon as the

last child had left the room Elizabeth hurried along the corridor to the Head's office, where she paused before knocking as she tried to still the beating of her heart.

"Come in," was the abrupt command and Elizabeth opened the door tentatively. To her surprise a man was seated in a chair at the side of the room. He did not make any effort to stand when she came in but looked at her unsmilingly.

"This is Mr. Bulloch," said the Head addressing Elizabeth and indicating the man in the chair. *Well named*, thought Elizabeth, noting the thick neck and open shirt where the black hairs stuck out aggressively. He had small protruding eyes that swept over her insolently.

"This is Miss Brookfield, Bruce's teacher," said Mr. Ray smoothly.

"Now, Miss Brookfield, Mr. Bulloch tells me that Bruce has reported to him that Tommy has been blackmailing Bruce into giving him lollies, with threats to beat him up after school if he refuses. It seems that Bruce has been taking different kinds of lollies for some time now because he is scared of Tommy. Have you seen anything suspicious happening in or out of school?"

Elizabeth thought quickly. *If she mentioned the fight she intercepted the other morning this could look bad for Tommy.*

"I have only had the class for less than one week, Mr. Ray, and I am still getting to know the children's names. As you know there are forty in the class. As regards Tommy, he has been early to school the last few mornings and has come to help me before school. I know for a fact that he left early for home yesterday, before most of the other children. As for Bruce, he sits in a group on the other side of the room from Tommy and there is no chance of their communicating in class. Of course, I do not know what happens in the lunch hour. I would like to mention though, that this morning I saw Bruce slip something into his mouth that was presumably a lolly."

"Did you say anything to Bruce about this, Miss Brookfield?"

75

"Not at the time, Mr. Ray, I was intending to speak to him at lunchtime."

Mr. Bulloch reddened and seemed on the verge of saying something when Mr. Ray said smoothly, "Thank you, Miss Brookfield; that has been very helpful. Would you like to go and have your morning tea now?"

Elizabeth escaped thankfully. She was conscious of Mr. Bulloch's angry little eyes boring into her back. *He was so like an adult version of his son, even more unpleasant though,* she thought.

In the staffroom she poured herself a cup of tea and took her mug across to the table to sit by Mary. "How're things, Elizabeth?"

"Oh, not so good, my uncle collapsed yesterday through working in the sun."

"The uncle we're meeting on Friday?"

"Yes," said Elizabeth slowly, "perhaps we'd better cancel that arrangement. You and David go to the pictures, I'll come another time."

David was sitting opposite them. At the mention of his name he looked up. "Did I hear my name taken in vain?"

"I was just telling Mary about Uncle Mal. He collapsed through heat exhaustion yesterday when he was clearing the tanning pits of gorse."

"Gosh, I'm sorry to hear that, Elizabeth." David's bantering tone changed to one of concern.

"And I think I'd better pull out of tomorrow's arrangements, but don't let it stop you and Mary going to the pictures."

David's face fell but seeing Mary's eyes on him he said quickly, "That's a real shame, Elizabeth, but you and I will still go, eh Mary?" He paused. "Look, Elizabeth, I'm not doing anything on Saturday. Perhaps I could come and bring some of my scouts round to help clear those tanning pits. That might help your uncle."

"I didn't know you were a scout leader," said Mary surprised.

"You don't know all my guilty secrets," and he grinned.

Elizabeth thought suddenly, *He is really quite attractive in a funny kind of way.*

"I'll come around to your place at about eleven," he said, turning to Elizabeth, serious once more.

Just then the bell went for the end of break and as Elizabeth hurried back to the classroom, thoughts of Uncle Mal receded from her mind. Her immediate concern was Tommy.

The call from Mr. Ray came soon after lessons had started. Tina arrived with a note requiring that both boys accompany her to Mr. Ray's office. As they stood up Tommy looked pale and frightened while Bruce had a defiant set to his jaw. As Elizabeth watched them leave the room her heart sank. Having met Mr. Bulloch she knew that he would do his utmost to incriminate Tommy and all she could do was wait for the outcome. The next hour passed slowly and by twelve o'clock the boys had not returned.

Tina came to the room just after the lunch bell. "Mr. Ray would like to see you in his office," she said to Elizabeth, her usually cheerful face serious. Elizabeth walked with her along the corridor. At Mr. Ray's door Tina left her and Elizabeth knocked hesitantly.

"Come in," was the brusque reply.

When Elizabeth entered the room she was surprised to see Mr. Ray standing at his desk, the two boys in front of him. Tommy was sobbing as though his heart would break but Bruce's face was white and set.

"I've spoken to both these boys," said Mr. Ray looking grim, "and I'm not at all satisfied with their stories. It seems that neither of them is prepared to tell me the whole truth. It is a fact that Bruce has been stealing sweets from his father's shop and he has admitted that. He maintains that he was bullied into it by Tommy who has been threatening to beat him up. Tommy denies this but he has admitted to threatening Bruce, if he speaks to his father."

"Anyway, Miss Brookfield, I have decided to suspend each

of the boys for a week, beginning from this afternoon. I regard theft and bullying as very serious offences and I hope this will teach both of them an important lesson. Would you please give them work to do at home for a week. They will remain here in my office while I ring their parents to collect them."

"My mum's not on the phone, Mr. Ray," blurted out Tommy between sobs.

"Well, in that case we'll have to contact her another way."

"I would be happy to go during the lunch hour and see her," said Elizabeth quietly.

Tommy looked up at her.

"Well, if you are prepared to give up your time," said Mr. Ray.

"Of course I am," said Elizabeth. Then looking at Tommy, "You will have to give me clear directions to your home," she said gently.

Tommy had now stopped crying but his face was stained where the tears had left furrows down his cheeks. Stumblingly he explained that his home was only a few streets away from the school.

"I'll go right away," Elizabeth said, addressing Mr. Ray who was watching her closely.

She went quickly from the room and out through the main entrance, glad that no teachers or children were to be seen. They would be eating their lunches during this first part of the lunch hour. It did not take her long to find Tommy's home. Even if she had not known the number she would have guessed that this was the one. It was a small house, in a row of others all identical, the flimsy sort that had been put up after the war to provide quick housing for needy families. It was even more ramshackle than its neighbours, with toys strewn over the front lawn, which looked as though it had not been cut in weeks.

The gate was hanging on one hinge and as Elizabeth pushed it open she was careful not to put too much pressure on it in case it fell over. Weeds straggled across the path and there were big cracks in the concrete where more weeds grew. Elizabeth picked her way carefully, stepping over a teddy bear that lay face downward on the front step. She knocked at the door and there was scuffling inside. Slowly the door opened and a grubby girl of about four stood looking at Elizabeth her mouth open.

"Who is it, Susie?" called a woman from somewhere at the back of the house.

"Don't know, Mummy," said the child. "It's a lady."

A young woman with a baby in her arms appeared behind Susie. Her blonde hair was strained back in an untidy pony tail and she had a thin worried face. *She must have been pretty once,* thought Elizabeth, *but she looks as though she has given up caring about herself.* She looked at Elizabeth questioningly.

"I'm Elizabeth Brookfield, Tommy's teacher," she began.

"Oh, nothing's happened to him has it?" The woman looked frightened.

"No, he's quite safe," said Elizabeth gently, "but I do need to speak to you about him."

"Come in. Please excuse the mess," and she looked round apologetically, "the baby's been sick this morning and I haven't had time to do any housework."

Elizabeth followed her into a frowsy living room with toys lying around the floor. The woman cleared off the dolls that sat in state on the settee and indicated to Elizabeth to sit down. She seated herself in a worn armchair opposite.

"I'm afraid there has been a bit of trouble at school," Elizabeth began.

"Oh dear, and I thought Tommy was doing so well this year," said his mother. "He can't stop talking about you," she said with a little smile. "He thinks you're wonderful."

"I am very pleased with him too," replied Elizabeth quickly. "He's been trying so hard with all his schoolwork and he's been very helpful as well, before and after school."

"Well, what can be the matter then?" asked the woman puzzled.

79

Elizabeth paused. "There's another boy in the class who has been stealing lollies from his father's shop. He says that Tommy has threatened him physically if he doesn't give him lollies."

"That can't be true," burst out his mother. "Tommy would never make another child steal for him. Tommy is as honest as the day. He's always promised me never to steal and he never lies to me."

"I believe you, Mrs. White, and I believed Tommy when he told me the other morning what had really been going on. I intercepted him and this other boy just as they were going to have a fight and I took them into the classroom. When Tommy was on his own with me he told me that the other boy had threatened to tell his father that Tommy had put him up to stealing the lollies, when in fact he had nothing to do with it."

"In that case, if you know the truth why should Tommy be in trouble?"

"The Headmaster has questioned the two boys and it seems he is not satisfied that they are telling the truth, so he is suspending both of them for a week."

A bitter look came into the woman's eyes. "I know what it is. Because Tommy's Dad is in jail for embezzlement everyone thinks that his son is tarred with the same brush. Well, I know that Tommy is no thief and I think you do too."

"I believe Tommy is honest but the trouble is that there is no proof. I think all we can do is reassure Tommy that we believe in him, but I'm afraid we have to accept the Headmaster's ruling in this case."

The woman looked at Elizabeth without speaking and said finally, "Thank you, Miss Brookfield, you've been very kind but I think we can't win, ever. People will always judge us because of my husband."

Elizabeth reached over and touched her hand. It felt thin and cold. "Would you be able to come with me to the school to fetch Tommy home now?"

"I'll have to bring all the children. There's no-one to look after them here."

"That's all right. I can help you. Would you like me to take the baby?"

Unceremoniously the woman pushed the baby into Elizabeth's arms and left the room. Elizabeth looked down at the sweet little face. The baby lay sleeping peacefully, her lashes like shadows against the pink cheeks.

Some minutes later Mrs. White returned with Susie and two toddlers about two years old, twin boys it seemed. They gazed at Elizabeth as they clung to their mother's side. "I'll put the twins in a push chair," she said. "Susie, you can push the baby's pram." Some minutes later the little entourage set off to the school.

When they reached the school gate, Elizabeth led them up the drive and through to the main entrance. She helped lift the pram and pushchair over the steps and into the vestibule. Tina came out of her office and smiled kindly at Mrs. White. "Would you mind waiting a moment while I let Mr. Ray know you are here?" she said, glancing down at the pushchair and pram. She disappeared and returned a few minutes later with Mr. Ray followed by Tommy. The headmaster came forward with his blandest smile and held out his hand to Mrs. White who just stared at him.

"Mum, I didn't do it!" burst out Tommy.

"No, I know you didn't and I've come to fetch you home."

"Mrs. White, I have been into the matter thoroughly," said Mr. Ray firmly.

Ignoring him she held out her hand to Tommy. "Come on, son, you're coming home with me. This school is no place for you." Tina and Elizabeth looked on dumbfounded as she turned on her heel and beckoned the children to follow her. Mr. Ray stood watching then shrugged slightly and turned away. Tina looked at Elizabeth.

"Well, I never did!" she exclaimed. Then remembering

practicalities she said, "It's nearly bell time. I suppose you haven't had time to eat your lunch. Go and get yourself a cup of tea, Elizabeth. Goodness, what a to-do!"

Elizabeth went into the empty staffroom and fetched her mug from the cupboard. With a shaking hand she poured herself a cup of tea and took a gulp. *Ugh, it was lukewarm.* She poured the rest down the sink, rinsed the mug and went out.

As she hurried down the corridor to her room she tried to steady her thoughts but the events of the last few minutes had shaken her profoundly. Never could she have imagined such a scene, where a mother defended her child against what she regarded as injustice and defied authority. Mr. Ray for once had lost his dignity, as he stood by helplessly while Mrs. White swept out of the school. Instead of Mr. Ray pronouncing sentence and suspending the child the mother had got in first and removed her son from the school. Something in Elizabeth made her feel like applauding Mrs. White.

When she got back to the children, who were waiting patiently in line outside the glass door, Elizabeth had somewhat regained her equilibrium.

At two o'clock Tina slipped into her room with a whispered message. "The bell is going at two thirty today for early dismissal because of the staff meeting."

It was already very hot in the room so Elizabeth decided to ignore the lesson planned in her workbook and to read the children a story instead. "Put everything away, children, and rest your heads on the desk while I read the next chapter of Treasure Island." A sigh of happiness went through the class. As she read Elizabeth was hardly following the story, her mind was so busy with thoughts of Tommy.

Promptly on the bell Elizabeth dismissed the children and then made her way to the staffroom. She was glad that she was the first one there. Though not aware of hunger pangs she was very thirsty. It was a relief to find a fresh pot of tea standing on the bench. When she had filled her mug she went and sat down about half way along the table. Almost immediately the rest of the staff arrived. Jeanette came and sat beside her.

"Thank goodness it's a short day," she said taking out her lighter. "These hot days we should all be getting out at half past two, even if it means starting school half an hour early."

"Why don't you suggest that, Jeanette?"

"Don't worry, I will," and she took a long draw on her cigarette.

By now everyone was seated around the table:- Mr. Ray at the head, Mrs. Ray on his right and Mac on his left. He coughed significantly and the buzz of chatter died down as everyone turned towards him.

"We have several matters to discuss this afternoon, but first and foremost is the issue of what to do during these hot days in February."

Elizabeth listened to him as he went through the difficulties arising from administration. She found herself losing concentration and beginning to feel drowsy. She fought against it and managed to keep her eyes open though she lost the thread of what he was saying. She found herself studying Mr. and Mrs. Ray. He reminded her of a sleek, well fed tom cat and his wife beside him, of a little tabby. *What a strange pair they are,* thought Elizabeth idly. She wondered what they were like at home.

Suddenly she heard Mr. Ray say, "Have any of you a suggestion to make?"

Jeanette immediately spoke up. "Why can't we begin school half an hour early and finish at two thirty for the next couple of weeks?"

"What do the rest of you think about that suggestion? Would it seriously affect any of you if we did start earlier?" Several made comments but generally most were in favour.

"Thank you for that very practical suggestion, Jeanette. As everyone seems to agree we will adopt this suggestion and send a note to parents tomorrow. Will you make a note of that please, Tina?" he said turning to the secretary.

After this there were only a couple more matters to discuss and the meeting broke up.

Elizabeth smiled across at David and Mary. "I have to go early tonight. See you tomorrow," she said and quickly left the room.

Cycling home alongside the brook Elizabeth was glad of the breeze she created. It was still very hot and she felt tired and sticky, also a little depressed. At the bottom of the hill she dismounted and pushed the bicycle the rest of the way. Clicking open the gate she felt once more, as though she were entering another world. Suddenly the silvery chime of a bellbird rang out through the still air.

Aunt Rose came out to meet her at the kitchen door carrying a jug of chilled ginger beer. "You look very tired, Elizabeth, and rather strained." She gazed into Elizabeth's face concerned.

"It has been rather a stressful day, Aunt Rose, and I'm glad to be home."

"Well, you just sit down and have a glass of this and tell me all about it."

"First, Aunt Rose, how is Uncle Mal?"

"Oh, he is quite improved. We insisted he come inside this afternoon and not sit out in that whare. We made him lie down on the couch on the upstairs verandah and he even managed to sleep for a couple of hours. At lunchtime I took a tray to him there and he seemed to enjoy it. He would go to milk Bessie at four o'clock even though Gertrude offered to do it. He's probably still out there."

"I'll go and see him as soon as I've finished my drink," said Elizabeth eagerly.

"Now you sit still for a few minutes, my dear. There's plenty of time," and Aunt Rose patted Elizabeth's hand. "Now tell me about today."

Elizabeth launched into her account of the two boys and her

visit to Tommy's mother. She omitted no detail and Aunt Rose listened carefully. After Elizabeth had finished Aunt Rose was silent for a few seconds.

"I think your headmaster was put into a difficult position, Elizabeth. He listened to the stories of both boys and he had no way of knowing which one was telling the truth so I suppose to be fair he had to punish them both equally. You and Mrs. White accept Tommy's word but you have no actual proof except your trust in him."

She continued, "I think it is unfortunate that Tommy's mother behaved the way she did, refusing to listen to Mr. Ray, but I suppose she is under a lot of strain with all those children and no husband to help her and so she is not able to act rationally. I just hope that she doesn't keep Tommy at home or the authorities will be after her."

"What would they do?"

"They might take Tommy away and put him in a foster home."

"Oh, that would be terrible, Aunt Rose. I must do all I can to stop that happening."

"You say you have to supply Tommy with work while he is suspended from school, then perhaps when you visit his home you can talk to his mother and persuade her to send the boy to school."

Elizabeth drained her glass of ginger beer and stood up. "Thank you for your advice, Aunt Rose. Now I really must go and see Uncle Mal."

She took the outdoor path that skirted the verandah and opened the gate leading to the back paddock. Here she paused for a moment enjoying the tranquil scene before her:- sheep grazing, white against the green grass, a stream meandering through the gorse and behind it all a backdrop of hills. She walked across the paddock to the brick shed feeling her energy return after the draining effects of the day.

As she came around the corner there was the familiar sight

of Bessie in her bail, her tail swishing away the flies and Uncle Mal leaning over a bucket rinsing out a cloth. He straightened up as he heard her footsteps. Elizabeth ran impulsively to him.

"Oh, Uncle Mal, I was so worried about you," she said, tears in her eyes.

"I'm all right, Missy," he said gruffly. "Look at me, perfectly well, a lot of fuss about nothing."

"I feel it was my fault. I shouldn't have made such a thing about the tanning pits."

"Don't you blame yourself, my dear, I was keen to get the job finished."

"Well, Uncle Mal, there is no need for you to do it. My friend David is a scout master and he has offered to come along on Saturday morning with some of the boys and clear the gorse from the remaining pits."

Martin smiled. "That is good of him." He gave Elizabeth a knowing look. "I think he must be rather keen on you."

Elizabeth coloured. "Are you finished here, Uncle Mart?"

"Will be in a few minutes, off you go, Bessie," and he gave the cow a light tap on the rump.

Elizabeth waited while Uncle Mal cleaned up from milking and then the two of them set off across the paddock to the house, Mal carrying the bucket of frothy milk. When they reached the whare he looked at her closely. "If you don't mind me mentioning it you look quite done in. Had a hard day at school?"

"Mm," she said, unwilling to go into details. "I'd better go into dinner now, it's nearly six o'clock."

Conversation at the table centred on the high temperatures of the past few days and Elizabeth told the aunts about the decision at the staff meeting to begin and finish school earlier.

"That sounds a sensible idea," commented Aunt Gertrude.

"Does that mean you will be leaving earlier tomorrow morning?" asked Aunt Rose.

"Yes, but I will probably be home at the usual time."

When she was at last in her bedroom Elizabeth sat by the

open window gazing down the valley and thinking through the events of the day. She thought back over Aunt Rose's comments on Tommy and his mother and she saw the logic behind them. Aunt Rose was really a very wise woman. *What a store of wisdom old people can draw on,* thought Elizabeth.

CHAPTER SEVEN

Elizabeth was deeply asleep when suddenly the alarm clock buzzed in her ear. She woke with a start and turned over to look at the time. It was already six o'clock. How she wished she could bury her head in the pillow and lapse back into unconsciousness. Resisting the temptation she sprang out of bed.

It took her exactly half an hour to get ready before going downstairs to have breakfast. She ate without appetite but she knew she had to have food or her energy would flag half way through the day. Her lunch, prepared by Aunt Rose, was in the safe as usual. Generally her aunt came to wave her off but today being half an hour earlier Elizabeth did not expect her to appear.

As she was wheeling her bicycle along the path she was startled to hear Aunt Rose's voice. "Have a good day, Elizabeth. Remember it's Friday and almost the weekend." Elizabeth laughed and waved. How perceptive the old lady was. All of a sudden Elizabeth felt light-hearted.

She enjoyed her ride to school through the fresh morning air. At the school gate Elizabeth dismounted and felt a slight pang when she thought of Tommy. At least she would see him this afternoon, but she would also have to visit Bruce's home and she recoiled at the thought.

In her classroom Elizabeth immediately began preparing for the day. All the work had to go on the blackboard that she had missed putting up yesterday because of the staff meeting. She was so absorbed she did not hear the door open. Somebody coughed behind her. She swung around and there was Mr. Ray.

"Sorry to startle you. I won't keep you a minute as you're busy, but I wanted to remind you about taking work to Bruce and Tommy. You will need to give them plenty to do to keep them occupied for the week. If you need help, please let Mrs. Ray know and she will give you some guidance."

The way he spoke grated on Elizabeth. He had an unerring way of making her feel inadequate. She said quietly, "I hadn't forgotten, Mr. Ray, and I will go round to both boys' homes this afternoon after school."

"Before you do, perhaps you would call in at my office so that I can see what you have prepared." With this he went out closing the door carefully behind him. Inwardly fuming Elizabeth returned to her work. After some minutes she settled down, and by the time she went outside to greet the children she was once more in command of herself.

The morning passed uneventfully and when the bell rang for break Elizabeth was ready for her cup of tea. All the staff seemed present this morning and there was a buzz of chatter.

Mary and David were sitting together and David immediately stood up, signalling to Elizabeth to take his seat. As she walked across the room balancing her mug in one hand she heard comments from all sides on the early start.

"You look your usual bright self, Elizabeth," commented David, "despite losing half an hour's sleep."

"I actually prefer early mornings. Everything is so lovely and fresh outside."

"Dew's on the rose, lark's on the wing etc." said David.

"Oh, we are waxing poetic this morning," said Mary. "Early mornings must agree with you too."

"Between ourselves, it's the thought of finishing early,

89

especially on a Friday. Pity you're not coming to the pictures, Elizabeth. By the way, how is your uncle?"

"He refuses to admit there is anything wrong with him, says it was all a big fuss over nothing."

"Oh, so he's an obstinate old codger. I'm looking forward to meeting him."

"He seemed quite touched that you and the scouts were prepared to go and work on the tanning pits. Anyway, you two enjoy the pictures tonight. I'll be thinking of you."

After break the children worked busily and seemed to have greater concentration this morning. The earlier hour evidently suited them too. When it was lunch time Elizabeth supervised them as usual then went back to her desk to prepare work for Bruce and Tommy. She made sure that she covered all the subjects and tried to align them with her own planning for the next week. She found this took her most of the lunch hour so she decided to eat her sandwiches at her desk and forgo a cup of tea. She finished with five minutes to spare, which gave her just sufficient time to hand in the work to Tina so that she could pass it on to Mr. Ray.

During the afternoon a pleasant breeze came through the open windows and for the first time that week the children seemed relaxed and happy. They worked with a will and Elizabeth found herself enjoying teaching in the latter part of the day. When she dismissed the class at two thirty there was almost a holiday atmosphere. Then Mr. Ray appeared at her door. Under his arm was the work Elizabeth had prepared. At the serious set of his face Elizabeth's heart began to beat faster. *Was he going to find fault with what she had prepared so painstakingly?*

"This seems quite adequate," said Mr. Ray grudgingly, "though you may have to spend some time explaining to the parents how you want the work spread out over the five days. I presume you are going to the homes this afternoon."

"I was intending to."

90

"Very well, Elizabeth, I hope you get through to Mrs. White better than I did. She is a most difficult parent. We don't have many like her fortunately."

Elizabeth was thinking, *I would have responded the same way if my child was accused of something he hadn't done*, but all she said was, "I'll do my best, Mr. Ray." He laid the work on the table, gave Elizabeth a brief smile and left the room.

As soon as he had gone Elizabeth gathered her belongings and was preparing to leave the room when to her surprise John Tamati appeared at the window.

"Just came to wish you a happy weekend, Elizabeth. Are you doing anything exciting?"

"Not particularly, though it will be nice to have a break from school."

"Yes, the first week back is pretty full, and you're new too. All the same, from what I can see you have coped very well, and shaken us up a bit. Taking the kids outside that day has brought about a few changes around here, but apart from school, Elizabeth, I'm glad you've come here. I look forward to seeing you each day."

Elizabeth blushed and looked down at the desk to hide her confusion. "Thanks, John. Look, I have to fly. I've got to go and visit a couple of homes to take work for the children. See you Monday. Have a great weekend." She scooped up her bag and fled.

Out at the bicycle stand she found her heart was thumping. *What was it about John Tamati that had this effect on her? Whenever David said anything personal or paid her indirect compliments she was quite untouched.* She stood for a moment trying to calm down. She had to give all her attention to the coming interviews and keep her wits about her.

She mounted her bicycle and was soon outside Tommy's house, which now seemed quite familiar. She pushed open the gate and wheeled her cycle along the broken path up to the front steps where she left it on its stand in the long grass at the

91

side of the path. At her first knock the door opened suddenly and Tommy was standing there. His face lit up when he saw her.

"Hello, Miss Brookfield. Have you come to see Mum?"

"Well, yes, Tommy, but to speak to you as well."

"I'll fetch Mum," he said and disappeared, leaving Elizabeth on the doorstep.

Mrs. White appeared a few seconds later. She looked enquiringly at Elizabeth. "Well?" she said.

"I've come with work for Tommy," said Elizabeth holding up her satchel.

"I suppose you'd better come in then," was the grudging reply.

Feeling awkward Elizabeth followed her into the shabby little sitting room. Mrs. White gestured towards the sofa and Elizabeth sat down. "First I want to say, Mrs. White that I believe…"

"That Tommy is innocent of the charges laid against him," interrupted Mrs. White.

"Well, yes, I suppose you could put it that way. At any rate, I believe that Tommy was telling the truth when he said that he had nothing to do with Bruce stealing from his father's shop. Unfortunately Mr. Ray has no proof. It is only Tommy's word against Bruce's."

"In that case he shouldn't be punishing Tommy if there is no proof."

"All the same, Mrs. White, Tommy did make physical threats to Bruce and he admitted it to Mr. Ray. I'm afraid that looked bad for Tommy. Anyway, both boys are suspended for a week so they are being treated alike. I think the best thing for Tommy is to accept his punishment and show Mr. Ray by his good conduct that he is actually a first rate pupil, as I believe he is."

All the time she was speaking Tommy did not take his eyes from her face. Elizabeth looked at him. "Are you prepared to accept this punishment, Tommy, and prove to everybody what a fine boy you really are?"

"Yes, Miss Brookfield," he said, sitting up very straight and squaring his shoulders. Despite his eight years he suddenly looked manly. His mother was gazing at him, pride in her eyes.

"OK, Miss Brookfield, if Tommy is prepared to take that attitude I will go along with it."

"Thank you, Mrs. White," said Elizabeth relieved. The tension had gone out of the atmosphere and Mrs. White even smiled as Elizabeth opened her satchel and took out the work. As simply as she could Elizabeth explained what had been planned for the week and how it should be apportioned daily. Both Tommy and his mother listened carefully.

At the end Mrs. White offered Elizabeth a cup of tea. "I'd love to stop," she said regretfully, "but I really have to go."

As she was bending down to pick up her satchel Mrs. White suddenly asked, "You wouldn't be connected by any chance to Miss Rose Brookfield who lives at the old house in the valley, would you?"

"Yes, I'm her great-niece and I'm actually staying with her."

"Well, I'll be jiggered. She used to be my Sunday school teacher at the Baptist church. She's a lovely lady and she was always kind to me. Please tell her I remember her well and all the Bible stories she used to tell us."

"I certainly will. I'm sure she'd be delighted to hear about any pupil she taught." A thought occurred to Elizabeth, "but she won't recognize your name."

"Of course not, tell her I was Karen MacNeish. I think I was about Tommy's age when I was in her class. Oh, and Miss Brookfield, you're welcome to come here any time and visit us. Tommy would like that wouldn't you, son?"

"Yes, Mum," he said fervently.

They both stood at the door to wave her off and as Elizabeth cycled away she felt happier than she had all day. Even the thought of visiting Bruce's home no longer filled her with dread.

She stopped outside the dairy, as the address she had been given indicated that the family lived above the shop. Dismounting from her bike she propped it on its stand and lifted her satchel out of the basket. Taking a deep breath she entered the shop. To her surprise it was empty so she pressed the bell on the counter and waited. After what seemed a long time, though it was probably only seconds, a woman entered quietly through a door at the back of the shop. She was small and mouse-like, with wispy brown hair and a sharp little face. She stared at Elizabeth and slowly recognition crept into her eyes.

"You are Bruce's teacher, aren't you?"

"Yes, I'm Elizabeth Brookfield and I've come with Bruce's work for next week." Elizabeth took the package out of her satchel and handed it across to the woman who took it from her silently. She turned it over in her hands then looked up at Elizabeth.

"My husband is very angry about all this," she said. "He thinks Bruce should not be punished because he stole out of fear, but I said that if Bruce was being threatened he should have come and told us, not taken the lollies, because that is still theft."

"I think you're right, Mrs. Bulloch. Bruce needs to learn that theft is theft, whatever the reason."

"It's making a lot of trouble in our home," and to Elizabeth's amazement the woman began to sob, great tearing sobs that shook her body.

Elizabeth leaned across the counter and took the woman's hand. "I'm very sorry," was all she could say.

Mrs. Bulloch straightened her shoulders and taking a handkerchief from her pocket dabbed at her eyes. "It's not your fault," she murmured, "though my husband blames you and me too. Oh, if you knew what hell it is here," and she sobbed again.

"Look, if there is anything I can do, Mrs. Bulloch."

The woman looked at her with bloodshot eyes. "No, there's nothing but if this goes on I'll leave him, I really will. I don't know how long I can bear this."

The woman seemed to have lost all control so Elizabeth

went behind the counter and put her arms around the thin shoulders. Mrs. Bulloch leaned against her like a child. "Can I make you a cup of tea?" Elizabeth said gently.

"That would be nice. There's a room behind here," and she indicated a door behind her.

They both moved into the small sitting room where a kettle stood on a sink. Mrs. Bulloch sank into an easy chair and Elizabeth put on the kettle. Everything was to hand and once the kettle had boiled she made the tea and poured it into two mugs. "Do you take sugar?" she asked.

"I shouldn't be leaving it all to you," said Mrs. Bulloch helplessly. "You are very kind."

"I just want to help you. It sounds as though you are under a lot of strain. Is there anybody you can talk to? Have you a sister or close relative?"

"No, not around here, we moved up from Christchurch a couple of years ago when we bought this shop and things have gone from bad to worse. We have a mortgage and the shop is not paying. My husband is very worried and this trouble with Bruce seems to have been the last straw. He's so angry and he takes it out on me."

Elizabeth looked at the poor woman in front of her and felt overwhelming pity. "Look, Mrs. Bulloch, please regard me as a friend. I'll do all I can to help Bruce and if you want to talk to me at any time just get in touch with me. Actually, I came to tell you how the work should be apportioned on a daily basis."

"Oh yes, of course, I should be attending to that," and the woman gave herself a shake.

Elizabeth opened the satchel and took out the papers. As she now had Mrs. Bulloch's attention she explained each piece of work slowly and carefully.

"You have prepared all that very thoroughly," Mrs. Bulloch said looking at Elizabeth gratefully. "When will you be coming back again to pick it up?"

"I'll come again on Monday after school. If you can start the programme on Monday morning then I'll have some work to mark. We must keep up Bruce's interest in school."

"Yes, he is only young and I do want him to be a good boy."

"Of course, and we will do our best for him, so I'll see you on Monday then."

"I'll look forward to that. You've helped me a lot," said Mrs. Bulloch trying to smile, though tears welled up in her eyes once more.

"I'll see my way out," said Elizabeth leaving the room.

As she went through the shop she looked around her. On the shelves were the usual small grocery items and on the counter were rows of packet sweets and chocolates. The shop was well stocked yet it had a forlorn air, but perhaps that was only her imagination, wondered Elizabeth.

Once she was outside she began to breathe freely again and the sense of oppression lifted from her as she mounted the bicycle. *How different this interview had been from what she expected. That poor woman was surely on the edge of a breakdown.*

As Elizabeth cycled home she felt older. Her experiences of the past few days had opened her eyes to the misery there was, even in a quiet place like Nelson.

CHAPTER EIGHT

Elizabeth woke with a start. The sun was well up and flooding the room with light. Elizabeth threw back the covers then suddenly remembered that it was Saturday. She sank back on to the pillow and for some minutes lay thinking about the day ahead. David said he would be coming with the scouts sometime after ten. Looking at the clock she saw that it was already eight thirty.

She thought what to wear today. It was already hot so she needed something cool and casual. Shorts and a shirt seemed the obvious choice, yet if she would be helping grub up the gorse her bare legs would get scratched in shorts. Jeans were the better option even if they were hot and tight.

Half an hour later Elizabeth went downstairs. The aunts were seated at the kitchen table. They looked up in surprise as Elizabeth appeared at the door. "You're up bright and early," said Aunt Rose. "We thought you would want to sleep in this morning, Elizabeth. You have to get up so early on school mornings."

"I've had an extra hour as it is," replied Elizabeth smiling. "Anyway, David and the scouts will be here any time after ten so I need to arrange with Uncle Mal about tools for them."

"I suppose you do. Make sure Mal doesn't try to help, Elizabeth. It's very hot today and he shouldn't exert himself at all." Aunt Rose's forehead puckered.

"No, I'll see that he keeps in the shade and doesn't do any work," Elizabeth said firmly.

"I'll make up a jug of ginger beer and give you sandwiches and biscuits to take out at midday. Young boys always have good appetites, especially if they've been working."

"Thanks, Aunt Rose; I'll help cut the sandwiches."

Shortly afterwards Aunt Gertrude left the room but while Elizabeth ate her breakfast Aunt Rose made a fresh pot of tea. As she poured it she commented, "You seemed very tired yesterday when you came home from school, Elizabeth, and you were a lot later than I would have expected, especially as you were finishing early."

Nothing much misses Aunt Rose, thought Elizabeth. She said, "I had to call on the parents of the two boys who are suspended for the week, to let them have the work they need to do. I went to Tommy's house first. His mother asked me if I was related to Miss Rose Brookfield and when I told her you were my aunt she said that you had been her Sunday school teacher. She said that her name was Karen MacNeish."

Aunt Rose looked thoughtful. "Yes, I remember Karen. She was a quiet little girl with fair hair. She was always very attentive and attended Sunday school regularly. Well I never, fancy her being married with five children of her own. Didn't you say something about her husband having been in prison?"

"Yes, he's still in prison and it looks as though she's having a struggle to keep going."

"It's not surprising. Poor girl, she can't be very old and to have to manage on her own with so many children…" Aunt Rose trailed off. Her expression was sad. "I wish we could do something for her, Elizabeth. I wonder…"

"Yes, Aunt Rose."

"I wonder if we could invite her to bring the children up here one day, to play in the garden while I talk to her. It wouldn't be much but it might help her to have someone to take an interest." Aunt Rose suddenly became brisk. "I'll write a note to her and next time you visit the home you could give it to her, Elizabeth." With that she stood up. "Well, dear, we'd better get on with preparing that tray for lunch," she said.

Promptly at ten thirty David appeared at the kitchen door. He was surrounded by boys in scout uniform who peered curiously through the open door. Elizabeth counted them. There were only six but it seemed like more.

"Hello, David," she said smiling. "I see you have brought a good number of helpers with you. Is this 'Bob a Job' day?"

"Well, it could be, eh, boys?"

"Yes, Sir," they chorused.

"If they do a good job, any contribution to the fund would be appreciated," said David promptly. "We are saving for a new scout hut at the moment. Anyway, lead us to the work place, Miss Brookfield."

"Follow me, everybody," said Elizabeth.

She led them round the front of the house to Uncle Mal's whare where he was waiting for them, leaning against the door his pipe in his mouth. An array of tools was propped up beside him in a couple of buckets.

Elizabeth made the introductions briefly. "Uncle Mal, this is David and his scouts who have come to help this morning."

Uncle Mal removed his pipe and held out his hand. "Call me Mal," he said, "Everyone else does." David shook his hand warmly.

"The tools are there," said Uncle Mal indicating the buckets. "Perhaps some of you could carry them." There was a scramble as boys pushed each other to get to the buckets. "Steady on," said Uncle Mal laughing. "You've got an eager bunch here," he said to David. "Now follow me and I'll take you over to the pits."

He set off through the gate into the paddock, the boys clustering around him asking questions nineteen to the dozen while David and Elizabeth followed. David was gazing interestedly about him.

"What an amazing place! That hill behind the house and the stream running all the way down through the property."

"It's called Sugarloaf."

"How descriptive! Have you climbed it, Elizabeth?"

"Give me a chance?" She laughed. "I've only been here a week and most of that time I've been teaching."

"I'd have been up it the first day. What a marvellous view you would get from the top." David's lean face was alight with enthusiasm.

By now they were nearly at the first tanning pit. Uncle Mal stopped and pointed into it. "This is the first of the eight tanning pits. As you can see I have cleared four of them, but there are still four to go. Do you think you can manage it, boys?"

"Yeah, easy!" said one and there was a murmur of assent.

"Now you take your orders from your master."

Mal turned to David. "I suggest that you use the clippers and cut low to the ground. There are a few pairs of gardening gloves for those who are going to drag the branches out. Be careful, gorse is full of thorns. If you make a heap of them we can set fire to them in a few days' time once they are dried out."

David listened carefully then told the boys to gather round. Elizabeth was impressed by the clear and simple instructions he gave. Then he divided the boys into teams to work on different sections. Already the sun was getting hot and she looked at Uncle Mal who was standing bare- headed.

"Shall we leave them to it, Uncle Mal and go and sit in the shade somewhere?"

"I want to see what they are doing," he replied firmly.

She looked around. A large cabbage tree was conveniently nearby. "We could sit under that. Look, there's a wheelbarrow. That would make a good seat for you. I'm happy to sit on the ground."

Uncle Mal took out his pipe and lit it, perching on the edge of the wheelbarrow. From there they could both watch the work going on. David had his sleeves rolled back and a thick lock of curly hair fell over his forehead. From time to time he wiped his brow, but still worked on, steadily hacking at the gorse and never looking up. The boys pulled and tugged at the untidy branches and steadily the pile grew.

At a quarter to twelve Elizabeth slipped away. Quickly she crossed the paddock and let herself through the gate. When she reached the kitchen she crossed to the table where there were a couple of trays covered with tea towels. Then she opened the fridge and took out two large jugs of ginger beer which she placed carefully on each of the trays.

Aunt Rose came through from the living room. "Are you able to manage all that, Elizabeth?"

"I'll make two trips, Aunt Rose." Walking back, while balancing the tray, was no easy feat and when she reached the shelter of the tree Elizabeth laid it on the grass thankfully. "I'm just going for the second one," she murmured, pleased to see that Uncle Mal was puffing quite contentedly at his pipe.

When she returned with the second tray it was already past twelve o'clock. She walked over to where David and the boys were working.

"Smoko!" she called. They all looked up, their faces red and glistening with perspiration. "Put your tools down and come and have some lunch." David straightened up slowly.

"I think you've done enough for today. It's getting too hot now." Elizabeth was concerned for him.

"OK, stop work, boys," said David.

Wearily they straggled across the grass and sat down under the tree. Elizabeth lifted the covers off the trays and there was a murmur of appreciation when they saw the plates of sandwiches and biscuits. Elizabeth carefully poured the ginger beer into plastic beakers and handed them around, beginning with Uncle Mal. Gratefully they downed the cool sweet liquid. She then passed the plates of sandwiches around, telling the boys to take two at a time. It was not long before all the

101

sandwiches were gone and then the biscuits. There was just enough ginger beer for everyone to have a second mugful.

"You haven't had anything yourself, Elizabeth," said David.

"I'll have my lunch later. I haven't been working like you."

After lunch the boys were eager to get started again.

"I think they should stop now," said Elizabeth. "We don't want them to get sunstroke. What arrangements have you made to get them home, David?"

"I'll take them back in the van and drop them off at their homes. Then, do you mind if I come back after that, Elizabeth? That will give me a chance to talk to your uncle. There hasn't been time so far." He addressed the boys. "Come on, lads, we'll be on our way."

"Oh, Sir, do we have to go now?"

"'Fraid so." He turned to Uncle Mal, "Would you mind if I brought the boys back another day? They're just longing to explore your place."

"You're very welcome. The boys have done a grand job. Look, here's half a crown for each of you." He pressed coins into the outstretched hands.

"Gee, thanks Sir," they said fervently.

"You can keep a shilling of that and put the rest into the fund," said David with a wink.

The boys ran ahead across the paddock full of energy, while the adults followed at a leisurely pace. Elizabeth stole a sideways glance at Uncle Mal. He looked relaxed and happy. The contact with young people obviously did him good and Elizabeth was glad that David had brought the boys with him.

When they reached the house and were passing in front of the verandah Uncle Mal said, "I think I'll sit down for a while and wait for you to return, David." The boys clustered around him.

"Thanks for a beaut day, Sir," said one.

"I can't wait to come back," said another.

Uncle Mal lit his pipe and smiled, his eyes twinkling under bushy eyebrows.

"Come on, boys," said David hustling them. "Bye for now, Elizabeth. I should be back in about an hour."

As they disappeared around the corner of the house Uncle Mal looked up at Elizabeth. "A fine young man that, Missy. You could do a lot worse. He's a worker, hardly stopped out there in all that heat."

Elizabeth looked thoughtful. "Yes, I noticed that too. I think I'll go and have a bite to eat. Would you like me to bring you a cup of tea out here?"

"A great idea!"

Elizabeth hurried off. In the kitchen Aunt Rose and Aunt Gertrude were both seated at the table finishing their lunch.

"Those lads certainly enjoyed themselves out there. We heard them chattering as they went past the door," said Aunt Gertrude. "He seems a nice enough young man, Elizabeth. What did you say his name was?"

"David, David Welch."

"Mm, he's not what you'd call handsome, but he looks pleasant."

"Handsome is as handsome does," said Aunt Rose, reprovingly.

Aunt Gertrude laughed then looked at Elizabeth shrewdly. "All the same, I have the feeling that Elizabeth has some romantic notions about men. Would I be right? I know when I was young I liked a man to be good looking."

"David's good fun to be with," said Elizabeth, immediately defensive.

"No doubt," said Aunt Gertrude ironically.

Elizabeth was glad to make the tea and escape to the verandah. Being with Uncle Mal was more relaxing than parrying the remarks of Aunt Gertrude. She found him puffing away at his pipe contentedly. Elizabeth sat down on one of the cane chairs and poured out the tea. Then she lay back and let the peace of the garden steal over her. There was no need to talk and gradually she felt her eyes close. She was not sure how long she sat like this but suddenly she heard footsteps. She sat up with a start as David appeared round the corner.

"Hello," he said cheerfully. "It didn't take me as long as I thought it would. Oh, is that a pot of tea, I see?"

"It'll be quite cold now," said Elizabeth quickly. "I'll go and make a fresh one. Sit down, David, I won't be long."

When she came back she found the two men deep in conversation. Uncle Mal was explaining the tanning process to David, who was sitting forward listening with rapt attention. Elizabeth poured the tea giving only half an ear to what was being said. She was more interested in studying David, as she thought of Aunt Gertrude's observations about him. Suddenly her attention was caught by something Uncle Mal was saying.

"If you are interested in history, here's something for you, David. The first railway in New Zealand was built in Nelson, just down the road from here."

"Which is that?"

"The Dun Mountain Railway, and here's something else of interest. It was opened almost exactly one hundred years ago, on the third of February, 1862."

"Why, that was a hundred years ago last Saturday!" exclaimed Elizabeth.

"That's right, Missy, and we were at the unveiling of the memorial plaque."

"That must have been just before I arrived in the afternoon."

"Yes, your aunts didn't want to put you off so they said nothing about it."

"Why was a railway laid here, of all places?" asked David.

"Well, they discovered copper and a large deposit of chromite up on Wooded Peak north-west of the Dun Mountain."

"What is chromite, Uncle Mal? I've never heard of it," asked Elizabeth.

"It's a mineral used as a dye. You know that the cotton

industry was very important in England last century. Well, chromite produced yellow and mauve dyes for the cotton."

"So they thought it was worthwhile to transport chromite all the way from New Zealand to Britain," said David thoughtfully.

"Yes, but because the mineral deposits were high up on the mountain they needed a railway to run from the mines down to the port."

"That must have been a huge undertaking in those days," said David.

"It was, and very costly too. A group of men got together and formed a syndicate but they had to go to England to raise the necessary capital. They got the money too. Their representative was a man called Wrey and he came back with the money and twenty-four miners."

"How long was the railway?" asked Elizabeth.

"At first it was intended to go through the Maitai Valley and according to the original plans it would have been almost ten miles."

"So what happened to change it?"

"Well, they sent in an engineer, a man called Hackett, to investigate the copper deposits and he found that there was not sufficient copper to make it worthwhile mining but that there was a good amount of chromite higher up on Wooded Peak. To reach it they needed to find a new and more direct route for the railway and that is when they settled on the Brook Valley."

"Did they use engines for the railway?" asked Elizabeth.

"Goodness no, it was all horse drawn. From Brook Street the horses drew the empty wagons up the incline to the mines on the summit. This was in the morning. Then the horses were returned to a base further down the mountain. When the wagons were filled they were put under the control of a brakeman who controlled the speed as they descended, using the force of gravity this time. They were only allowed to go four miles an hour, otherwise they would have run the risk of being derailed."

"What happened when the wagons reached the bottom of the hill?" asked David.

"They had enough momentum to continue all the way to the corner of Hardy Street and Rutherford Street. Then they were hitched to horses that pulled them through the city and all the way to the port."

"So there would have been railway lines right through the centre of Nelson. Did they ever use it to carry passengers?" asked Elizabeth.

"Oh yes, but that was mainly after the mines closed in 1866."

"Gosh, that was only two years after they opened!" exclaimed David. "What happened?"

"There were two reasons really," said Uncle Mart slowly, drawing on his pipe. "First, the chromite deposits began to run out and the ore that was left was poor quality. Then the cotton mills stopped production because their supplies of cotton from America were blocked because of the Civil War."

"Couldn't they import cotton from other places?" said David.

"I suppose they tried, but the cotton from Egypt and India was not of the same quality as the cotton from the southern states and so gradually the mills closed down. As you probably know, there was a lot of hardship among the mill workers once they were laid off."

"Oh yes, I remember when I was studying English at University we had to read 'Hard Times' by Charles Dickens and 'North and South' by Mrs. Gaskell. Both those books were set against the background of the strikes by cotton mill workers. It's strange to think that a railway so far away in New Zealand was affected by what was going on the other side of the world," said Elizabeth.

"So what happened to the railway after that?" persisted David.

"Since there was no further need for a railway up to the mine that part of the line was dismantled, but the remainder from Brook Street into the city was retained for passenger services. A horse drawn tram was bought from an Australian company and this was called The Dun Mountain Bus and it operated across the city. It was not supposed to go more than four miles an hour but in practice it often did more than that. Anyway this was the first city tramway in New Zealand and it operated until 1901."

"What an amazing history!" said David, "and to think it all took place virtually on your doorstep."

"You know an awful lot about it, Uncle Mal," said Elizabeth looking at the old man admiringly.

"That's not surprising, Missy. My mother and father used to speak of it constantly. In 1862 when the Dun Mountain Railway was opened my father built this house, so the house and the railway had the same beginnings."

David stood up. "I really must go," he said glancing at his watch. "I'm expected back for dinner. My landlady gets ropable if I'm late and her carefully prepared meals are cold. Thank you so much for an interesting day, Mal. You are very lucky to live here, Elizabeth." He smiled at them both and disappeared round the corner of the house. Elizabeth sighed. With his going it seemed suddenly too quiet. Uncle Mart seemed to sense it too.

"Pity he had to go so soon. It's good for you to have young company."

"I'm very happy the way things are," Elizabeth said quickly.

"Now, I'm going to milk Bessie," he said gruffly. "You go and see what those aunts of yours are up to." With that he stood up stiffly.

As Elizabeth collected up the tea things her thoughts were busy with the events of the day and all that she had been hearing. Suddenly a bellbird called, the clear notes rising and falling in the still air. Elizabeth stopped and listened. *How many others like her over the past hundred years had stood in this place and heard the same bird song?*

CHAPTER NINE

Sunday morning was misty. When Elizabeth woke she was surprised that for the first time in a week the room was not bright and sunny. She lay for a few minutes thinking over the events of yesterday then her mind switched to the day that lay before her. Last night she had decided that this Sunday she would attend the Baptist church with her aunts and uncle. It would be a way of showing that she regarded herself as part of the family. Also their reaction last week showed how much attendance at a Sunday service meant to them, but even beyond this Elizabeth felt it was important to show some respect for the God she had pleaded with when Uncle Mal was ill. Going to church was one way of showing gratitude.

Slowly and thoughtfully she chose her clothes for the day. She would wear her best outfit, a slim fitting dark blue dress with a dropped waistline. It was the kind of dress that would look right for any occasion and one she felt comfortable in.

When Elizabeth went downstairs her breakfast was laid as usual but the rest of the table was clear. She was just making herself a cup of tea when Aunt Rose appeared at the door. "You do look nice, Elizabeth. Are you dressed for church?"

"Yes, I would like to come with you this morning, if that is alright."

"Of course, it will be a little squashed in the back of the car, if you don't mind. Mal drives and I usually sit in the front with him: order of seniority, in other words being the eldest and most decrepit," she added with a smile.

"What time do you leave, Aunt Rose?"

She glanced at the clock, "Oh, in about twenty minutes."

"I'll make sure I'm waiting here on the dot," said Elizabeth firmly, more to herself than Aunt Rose.

She went upstairs to see that she had everything ready:- handkerchief, collection, Bible. Last of all she checked her hair and makeup. Allowing herself an extra five minutes she went downstairs and waited just outside the kitchen door. By now the mist had lifted except for a few wisps that still lingered in the orchard. There was a Sunday stillness over everything, even the birds seemed hushed this morning. Suddenly Elizabeth heard footsteps and the next moment Uncle Mal appeared around the corner of the house. Elizabeth stared. Could this upright man in the smart navy blue suit, white collar and striped tie be the same person who slopped around in worn old clothes every day of the week? He saw her look of astonishment and chuckled.

"You didn't expect me to go to the Lord's house in my working clothes, Elizabeth?"

"Well, no, but you look so different."

"That you didn't recognize me, eh? Just remember, Missy, 'fine feathers make fine birds.' You look very nice yourself," he added. "Are you coming with us this morning?"

"Yes, if I may."

Just then the two aunts appeared; Aunt Rose in a pale blue floral dress that brought out the blue of her eyes and Aunt Gertrude in a mauve linen suit that emphasized her slimness. *They both look extremely smart,* thought Elizabeth.

"Your chauffeur is ready," said Uncle Mal, and Elizabeth was struck by his change of manner. *He seems almost skittish, if that was the word.*

While they waited on the path outside the kitchen Uncle Mal

went into the garage and a few seconds later they heard the car starting up. Elizabeth followed the aunts through the gate into the drive. Uncle Mal opened the doors for each one of them, paying particular attention to Aunt Rose whom he helped into the passenger seat. As she eased herself into the back seat Elizabeth noticed how spotless the interior was. The faint sweet smell could have been from a cleaner or there again it could be perfume. She moved slightly forward to make more room for Aunt Gertrude.

Uncle Mal drove carefully along the now familiar roads and minutes later drew up outside the plain wooden building that was the Baptist church. It stood well back from the road with a large asphalt area at the side for parking. There were no trees to relieve the starkness, only a large notice board which announced the times of the morning and evening services and underneath in smaller lettering the name of the minister.

Uncle Mal handed out Aunt Rose first and then Aunt Gertrude, leaving Elizabeth to see to herself. While he locked the car the aunts and Elizabeth waited. Then they walked together towards the entrance. At the door they were greeted by a balding middle-aged man with a florid complexion, who handed each of them a hymn book and a notice sheet. He looked inquiringly at Elizabeth.

"This is Elizabeth, our great-niece from Auckland, who is staying with us," said Aunt Rose.

"Welcome to Nelson, Elizabeth," said the man warmly as he clasped her hand.

"Thank you," and Elizabeth smiled back at him.

There were two aisles dividing the pews. Elizabeth followed her aunts and uncle as they walked purposefully down the left aisle and into one of the front pews. Elizabeth sat down feeling self-conscious. She told herself not to be silly. Many strangers probably visited the church and there was no reason why people should be particularly interested in her. Nevertheless, she could feel the back of her neck growing hot.

Some minutes later she heard footsteps behind them and

turning slightly was amazed to see Tommy and his family filing into the pew on the opposite side of the aisle. As they sat down Mrs. White gave Elizabeth a quick smile then bent her head to say something to Tommy who was sitting next to her. He leaned over and smiled shyly at Elizabeth. The aunts appeared not to have noticed them. Aunt Rose's eyes were closed and Aunt Gertrude was studying her hymn book. Beside Elizabeth Uncle Mal was gazing thoughtfully in front of him.

Suddenly the man sitting on his own in the front pew stood up and went forward to stand in front of the congregation. He was tall and angular with thinning hair. There was nothing attractive about him, yet when he began to speak Elizabeth was arrested by his voice. It was rich and mellow, curiously at odds with his appearance.

"Welcome to you all this morning," he began, "especially to our visitors today. We are very glad to have you join us for worship and I hope that when you go away you will feel that it was good to be here." The words were ordinary enough but they were said with a depth of sincerity that made Elizabeth feel he was speaking directly to her.

He announced the first hymn and the organist played the opening verse. Elizabeth was struck by the words: "God moves in a mysterious way, His wonders to perform." *How true that was*, she thought. *What a curious chain of events had brought Tommy and his mother to be at the service this morning.*

As the hymn progressed she was arrested by verse four: "Behind a frowning providence He hides a smiling face." *Was that the way to look at misfortunes then? Was God really behind everything that happened, good and bad?*

They came to the end of the hymn and everyone sat down. The minister went to stand behind the lectern. "I'm going to read from Joshua, Chapter Two," he announced in his resonant voice. Elizabeth listened fascinated to the story of Rahab, the prostitute who hid the Israelite spies that came to her city on a reconnaissance mission. Through her help they were able to evade the soldiers who were sent to find them. Rahab also provided the spies with valuable information that they could carry back to their leader Joshua.

The minister paused at the end of the reading. "God often surprises us by the people he uses to accomplish his purposes. Rahab was a prostitute, a woman of the streets, yet she recognized that the God of the Israelites was the one true God and she was prepared to follow him, come what may. Eventually Rahab married an Israelite and she became the great-grandmother of David the psalmist. She is also mentioned as being in the genealogical line of our Lord and she is listed in the book of Hebrews among the great men of faith. How many of us would imagine a woman like that could be used by God? Yet He does not look at people the way we do. He is not impressed by outward respectability. He knows what is in our hearts. Those people around you that may appear in your eyes to be of no consequence, in God's eyes could be the most important of all."

Elizabeth stole a look at Mrs. White. She was sitting forward, her eyes fixed on the preacher. He did not prolong the sermon, obviously believing in brevity. *Yet nobody who heard the sermon this morning could go home unsure of the message,* thought Elizabeth.

After the last hymn and the benediction the service came to a close. Aunt Rose leaned forward to pick up her handbag and Elizabeth moved out of the pew. She noticed Mrs. White was bending down to speak to the twins.

Tommy came forward and said shyly, "Hello, Miss Brookfield."

"Hello, Tommy, it is lovely to see you here. I was very surprised when you all came in."

Mrs. White turned around when she heard Elizabeth's voice. "Oh, hello, Miss Brookfield, I was hoping to have a word with your aunt."

Elizabeth saw that Aunt Rose was talking to an elderly lady with a cane.

"I'll tell her you're here," replied Elizabeth. She went and stood quietly beside Aunt Rose who took her arm and drew her forward.

"This is Elizabeth, my great-niece. I was just telling you about her."

"Hello, Elizabeth, I remember your father when he was a small boy and used to come to Nelson." It was clear the lady was about to launch into a series of reminiscences so Elizabeth listened politely for a few minutes, waiting for a pause, then said quickly, "Aunt Rose, there is someone who would like to speak to you."

"Oh is there? Who could that be?"

"I'll just go and fetch her."

She left the two old ladies gazing after her and she went back to where Mrs. White stood holding the baby, with the children clustered around her.

"Mrs. White, Aunt Rose is just over there," said Elizabeth pointing.

"Come on children," said Mrs. White and she moved down the aisle towards Aunt Rose, the children straggling behind her.

"Miss Brookfield," she said shyly, "You probably don't remember me but I used to be in your Sunday school class."

"Oh yes, I do. You were Karen McNeish. Elizabeth told me that your little boy Tommy was in her class. This is Tommy isn't it?" she said looking down at him with a kindly smile.

"Say hello to Miss Brookfield, Tommy," prompted his mother.

"Hello, Miss Brookfield," he replied, gazing up into Aunt Rose's face.

"I've heard such good reports of you from my niece, Tommy," said Aunt Rose, "and I'm so glad to meet you." At her kind words Mrs. White beamed. "And you, my dear, it is so lovely to meet you after all these years. I wouldn't have known you, of course. You were only a little girl when you were in my class."

"Yes, I would have been about the same age as Tommy."

"And you've got all these other children too. What a lovely baby. She hasn't made a sound through the service, nor have

113

the other children. They have been so good," and Aunt Rose bent down to smile at the twins and Susie, who gazed back at her.

Aunt Rose straightened up and looked into the young mother's face. "I was wondering, my dear, if you weren't too busy today whether you would like to come and have tea with us this afternoon. My brother would fetch you in his car."

There was a pause then Tommy spoke. "Please, Mum, could we?"

"Well, that seems to be our answer. Yes, we'd love to come. Are you sure it isn't too much for you to have the whole lot of us?"

"I think we're used to children," replied Aunt Rose with a twinkle in her blue eyes. "There used to be nine of us and there were always cousins as well. Shall we say three o'clock then?"

"We'll look forward to that. Come on children, we'd better get along home." Mrs. White gathered her children like a hen her chickens and moved towards the door.

"Well, we'd better get along too, Elizabeth. Sorry I haven't been able to speak much to you, Jane." Aunt Rose addressed the old lady who was still sitting in the pew leaning on her stick, "but we'll catch up during the week at the Women's Meeting." With that she moved briskly towards the door with Elizabeth following.

As they passed through the vestibule several people greeted Aunt Rose and looked curiously at Elizabeth. "I expect Gertrude and Mal are waiting in the car," murmured Aunt Rose. Sure enough they were, Gertrude looking impatient and Mal staring straight ahead of him.

As soon as they arrived home the aunts put on aprons and began preparing lunch. As usual, on a Sunday there was cold meat and salad with hot potato. Elizabeth helped set the table in the living room, which doubled as a dining room as they had most of their meals there. When everything was ready they sat down in their usual places. Uncle Mal said a brief grace then began carving meat from the cold lamb joint.

At the end of the meal Aunt Rose looked up and said, "We are having visitors for tea."

"Oh, who is that?" asked Gertrude.

"A former Sunday School pupil of mine, Karen MacNeish. She is bringing her family with her. They all seem to be very young. What ages are they Elizabeth?"

"Tommy's the oldest. He's eight. Then there is a little girl of four and the twins who are two years old. Oh, and there is the baby as well."

"Quite a brood! She must be very busy with all those kiddies under five," remarked Aunt Gertrude. "I've never heard you mention that name, Rose. How is it that you have suddenly come into contact with her?"

"She happened to be at church this morning."

"Oh, that was the family in the pew opposite ours. What time are they coming this afternoon?"

"Not until three. I wondered if you would go and collect them, Mal. Elizabeth will give you the directions." He nodded and looked enquiringly at Elizabeth.

"I'll write the address down for you," she said.

"What are you giving them for tea, Rose?" asked Gertrude.

"We've got plenty of cake and biscuits. I'll make a pile of sandwiches and a red jelly for the children. That with some ice cream should go down well."

"Sounds just right, Aunt Rose," said Elizabeth enthusiastically. "I'll help cut some sandwiches after lunch."

By two o'clock everything was ready and on plates covered with tea towels. The aunts went off to their rooms and Uncle Mal to his whare. Elizabeth decided to sit on the verandah with her book but it wasn't long before the warmth of the afternoon sun lulled her into a state of lazy reverie.

Promptly at quarter to three Uncle Mal appeared round the corner of the verandah and Elizabeth handed him the piece of paper on which she had written the address. He took it from her and scanned it briefly. "Ah yes, I know exactly where that is." He smiled and set off smartly along the path. Elizabeth stood and watched him, wondering at the change in him since the day she had arrived. Thoughtfully she went upstairs to her room. As she was combing her hair and applying fresh lipstick Elizabeth wondered about the afternoon to come and this unusual tea party.

Downstairs she found the aunts bustling about in the kitchen. "There they are now!" exclaimed Elizabeth as she heard the car pulling into the drive.

She ran down the path and opened the gate just as Uncle Mal was helping Mrs. White from the car. She had the baby in her arms and was awkwardly clutching a large cloth bag.

Elizabeth said quickly, "Let me take the bag," and Mrs. White handed it to her gratefully.

Elizabeth bent down peering into the back of the car where the four children were sitting, Tommy and Susie gazing around them wide-eyed, the twins bouncing excitedly on the seat. Uncle Mal opened the door and they all seemed to tumble out at once. They looked up shyly at the old man as he smiled down at them from under his shaggy brows.

"Come and meet the rest of the family," he said to the children, then turning to Mrs. White, "Of course you know my sister Rose."

"Oh yes."

They all followed Uncle Mal as far as the kitchen door where Aunt Rose stood waiting to welcome them. "What a lovely family!" she said looking down at the children who clustered around their mother. "Do all come in," and she led them through the kitchen and into the parlour where Gertrude was sitting. She rose gracefully from an easy chair and came forward to meet the little crowd as they stood hesitantly at the door.

"This is my sister, Miss Gertrude Brookfield," said Aunt Rose. All eyes turned to her.

"And you must be Karen, my sister's past pupil," said

Gertrude with a warm smile. "Do sit down," and she gestured towards one of the chairs. "What a beautiful baby! Do you think she would mind if I held her? I adore babies." She said this sincerely.

Elizabeth looked at her amazed. This was a side of Aunt Gertrude she would never have suspected. Mrs. White handed over the baby and Gertrude took her easily into her arms, while the children watched open-mouthed.

Uncle Mal had been standing behind the group but now he cleared his throat. "While all this baby adoration is going on perhaps the other children would like to come with me and see something of the farm."

"Oh, yes please," said Tommy and Susie together. The twins were standing with their fingers in their mouths, mesmerized by their new surroundings.

"Well, you two come with me," he said to the older two.

"And we'll take care of the younger ones," said Aunt Rose quickly. "I'll get some toys for them."

She left the room and was back within minutes with a box full of small toys of all kinds. She put this in a corner and immediately the twins began rummaging in it.

"You sit down, Aunt Rose, and I'll make a cup of tea," said Elizabeth moving towards the kitchen.

When she came back some time later with the tea things on a tray she could see that the ice was broken and the three women were chattering unreservedly.

After they had finished their tea Aunt Gertrude got up with the baby in her arms. "Look, she's fast asleep. Would you like me to lay her on the settee?" She looked at Mrs. White. "I can arrange some rugs and make her comfortable. That way you won't have to hold her all the time. It must make you very tired." While she was speaking Gertrude was busy placing rugs into position and then she laid the sleeping baby on them. "There, she'll be fine now," she said. "I'll leave you to talk about old times for a while," and she left the room through the door into the passage.

Aunt Rose drew her chair closer to Mrs. White. "Now, Karen, tell me all about yourself. I think the last time I saw you, you were about eight. A lot of water has gone under the bridge since then."

"It certainly has. Well, where shall I start? My parents moved to Blenheim from here and life changed for us. Dad lost his job and times were hard. I had to leave school at fifteen and went to work in a haberdashery. I was disappointed because I really wanted to train as a nurse but we needed the money. Anyway, I stuck that out but I wanted to get away from home. Dad was drinking quite heavily and he often came home violent after he'd been to the pub. Well, I met this guy who seemed quite nice and respectable. He was a builder and had a good job. He wanted to marry me and though I wasn't what you would call 'in love' I thought it would be better living with him than staying at home, so we got married. Tommy came along almost straight away."

"What was your husband's name?"

"Oh, didn't I say? Barry White is his name. I did tell you that he worked for a building firm didn't I? Well, it turned out that the owner of the business was unwell and so he passed on a lot of the paper work to Barry because he had a good head for figures. We were trying to save for our own home at the time and were having a struggle."

"Well, to cut a long story short, Barry began to fiddle the books and embezzled quite a large sum of money over a few months. I knew nothing about it. He just said that his wages had gone up and I didn't ask any questions. Anyway, when the accountants came in to check the books they found there was money missing and they discovered that Barry was responsible. Of course, there was a court case and he went to jail about a year ago, before the baby was born. So there you have it, my life story." She said this with a bitter twist of her mouth.

Aunt Rose had been listening carefully to every word. "You've had a hard time, Karen, but you do know that difficult circumstances are sent for a reason."

"You mean, 'Behind a frowning providence God hides a smiling face.'"

"The words from the hymn this morning; I noticed them too and it made me think over my past life. Times have not always been smooth for me either, nor for my family. I won't go into that now, because I don't like to dwell on the past, but we had something like that happen in our family and it can be very hard to recognize that behind it is a loving God, but I can assure you, He is there."

"Do you really believe that, Miss Brookfield? I wish I could. Everything seems to be bad at the moment." There was a sob in her voice.

"I think all you can do is trust God, hard as it is and pray to him. You know prayer can bring about miracles. I have seen it happen, in my life and in others." She laid a hand on Mrs. White's shoulder. "Do you mind if I pray with you now?"

"No, please do."

Aunt Rose's prayer was simple but as she spoke peace seemed to descend on the room and when she finished there was a different look on Mrs. White's face.

"Now I think we ought to call the children in for tea, Elizabeth," said Aunt Rose suddenly becoming matter of fact.

"I'll go and fetch them," Elizabeth replied. As she left the room she glanced at the corner where the twins were playing happily. There was a change in the whole atmosphere. Glancing at her watch she saw that it was four thirty. Uncle Mart would be finishing the milking by now and no doubt Tommy and his little sister were there watching him.

True enough, when she reached the woolshed Uncle Mal was just cleaning up and Bessie had already left the shed. As she came in the children looked at her with shining eyes.

"We've had a super time, Miss Brookfield. Uncle Mal even let us milk Bessie."

"Did he? Well, if you come to tea now you may even have some of Bessie's milk."

"You go on with the children, Elizabeth, I won't be long," said Uncle Mal.

They left him finishing the cleaning and all across the paddock the children chattered excitedly about their experiences that afternoon. Elizabeth tried to attend to them but her mind was on what had taken place in the parlour. It was the same over tea. The children ate ravenously of all that was on the table but Elizabeth was more occupied with watching their mother, who in a subtle way, seemed quite different.

After they had all gone, driven home by Uncle Mal, Elizabeth and Aunt Rose talked quietly about the events of the day. "Do you know," commented Elizabeth, "I would never have believed such a change could come over anybody. Mrs. White seemed a different person from the woman I visited during the week."

"It's amazing the difference prayer can make," said Aunt Rose quietly. "I've seen it happen time and again."

CHAPTER TEN

The next week went very quickly for Elizabeth. Life at school had settled into a routine and even Mr. Ray left her alone. Each afternoon John Tamati stopped at her window and chatted for a few minutes. Elizabeth found herself looking forward to seeing him at the end of the day although she told herself that there was nothing in it, John was merely being friendly. In the staffroom he kept aloof from her, usually talking with Mac or one of the other men teachers, though now and again she caught his eye on her. Then she would smile and look away.

David and Mary always reserved a seat for her in the staffroom where the three of them sat each day. On Wednesday morning at break David brought up the subject of Friday night.

"Look, Elizabeth, you missed out last week on going to the pictures. Why don't we all go this Friday? I see that Westside Story is showing at the local bughouse and you, Mary, you could make it couldn't you?"

She looked crestfallen. "Actually I can't. I'm going away for the weekend to visit my cousin in Blenheim."

"Oh well, it looks as though it will have to be a twosome again, eh Elizabeth?" he said chirpily.

Elizabeth glanced at Mary and said quickly, "I think we should ask Jeanette. She might be at a loose end this Friday."

"OK, you ask her."

When Elizabeth approached Jeanette later in the day she said, "Sorry, can't make it. I've got to finish a dress I'm making for a dance on Saturday night." So that left herself and David after all. Mentally Elizabeth shrugged.

Friday was the day she would be visiting Tommy's home and then Bruce's. She had thought a lot about Mrs. White's visit the previous Sunday and the memory of the day was like a shaft of sunlight. With Mrs. Bulloch it was different. Every thought of her seemed to be overlaid by a cloud. Elizabeth had never before encountered misery like hers and she dreaded making a return visit to the home.

Inevitably Friday arrived. At the end of the school day Elizabeth dismissed the children and gathered up the books she needed for lesson planning. She crossed the room to the window and saw coming across the playing field towards her, John Tamati. He looked as though he had something on his mind. When he reached the open window he stood for a moment his dark eyes fixed on hers.

"Look Elizabeth, I've been wanting to speak to you about a rather personal matter but I suppose you are in a hurry to get home, being Friday." He glanced at her satchel which lay on a desk near the window.

"I do have to make a couple of visits," she said hesitantly, "but never mind about that."

"It's just that I wanted you to know things have not been easy at home for quite some time." He paused. "In fact, my wife left me yesterday."

"Oh John, I'm so sorry." Elizabeth was genuinely concerned.

"Thank you, but it's been coming on for some time now. We're going for a divorce. That's the best way all round. She's gone home to her parents and once we have seen our lawyers we will come to some settlement. It's all very amicable and fortunately there are no children." Elizabeth did not know what to say.

"I suppose you're wondering why I have told you this," he

continued. "It's rather hard to explain but ever since I met you, I've felt you and I were on the same wave length, Elizabeth." He paused. "I wanted to let you know the true state of things, just in case you thought that because I'm married you shouldn't have too much to do with me." Looking into his face Elizabeth could see he was deadly serious.

"I think you realize that you mean a lot to me, Elizabeth." He paused as though waiting for a response.

Her heart was thumping so much all could say was, "Thank you for telling me this, John, but I really need to go away and think about it."

"I understand, Elizabeth." His eyes, as he gazed into hers, were pleading.

Elizabeth watched him as he walked slowly away from her, his shoulders sagging. Her chest felt tight and breathing was difficult so she sat down on the one of the children's chairs. There she remained for some time simply staring out of the window but seeing nothing. Thoughts chased each other through her brain until at last she mentally shook herself. *This is no use. I have to get going and make those visits. I'll think about all this later*. Resolutely she picked up her satchel and left the room. Glancing at her watch she saw it was already three forty-five and she had meant to leave promptly after three.

As she went out of the building nobody seemed to be around and the school had that curiously forlorn air which comes when the children have left. Elizabeth was glad to mount her cycle and leave the school grounds. It did not take her long to reach Mrs. White's. Tommy must have been watching for her, because as soon as she stopped outside the gate he came running down the path.

"I've done all my work, Miss Brookfield, and a bit extra as well." His eyes were shining under his neatly trimmed fringe.

"Well done, Tommy. I'll look forward to seeing it. Is Mum around?"

"She's in the kitchen. I'll go and tell her you're here."

He ran inside leaving Elizabeth to walk up the path. She noted with surprise that the garden looked much tidier; the lawn had been mown and there were no toys lying around. When Mrs. White appeared at the doors Elizabeth could only stare, she looked so different. Her blonde hair had been cut to shoulder length and framed her face becomingly. She was wearing makeup and as she stood in the doorway she looked girlishly pretty.

"Hello, Miss Brookfield. I was expecting you. Do come in and have afternoon tea with us. I made a sponge especially."

Tommy was standing behind her in the hallway and added, "Please do, Miss Brookfield."

Elizabeth had not intended to stay longer than a few minutes but it was impossible to refuse such an invitation. As she entered the house she looked around her amazed:- no toys lay on the floor, everything was spotless and there were even flowers on the hall table. Mrs. White led her into the sitting room and it too looked colourful and fresh - bright covers had been laid over the settee and easy chairs to hide the worn upholstery.

As Elizabeth looked around her Mrs. White laughed gaily. "Looks a bit different from the last time you saw it, eh? I decided to have a good spring clean outside and in. We've been in a muddle for too long." She leaned forward dropping her voice confidentially. "It was after visiting your aunts and uncle last Sunday. Everything changed. I felt happy for the first time in years and well, I saw that I had let things go. Anyway, I set to work and there you are?" She waved her arm around the room.

Elizabeth smiled. "I've never seen such a transformation. I will tell Aunt Rose. She will be so pleased."

Mrs. White excused herself and returned with a tray laden with tea things. She handed Elizabeth tea in a dainty china cup and offered her a slice of sponge cake.

"Where are the twins this afternoon?" Elizabeth asked.

"Oh they're having their afternoon sleep and so is Susie."

Then she began telling a story about the twins that made Elizabeth burst out laughing.

At last she stood up. "Thank you for the tea and the sponge cake. It was really delicious."

"Oh do you have to go already?" said Mrs. White.

"I'm afraid so. I have another visit to make this afternoon."

"Oh well. Tommy, go and fetch your work to give to Miss Brookfield. By the way, he will be coming back to school next Monday and I'll send a note of apology to Mr. Ray for the way I spoke to him."

Seeing Elizabeth's look of surprise she added, "I've had a change of heart since last Sunday you know." Elizabeth smiled back at her.

Tommy came running up with a large envelope and handed it to her. As she took it Elizabeth said gently, "I'll look forward to seeing you on Monday, Tommy."

A few minutes later she was on her bicycle and looking back, saw that Tommy and his mother were in the doorway waving to her. Still thinking about them and the huge change in Mrs. White Elizabeth drew up outside the Bullochs' dairy. She put the bicycle on its stand and went into the shop. As before, there was nobody behind the counter so she rang the bell. There was no response so she pressed it again. After a couple of minutes she decided to venture through the curtain at the back of the shop. The small room was empty and it did not look as though it had been used that day.

Elizabeth hesitated, wondering what to do next. There was something deathly quiet about the whole place. Taking a deep breath she put her foot on the stairs. *Here goes,* she thought. As she climbed, her footsteps sounded loud in her ears. On the landing she called out, "Is anyone home?" There was no reply. *Perhaps Mrs. Bulloch had just slipped out for a few minutes but surely she wouldn't leave the shop and house unattended.*

There was an unnatural stillness everywhere that made Elizabeth feel she should investigate further. *Could Mrs. Bulloch have met with an accident*? With this thought Elizabeth was emboldened to look into the rooms. The door on her right was closed. Tentatively she turned the handle and opened it. Lying sprawled across the bed was a woman, face downwards, her skirt rumpled up to her thighs. A smell of vomit tainted the air. Elizabeth stood, shocked for a moment, then crossed to the bed dreading what she would find. She looked down at the distorted features of Mrs. Bulloch, vomit oozing from her mouth. The woman's face was deathly pale but at least she was breathing, with slow rasping breaths.

Elizabeth glanced at the bedside table. An empty pill bottle was lying where it had fallen. Instantly Elizabeth took in the situation. *Mrs. Bulloch had taken an overdose and needed urgent medical help. Where was the phone?*

She fled from the room and into the hallway. Right in front of her was a telephone on a small table. She picked up the receiver and dialled 111. Immediately, a calm voice answered, "Would you like police, fire or ambulance?"

"An ambulance please, this is an emergency. A woman has taken an overdose and needs help desperately." Elizabeth gave the address and replaced the receiver. Now all she had to do was wait. She went downstairs and stood at the door of the shop.

It seemed like hours but in fact it was only a few minutes before the ambulance drew up outside. Two men in uniform hopped briskly out of the cab and went to the back of the van drawing out a stretcher. Elizabeth directed them upstairs to the bedroom. Expertly the men lifted the inert body onto the stretcher, securing it with a strap. Then they were down the stairs once more and lifting the stretcher into the van. The whole operation took less than five minutes.

"Are you accompanying the patient to hospital?" asked one of the men briefly.

"No, I'll stay here thank you." Elizabeth had already decided that she ought to be present when either Bruce or his father arrived home. Furthermore, the shop should not be left unattended. She could always ring the hospital to find out news of Mrs. Bulloch. She had noticed a few people gathering outside the shop when the ambulance was being loaded into the stretcher. As she went back inside a gaggle of women followed her.

"What's the matter with Mrs. Bulloch?" asked a thick-set woman with greasy black hair hitched behind her ears. *She seems more curious than concerned* thought Elizabeth, *probably one of the local gossips.*

"She had a bit of a turn so I rang the ambulance," replied Elizabeth. *There was no way that she would give this woman fuel for scandal.*

The other women were listening closely. "She never looked very healthy," said one, "such a thin woman and so pale."

"Never had much to say either," remarked a coarse looking woman, who was very pregnant.

Elizabeth wished they would go away. It was clear that they were not friends of the Bullochs and she did not want to ask them if they knew where Mr. Bulloch might be. Elizabeth suspected that he was at the pub, but if so where was Bruce? Eventually the women left, talking excitedly among themselves and ignoring Elizabeth.

After they had gone she leaned against the counter feeling suddenly exhausted. A quarter of an hour passed and there was still no sign of Bruce or Mr. Bulloch. Just as she was on the point of ringing the hospital for news, a large blonde woman burst through the door, Bruce following sheepishly behind.

"I found this kid down the road throwing stones at cars and I managed to get it out of him where he lived so I brought him home?" She looked Elizabeth up and down, evidently deciding she couldn't be his mother. "Do you know him?"

"I do actually. I'm his teacher."

"Poor you, I know what I'd do to him if he was in my class," the woman said grimly.

"Well, thank you for bringing him home. I'll take care of him now."

The woman stalked out and Bruce stood with his head down. Elizabeth paused, unsure how to proceed. She said seriously, "Is that right, Bruce, were you throwing stones at cars?"

"Yes, Miss Brookfield."

"You realize that is very dangerous, don't you? You could hurt someone, perhaps make a driver swerve and hit another car. Then there is the damage to the car as well. That could cost the driver a lot of money to get it repaired. You were very thoughtless, Bruce, and I am disappointed in you. What have you got to say? Look at me, Bruce."

"I'm sorry, Miss Brookfield."

"Will you promise me never to do it again?"

"Yes, Miss Brookfield."

"Good, then we'll say no more about it." She looked down at his face and felt compassion for him. Very gently she said, "Bruce, there is something I have to tell you. Your mum was very sick this afternoon and had to go to hospital."

His head shot up, his eyes frightened. "What's the matter with her?"

"She had difficulty breathing. I called an ambulance and they came and took her to the hospital straight away. Now it is important that we get hold of your dad and let him know. Do you have any idea where he might be?"

Bruce looked at her embarrassed. "I think he might be at the pub. He goes there most afternoons."

Elizabeth considered for a few moments. "Do you think you could take me there, Bruce? Is it far away?"

"No, not really."

"Well, let's go together straight away." She wanted to keep Bruce from going upstairs in case he should look in his mother's room.

Without ado she took his hand and together they went out of the shop. Once outside he let go of her hand and they walked

128

side by side along the quiet street as far as the corner. "The pub is just at the end of this street," said Bruce pointing.

A few minutes later they reached the hotel which was built in the manner of all such buildings at the turn of the century, having a verandah extending on all sides, supported by wooden pillars with a fretwork design in the corners. From the open doorway raucous laughter and male voices reached into the street.

Elizabeth quailed inwardly. *At this time of day the 'six o'clock swill' would be in full swing, and a pub was no place for a woman. Still, there was nothing for it; she had to find Mr. Bulloch.* She lowered her voice as she looked down at Bruce who appeared hesitant as well. "We have to go inside, Bruce, and find your dad."

She walked firmly up the steps and onto the verandah, Bruce following, then through the door. As she entered the noise stopped for an instant and all heads turned. Elizabeth marched up to the counter keeping her eyes fastened on the barman who goggled at the sight of a woman invading this male sanctum. Trying to ignore the unwelcome attention of the men leaning over the bar staring at her, Elizabeth said firmly, "I'm looking for a Mr. Bulloch. It's very urgent."

"He was here a few minutes ago, love," said a voice near her, "probably gone for a pee."

There were loud guffaws at this, but when Elizabeth looked around at the speaker she could see that the eyes were kind in the rough unshaven face.

"Wait, I'll go and have a look." He disappeared and as Elizabeth stood at the counter the noise resumed once more, as the men got down to the serious work of drinking. The fug, with its mingled smell of beer and cigarettes, made her eyes smart.

She looked down at the child standing close beside her. "Won't be long now, Bruce."

The words were scarcely out of her mouth when the man returned, Mr. Bulloch behind him looking truculent.

"Oh it's you!" he exclaimed, surprise and resentment in his voice, "and what's Bruce doing here?"

"I had to bring him, Mr. Bulloch. Your wife is in hospital. It's very urgent. I had to call an ambulance."

His manner changed instantly. "Where is she, in Casualty?"

"Yes."

"I must go there at once. I'll take a taxi."

He looked across at the barman, "Bob, ring a cab for me, will you? I'm going to the hospital. Bruce, you're coming with me."

"I'll go back to the shop then, shall I?" asked Elizabeth. "Would you like me to lock up?"

He fumbled in his pocket producing a key. "Just drop it through the door when you go out, thanks." He took Bruce's hand, murmuring something to him. He seemed to have forgotten Elizabeth already so she hurried towards the open door, relieved to escape from the smoky atmosphere.

When she reached the shop some few minutes later she glanced quickly around. Everything was as before. She hesitated for a few moments. *It seemed dreadful to leave the bedroom in the state it had been, with the vomit on the sheets and the general disarray. What should she do?* Quickly she made up her mind. Running up the stairs she stopped outside the bedroom door then pulled it open. Holding her breath she went over to the bed and pulled back the soiled sheets, bundling them together. She then folded the blanket and placed it on a chair. Last of all she pulled up the coverlet. Giving a quick glance around before shutting the door she was satisfied that the room looked tidy at least. She was glad to descend the staircase and leave the shop. After turning the key in the lock she dropped it through the letter slit. Her bicycle was still on its stand outside the shop. Thankfully, she mounted it and began pedalling as fast as she could, with a sudden longing to reach the sanctuary of the old home.

When she walked into the kitchen Aunt Rose looked up in surprise, "You're so late, Elizabeth, I was wondering what could have happened to you. My dear, you don't look at all well."

"I've got an awful headache, Aunt Rose, and I feel a little sick. I think I'll go up to my room and lie down. Oh, but before that I need to ring David. I was meant to go out with him this evening but I couldn't face it now."

"You go right ahead, my dear, and ring him."

When she spoke to David Elizabeth was brief. "Look David, I'm not feeling well. I'd rather not go to the pictures tonight if you don't mind. Sorry to let you down at the last moment."

"Oh that's all right. I understand. I'll ring you tomorrow to see how you are. Bye."

Elizabeth replaced the receiver and went up to her bedroom. She pulled back the cover and lay down on the bed just thankful to be still and quiet. Gradually her head stopped thumping and she felt herself drifting. In a few minutes she was sound asleep.

CHAPTER ELEVEN

Elizabeth woke suddenly. It was very dark and she could barely make out the illuminated figures on her bedside clock. Peering at it closely she saw it was two thirty. *What had wakened her?* Then she heard a noise coming from beneath her, like busy footsteps walking to and fro. This was accompanied by a curious humming sound, similar to the whirr of a machine. She lay scarcely breathing, listening intently. Then all went quiet. She waited for the noise to start up again but there was nothing, only a faint ringing noise in her ears, the kind that comes when there is deep silence. She must have been dreaming, but no she knew she had been wide awake. Mystified, Elizabeth turned over and very soon was fast asleep.

When she woke up it was morning and the sun was streaming into the room. She lay, thinking about the events of yesterday and what was ahead of her today. *First of all she must ring the hospital and enquire about Mrs. Bulloch. Then there was Bruce. Although he had his father to look after him, how capable was Mr. Bulloch of caring for a child?* While she was washing and dressing many thoughts raced through Elizabeth's mind.

Once she was downstairs she went through to the kitchen where Aunt Rose was busy at the sink. She looked up as Elizabeth came in. "How are you feeling this morning, dear?

You certainly look better. I came up to your room shortly after you went upstairs, with a cup of tea, but you were sound asleep and I didn't want to disturb you so I left you."

"Thank you, Aunt Rose. I think I was very tired and that is why I had a headache. Anyway, I feel fine this morning. Do you mind if I use the telephone? I need to ring the hospital."

At the look of enquiry on her aunt's face Elizabeth said quickly, "I'll tell you all about it as soon as I've made the call."

"The hospital number is on the pad by the telephone," said Aunt Rose.

Elizabeth went through to the parlour where the telephone stood on a small round table. She dialled the number and was through to the hospital immediately.

"I'm enquiring about a Mrs. Bulloch who was brought into Casualty yesterday. Can you give me any news of her please?"

"Hold the line while I make enquiries." Elizabeth waited.

"She's been transferred to Ward 33. She's making good progress."

"Can you tell me what ward that is?"

"Emergencies."

"How long is she likely to be there?"

The voice was curt. "I can't say, possibly two days or maybe more. It all depends on her assessment."

"Thank you," said Elizabeth and put the phone down slowly. She went back into the kitchen.

"I've made you a cup of tea, dear," said Aunt Rose and Elizabeth noted how trim and tidy she looked in her floral print dress and crisp white apron. "Now, while you're drinking it tell me why you had to ring the hospital."

So Elizabeth recounted what had happened, from the time she entered the Bullochs' shop to when she went into the pub. A horrified look crossed Aunt Rose's face at this stage of the account. "I suppose you did have to go into that place, Elizabeth, but oh dear, it is no place for a woman. All the same you managed to find him."

"Yes." Elizabeth was inwardly amused at Aunt Rose's reactions. The old lady had hardly turned a hair at the description of Mrs. Bulloch lying near to death, yet was scandalized by Elizabeth's entering a pub.

"So what is the news of Mrs. Bulloch today?"

"She's been transferred to an emergency ward where she will have to be assessed. What will happen to her then, Aunt Rose?"

"Unfortunately, she'll probably be sent home, back into the same situation. We can only hope that some relative will come and stay with her for a few days."

"There are none here in Nelson," said Elizabeth. "The family moved up from Christchurch. That is what Mrs. Bulloch told me herself."

Noting Elizabeth's anxious face Aunt Rose said soothingly, "Now you're not to worry, dear. God's in control and we must leave it all with Him. Now you have some breakfast."

Elizabeth looked at her. *What a wonderful philosophy of life the old lady had. It was no wonder she had such a serene and lovely face.*

After breakfast Elizabeth said, "I think I'll go out into the garden for a while. It's such a beautiful morning." As she walked down the path into the orchard Elizabeth breathed in the mingled scents of stock and roses. A fantail flitted through the branches of an apple tree as she passed beneath it, the little bird with its fanlike tail darting after invisible insects. A thrush banged a snail shell against the path in front of her and she stopped to watch it. The air seemed full of sound, birds calling from the trees above her and bees humming around the lavender bushes. There was a peace here that soothed and quietened her.

Slowly Elizabeth wandered among the trees until she came to the path that led back to the house and which followed the fence dividing the orchard from the paddock. It was very shady here as the branches met overhead. The path continued up a slight rise to where the trees thinned out and dappled patterns of sunlight and shadows shimmered on the asphalt. Elizabeth was glad to emerge once more into the light and warmth of the morning sun.

As she passed the whare she noticed that the door was open and the next moment Uncle Mal appeared in the doorway. He smiled at her with obvious pleasure. "Hello, Elizabeth, I'm glad to see you up and about. From what my sister said I thought you were quite unwell yesterday."

"I just had a bad headache. It had been a strenuous day. Anyway, I feel fine this morning. I thought I'd stay around here, maybe even try to climb Sugarloaf."

"Well, before you do that, come and have a cuppa with me. There is something I want to talk to you about." There was an urgency in his manner and as Elizabeth followed him into the whare she wondered what it was he wanted to say.

He gestured towards the old easy chair and she sat down, watching him as he made the tea. He poured hers into a cup with a matching saucer but took a mug for himself. Then he sat back and looked at her thoughtfully.

"I've been thinking, Elizabeth, these last few days, about my promise to leave you that trunk full of personal bits and pieces. For many years I've not looked into it but last night I was going through my papers. There's a lot of stuff that would be of interest to no one except myself, but there are some old journals that you might like to read, as you are keen to know more of the family history. I have not read them myself. They were given to me by my sister Katey before she went to China. Anyway, I would like you to have them."

"What about the aunts, Uncle Mal? Wouldn't they want to have their sister's diaries?"

"Not they. Neither of them is interested in digging up the past."

"I had noticed that; whenever I try to get them talking they just clam up."

"So, you see, those old journals would just be put to one side if I gave them to my sisters. They might even throw them away."

Elizabeth looked at him, uncertainly. He touched her arm. "You take them, Missy. I know my sister Katey would have liked you to have them. You are so very like her it is uncanny," he added.

Elizabeth said simply, "Thank you Uncle Mal, I will treasure them." He sat back looking relieved.

A thought occurred to Elizabeth, prompted by this talk of the past. "Uncle Mal, something strange happened last night. I woke up between two and three o'clock and heard strange noises coming from the room beneath me, which is the living room."

"What kind of noises?" He leaned forward tense, his eyes fixed on hers.

"Well, it sounded like footsteps hurrying backwards and forwards and then there was a whirring noise like a kind of machine. All of a sudden it stopped and that was all. I thought I'd been dreaming but I know I was fully awake."

Uncle Mal said slowly, "So you've heard it. I've only known one other person who reported hearing those noises, such as you describe." He seemed to be speaking more to himself than to Elizabeth. "You won't know this, but in my grandfather's time the spinners used to work in a shed on the site where the house is now."

"You mean that I was hearing ghostly noises," said Elizabeth shivering.

"Could be, but it's nothing to worry about. All old houses carry some remnant of the past. There is even a theory that sound waves are trapped in the walls and instead of disappearing into outer space they can be released under certain conditions."

Elizabeth did not know whether to be comforted by this explanation. She did not relish the idea of the house being haunted.

"I wonder if there is any significance in my hearing those noises last night, such as a warning about some event."

Uncle Mal looked at her quizzically. "Now I think you are being imaginative. You've probably been reading horror stories. Anyway if there are any ghosts in the house they will all be friendly ones." His eyes twinkled. "Now if you're going to climb Sugarloaf you need to wear protective clothes. There is a lot of gorse and brambles up there and you could get nasty scratches." Elizabeth stood up. "Now don't forget to take these journals with you," and he handed her two leather bound books. Though the covers were dusty and the corners worn they looked in fairly good condition. Elizabeth opened the topmost one. The handwriting was clear although the ink was slightly faded. Uncle Mal leaned over her shoulder.

"That's my sister's writing all right. Seeing it brings her back." He frowned. "You take them, Elizabeth, they're yours. I'd rather not read them."

Elizabeth thanked him once more and left the whare clutching the books to her chest. She went up to her room and put them on the bedside table. She dearly wanted to sit down and begin reading right away, but instead she changed into her jeans and put on her stoutest shoes. When she was ready she went down to the kitchen. Both aunts were busy.

"I'm off to climb Sugarloaf," she announced. "Don't bother to keep lunch for me; I'll eat when I get back sometime."

Aunt Gertrude looked wistful. "I remember when I used to climb Sugarloaf, usually when I needed to get alone and think. You'll love it when you reach the top. The view's magnificent. You can see right down to the port."

"I'm glad to see that you've got on some sensible clothes," said Aunt Rose. "It's pretty rough up there. Look, take a couple of biscuits with you." She went to the safe and unscrewed a jar of biscuits, taking out two and wrapping them in greaseproof paper. She handed them to Elizabeth. "I don't like to think of you not eating."

Elizabeth laughed and lightly kissed her cheek. "You're very kind, Aunt Rose." She left the room quickly.

Outside she looked up at the hill which seemed to tower above her. In a corner of the paddock by the stream was a gate and Elizabeth made her way to it. She lifted the rope, which was slung over a post and the gate swung open. Elizabeth was careful to close it behind her, remembering how farmers hated gates being left open. In front of her was a path leading up the slope.

With a sense of excitement she began the climb. It was gradual at first, but as she had been warned, there were clumps of gorse growing beside the path and often she brushed against them and was thankful for the thick denims. The path led around the side of the hill and as she mounted higher she looked across at the paddocks on the opposite side of the stream and the backdrop of bush-covered hills. By now she could see nothing of the house. The path grew steeper, but rather than becoming tired, Elizabeth seemed to gain extra energy. A sense of freedom took hold of her and the world below seemed very far away.

Then she heard the call of a bellbird, not in the distance now, but very close at hand, the clear notes rising and falling. Ever afterwards the sound of the bellbird brought back those rare moments of carefree joy she felt when climbing Sugarloaf Hill that Saturday morning.

The final stages of the climb were not easy. The path dwindled to nothing and as she stood gazing below her the breath caught in her throat: the scene was unutterably beautiful. All around were hills, some so far away they melted into a blue haze, while others were like cut-outs against the deep blue of the sky. Far below the sea sparkled in the distance. The rows of houses beyond Brook Street were like models on a papier-mâché base. Nothing looked real from up here.

At the foot of the hill Elizabeth caught a glimpse of the red roof of the old house, partially hidden by trees. Elizabeth thought of the three old people who had been born in that house and would in all probability die there. *What family secrets would they take to their graves? Perhaps the journals that had been pressed upon her would reveal some of their mysteries.* Whatever they did reveal Elizabeth vowed she would keep to herself.

She sat down in the shade of a thick gorse bush. It was now midday and the sun was almost overhead. Elizabeth lay back against the support of a grassy mound so that she could gaze down the valley. Her thoughts became dreamlike. Suddenly unbidden came John Tamati's face across her inward vision. He had the same intense expression he had worn last night and Elizabeth knew that she was required to reach some decision regarding her future relationship with him. If only she could drift along enjoying the few moments she spent with him at the end of each day with no thought of the future, yet it was clear he was wanting more than this. While he was married there had been a natural barrier between them that was like a protection, but if that was removed she had to come to a decision about their relationship. Elizabeth was forced to confront the significance of what he had told her. *If his wife had left him then wasn't it permissible for her to form a relationship with him? After all, it was not as though he was being unfaithful to his wife.*

She thought of her aunts' reaction if she were to announce that she was seeing a man who was separated or divorced from his wife. She shuddered. Their disapproval of such a liaison would make it impossible to go on living with them. If she were honest with herself, she had to admit that she was uncomfortable at the thought of becoming involved with a divorced man. However much she was attracted to him, it didn't seem right somehow.

Sitting there on the summit of the hill Elizabeth wrestled with the problem. Surely, if she cared enough for John and he for her, none of these objections would matter but the fact remained that she had only known him a few days and in that time had spent hardly half an hour consecutively with him. On such a flimsy basis how could she make a far-reaching decision about him? *Why couldn't he be content with things as they were? Why was he trying to force an issue? No, she would not make any decisions about John Tamati, yet.*

Elizabeth lay back and closed her eyes, letting her mind drift like the clouds above her. It was just after three o'clock when she woke from a long doze and reluctantly stood up and began to make her way down the hill.

When she entered the house there was no sign of the aunts and Elizabeth guessed that they would be having their afternoon nap. She immediately went to the fridge and took out the jug of lemonade that was always kept full. She was very thirsty and gulped down a glass of the cool sweet liquid then poured another. Once her thirst was slaked she went upstairs to wash and change out of her jeans which were clinging to her legs. Her shirt too, was damp with perspiration. While she was pulling on a cool cotton dress her eyes fell on the journals that she had placed on the bedside table when she came back from the whare. She promised herself that when she began reading them, it would be when she had a good stretch of time ahead of her.

CHAPTER TWELVE

Elizabeth was now familiar with the Sunday routine at Brookfield House and she was ready punctually at ten o'clock outside the kitchen door waiting for the aunts and Uncle Mal. It was very pleasant to stand in the early morning sunshine feeling the warmth on her bare arms and hearing the birdsong all around her.

They set off at a leisurely pace through the quiet streets and when they arrived at the church Uncle Mal parked in his usual place. As they entered the building the same man was at the door handing out hymn books and a notice sheet. This time he greeted Elizabeth by name and gave her a friendly smile.

She followed the aunts and Uncle Mal down the aisle to their customary pew and glanced quickly around to see if Mrs. White was there with the family. There was no sign of them, but there were still five minutes before the service was due to start. When the family did not appear Elizabeth was surprised and faintly disappointed. Although there could be any number of reasons for their absence somehow she had taken it for granted that Mrs. White would make a point of attending church this morning.

Elizabeth mentally shrugged and gave her full attention to the preacher. He began reading Psalm Twenty-three in his mellifluous voice and as she listened it seemed to Elizabeth that she was hearing the words for the first time.

At the end of the reading the minister announced, "I am going to take as my text the first five words of the Twenty-third Psalm: 'The Lord is my shepherd.'

As he proceeded, Elizabeth was captivated by the range of meaning he drew out of these simple words:- "There is something intensely personal about the use of the pronoun 'my,' he said. "It shows David's intimate relationship with his God. How many of us can say the same? How well do we know the Lord? We might pray to Him when we are in trouble and have nowhere else to turn, but do we spend time alone with Him, just seeking to get to know Him, by reading his word and praying? If you have a close friend you usually want to spend time with them and share your inmost concerns, yet God is closer to us than any friend and cares more deeply. I suggest to each one of you that it is worth spending time to get to know Him."

He went on to say much more but these words made an impression on Elizabeth. Finally he announced the closing hymn: "What a friend we have in Jesus all our sins and griefs to bear, what a privilege to carry everything to God in prayer."

As Elizabeth joined in the singing her mind was on the sermon. She knew that her own relationship with God was far from intimate and that she usually turned to Him in emergencies and rarely for any other reason. *Perhaps it was time she began sorting out her priorities and setting aside time to get to know Him.* In the car going home she was still thinking deeply.

At lunch Aunt Rose commented, "I was sorry that Mrs. White was not at the service. I fully expected to see her there this morning after what you had told me, Elizabeth."

"What was that, Rose? Have I missed something?" Gertrude looked inquiringly at Elizabeth.

Elizabeth said slowly, "It was just that when I called at her

142

place on Friday, everything looked so different. The house and garden were all spruced up and Mrs. White told me she had had a change of heart."

Gertrude's eyebrows shot up, "Well I never, so her visit here had that effect?"

"Oh, and what she heard in church as well," said Aunt Rose. She added thoughtfully, "There must be some good reason why she was not in church today. I hope none of the children is sick."

Suddenly the telephone rang and everyone jumped. "I'll take it if you like," said Elizabeth springing up, "It'll save your legs," she added, glancing from one old lady to the other.

She hurried to the parlour and lifted the phone. "The Brookfield home, Elizabeth speaking," she said.

"Oh, Miss Brookfield, it's Karen White here. I just wanted you and your aunts to know our news. The reason we were not at church this morning is because my husband has been given parole. He is now home for good." Her voice was tremulous.

"Oh that is wonderful news. You must be thrilled. I know Tommy will be so glad to have his dad home."

"He certainly is. He follows him round like a shadow. By the way, he'll be back at school tomorrow. I expect he'll tell you all about his dad." She added anxiously, "Please let your Aunt Rose know that this is little short of a miracle. Barry was not due to come out for another six months but the parole board shortened the sentence for good behaviour. I am so grateful for your aunt's prayers."

"I'll let her know right away," Elizabeth promised. She went through to the dining room. The aunts and Uncle Mal looked at her questioningly.

"That was Mrs. White," Elizabeth said smiling. "Her husband came home this morning. He was released six months early for good behaviour." She turned to Aunt Rose, "Mrs. White says to thank you for your prayers. She sounds very happy."

"Well, that is good news," exclaimed Aunt Rose. "How glad she will be to have her husband home once more. It was really too much for her looking after all those children on her own."

"I wonder if he will manage to get a job," said Gertrude. "It's not easy for ex-prisoners."

Aunt Rose looked at her sternly. "If the Lord has released him from jail early He can find him a job. Nothing is too hard for the Lord."

Gertrude shrugged and looked significantly at Uncle Mal. Elizabeth caught the look and remembered the scene between them that she had overheard.

As soon as the lunch dishes were done and the aunts had gone for their rest Elizabeth went upstairs to her room and settled herself comfortably on the bed with a couple of pillows at her back. She opened the topmost journal. The first entry was dated the 18th April, 1890. Although the handwriting was a child's it was clear and well formed. Elizabeth began reading.

For the next couple of hours she was absorbed by the glimpses she had into the life of Katey and her family. She learned that in the year 1890 only five of the nine children born to Enoch and Sarah were living at home. The two eldest boys, Edward and Arthur, had moved to Blenheim and bought a farm together, while the oldest girl Alice had married and gone to live in Wellington. Of those still at home, Walter was the eldest at twenty-three and helped his father in the tannery, although he was preparing himself to be a missionary. Then came Malcolm who was fifteen and a pupil at Nelson College. There were only two years between Katey and Rose, who were twelve and ten respectively and appeared to be very good friends. Last of all was Gertrude, who at three years old was the baby of the family. There had been one other child, a boy named Percy, who had died of a severe asthma attack at the age of nine. This was a great sadness to Katey as they had been very close and she still treasured a picture he had drawn of her cat Fluffy.

Elizabeth read with particular interest the vivid descriptions of the school that Katey and Rose attended, the Hardy Street School for Girls, which Elizabeth passed each day on her way to school.

One entry, dated Tuesday, 14th October, recorded how Katey had been given a message to deliver to the infant teacher. She described vividly her impressions of what she saw in the infant classroom:-

Mr. Sutton took me along to the infant classroom and as we went in there was such a noise. All the children were chanting the ABC and the room was very crowded and hot. Without counting I guessed there must have been above sixty infants in a room that was clearly designed for half that number. They sat on benches quite close together and many of them looked flushed and hot. There was also an unpleasant smell that made me want to go outside and take gulps of fresh air.

Yet, on that day was born her desire to be a teacher. Elizabeth sat thoughtfully gazing down at the page on which this entry had been made over seventy years before. The words sprang out fresh and clear and it seemed as though the girl Katey was standing before her. Although she had not seen a photograph Elizabeth pictured her as having large grey eyes set in an oval face, with a sweet and serious expression and an abundance of wavy brown hair worn in a thick plait.

From that point on, Elizabeth followed with interest Katey's struggles to obtain a secondary education. She had set her heart on Nelson College for Girls which had been opened ten years previously. The founding principal was Miss Kate Edgar who had distinguished herself by being the first woman to obtain a university degree in the British Empire.

145

For Katey the main opposition came from her father who was dubious about the value of further education for girls. One night after supper he called her into the parlour. "Katey," he began, "Your mother and I have given serious consideration to the subject of your sitting the Scholarship Examination. If you should pass you will have entry to the Nelson College for Girls and then your education will continue for the next three years until you sit the matriculation examination. During this time we will have to support you. As you are aware, most girls leave school at the age of twelve and are able to assist their mothers in the day to day running of the household. However, we know you are an able scholar and that you are hoping to become a teacher."

He had sighed and added, "Life for women is changing in this country and more of them are becoming educated. Having taken all this into consideration we have decided to let you sit for the examination."

Katey enthused to her brother Malcolm about the subjects she would be studying at the college, particularly Latin and French. He laughed scornfully, "That won't help you much, Kate, when you get married. Surely cooking and sewing would be more suitable for a girl. You don't want to become a blue-stocking do you, and end up an old maid?"

Elizabeth smiled at this, yet even in 1962 some men still held to the idea that "a woman's place is in the home" and if they were only going to get married anyway, what need did they have for anything more than a basic education? *Thank goodness her own parents were more enlightened and had encouraged her to go to university.* All the same, even in 1962 in New Zealand there were not many openings beyond teaching for educated girls. Some few became doctors or dentists or even vets, yet the training was long and largely dependent on parents being willing to support their daughters. Elizabeth thought of the sketchy careers advice she had received in her last year at school. The three options presented

146

were:- teaching, nursing and secretarial work. It was fortunate that she had wanted to be a teacher above all.

Elizabeth closed the journal with a sigh. She felt she had read enough for today. She reached for her writing pad and picked up her pen to write her usual weekly letter to the family.

CHAPTER THIRTEEN

As she cycled to school on Monday morning Elizabeth felt as though she had been away for a very long time. In a sense she had, for had she not been transported back to 1890 through reading Katey's journal? Somebody once said that "the past is another country," and that is how it seemed.

Cycling along the familiar streets Elizabeth looked at them through new eyes, imagining how they must have appeared to Katey, as she walked to her school in Hardy Street so long ago. The old wooden building was still standing, although today it was no longer a school but headquarters for a government department.

Thoughts of the past still occupied Elizabeth as she drew up outside the school entrance. The usual gaggle of children clustered outside the gate and yes, Tommy was there. He came forward to meet her with a happy smile. "Good morning, Miss Brookfield. See I'm here early so I can help you get the classroom ready."

"I'm really glad to see you, Tommy," said Elizabeth sincerely.

As they walked along the corridor together he kept up a stream of chatter until they reached the door of the classroom. Here he stopped and looked up into Elizabeth's face anxiously. "Miss Brookfield, will Bruce be back this morning too?"

Elizabeth was not sure how she should answer. She said

slowly, "I don't know for certain. His mother was very sick over the weekend and she had to go to hospital. If Bruce is back in school we shall have to be very kind to him."

Tommy nodded sagely. "Oh I will, Miss Brookfield. Mum has talked to me a lot about the way I am to treat Bruce. She says I must take no notice if he is rude to me and to answer him kindly at all times."

Elizabeth looked at the boy wonderingly. His eyes were clear and earnest as they gazed into hers. "That is quite right, Tommy. Now let us get down to work shall we? You give out that pile of books while I put the day's work on the blackboard."

Half an hour passed quickly and soon it was time to bring in the children from outside. As they stood in line before her Elizabeth glanced along the faces. As she expected, Bruce was missing. The children filed into the room and once they were seated lessons began. The morning went quickly and Elizabeth was surprised when the bell rang for break.

She walked into the staffroom to be met by the usual hubbub and wreaths of smoke. David came across to her. "Hi, Elizabeth, you're a fine one, standing me up two Fridays running. You pleaded the usual female reason, a headache." His tone was bantering but there was a serious look in his eyes.

"I really did have a bad head, David, a real thumper. The last thing I wanted to do was sit through a film. Wait until I tell you what happened that Friday night."

Just then Mr. Ray approached them. "Elizabeth, do you mind if I have a word with you?" he said pleasantly. He beckoned her to one side and lowered his voice. "I have just had a phone call from Mr. Bulloch. It appears his wife is still in hospital in the emergency ward. He told me how you got her to the hospital just in time on Friday night and said that without your quick action she would probably have died. He is very grateful to you, Elizabeth. He also said that he is keeping Bruce at home and his aunt is coming to look after him until Mrs. Bulloch is released from hospital."

Mr. Ray paused and looked at Elizabeth with a twinkle in his eye. "You seem to have been something of a ministering angel all round, Elizabeth. I also had a letter from Mrs. White apologizing for her conduct the day she came to the school. She spoke very warmly about you and how you had helped her."

Elizabeth felt embarrassed. She was not sure how to react to Mr. Ray. He seemed to have unbent to her completely. She was even more surprised when he said, "Mrs. Ray and I would like to invite you to dinner with us, Elizabeth. Would tomorrow night be convenient? There is also an interesting programme on television at 8 o'clock."

Elizabeth was lost for words. An invitation to dine with the headmaster and his wife! It was incredible. "Thank you, Mr. Ray," she managed at last. "I would like that very much."

"Good. We will expect you at six o'clock then. You know where we live, just behind the school at number 6." He moved away leaving Elizabeth feeling dazed.

David came up to her. "What was all that about? You look shocked. Been sacked, eh?"

"Just the reverse, Mr. and Mrs. Ray have invited me to dinner tomorrow night."

"What! In living history I've not heard of anyone being invited there to dinner. You must have distinguished yourself in some way, Elizabeth. Is it linked with what happened on Friday night?" Just then the bell rang.

"I'll tell you later," she said hurrying away.

For the rest of the day Elizabeth saw nothing of David and it was not until after school when she went to the staffroom that she was able to speak to him. He was sitting with Jeanette and Mary and the three of them looked at Elizabeth curiously. David was the spokesman. "Now tell us what happened on Friday, Elizabeth. We are all agog to know what it is that has gained you special distinction with the Rays."

Elizabeth laughed. "I only did what anybody would do

under similar circumstances," and she explained how she had found Mrs. Bulloch after she had taken an overdose of sleeping tablets. They listened to her account without interrupting and there was a general laugh when she described how she had entered the pub at the busiest time.

"I feel sorry for Bruce," said Jeanette thoughtfully. "He might be a little tyke but it is hard on any kid to have a mother who is depressed enough to want to take her own life. I hope that her sister looks after her for a while, though personally I think she needs psychiatric treatment."

Then there followed a discussion on psychiatric hospitals. Elizabeth excused herself and slipped out of the room. Back in her classroom she immediately tackled the backlog of marking and worked on it until five thirty. Then she began packing up and went over to lock up the windows. She looked out expecting to see John Tamati on his usual training run but this night the playing field was empty. A pang of disappointment went through her. Although John had not been in the staffroom all day she had expected to see him after school.

She was still feeling flat as she rode home, although the sun was shining and a pleasant breeze fanned her face as she cycled along Brook Street. Once she had parked the bicycle in the shed she went straight into the kitchen where Aunt Rose and Aunt Gertrude were busy preparing the meal. They looked up as she came in and Aunt Rose wiped her hands on her apron then reached into her pocket producing a letter.

"We've some interesting news, Elizabeth. Next weekend we're having a visit from our niece Marion and her son Richard. They're coming over from Wellington to stay for a few days. Marion wants to catch up with some old friends and attend an art exhibition and Richard has a week's holiday."

Elizabeth was surprised. "I haven't seen Richard since we were children, when they were living in Auckland, though Aunt Marion has popped in to see Mum and Dad a few times." She smiled. "Richard was a terror. I remember the time he put tar in the hair of a little girl who lived along the road from them. Her parents were very rich and owned the biggest house in the neighbourhood. They even had a ballroom with a polished floor that we used to skate on. Glenis's mother was furious when she saw her daughter's hair and I think Richard had a hiding for that." The aunts laughed.

"That sounds like Richard alright," said Aunt Gertrude. "When he came here as a child he was always getting into mischief but he was always very sorry afterwards."

'Yes, we used to make him sit on the stool of repentance for a while until he promised to be good," added Aunt Rose. Elizabeth was amused at such a quaint and old fashioned punishment.

"I can't imagine what he would be like now," said Elizabeth. "He must be about twenty-four."

"Oh, Richard is quite respectable these days. He's a lawyer with a very reputable firm in Wellington," said Aunt Rose. She walked over to the range and lifted off a pot. Elizabeth could see that she wanted to get on with the meal so she asked no further questions but went upstairs to her room to freshen up for dinner.

Over the meal conversation returned to the visit of Marion and Richard. "Where will they sleep?" asked Elizabeth.

"We thought that Marion could be in the room next to yours and Richard in what used to be the boys' room across the landing. It will be a change for you to have company upstairs," added Aunt Gertrude.

This seemed a good time to ask one or two questions about the past. "Was the room behind mine where you used to sleep, Aunt Rose?"

She paused before answering. "Yes, that is where I used to sleep with Katey, until she left home. Gertrude was very small at the time and we used to be careful not to wake her as she always went to bed early." Aunt Rose became brisk. "But that was all a long time ago. Now, how do you like your pudding,

Elizabeth? That was a recipe I picked up from the radio today." It was obvious that she did not want to pursue memories of the past for she added, "How did you get on at school today? Was Tommy back in class?"

"Yes, and he was there early to help me. He said that now his father is back home they are all very happy and that his dad was going for a job interview today at the port."

"Probably at the fish canning factory," said Aunt Gertrude. 'There's always work available there. It's good that he wants to get a job straight away."

"But what about Bruce?" asked Aunt Rose. "Was he back at school?"

"No, Mr. Ray told me that Mr. Bulloch rang to say that Bruce's aunt was coming to look after him until Mrs. Bulloch is discharged from hospital. It sounds as though they may be going back to Christchurch." Elizabeth paused. "The amazing thing to me is that Mr. and Mrs. Ray have asked me to dinner tomorrow night." Both aunts stared at her.

"You mean that headmaster who has been so unsympathetic to you has asked you to dinner?" said Aunt Rose, disbelief in her voice.

"Yes, it seems he has been impressed by what Mr. Bulloch said to him on the phone, something about if it hadn't been for my quick action Mrs. Bulloch would have died, but I only did what anybody would have done," added Elizabeth.

"Well, wonders will never cease," said Aunt Gertrude. "It should be an interesting evening for you, Elizabeth. I don't expect many teachers are invited to the headmaster's home socially."

"No, I must say I was surprised, astounded actually, and Mr. Ray was so friendly."

"It's time Mr. Ray realized your worth," said Aunt Rose loyally. "I hope from now on he will have a different attitude towards you."

Nothing more was said about the invitation from the Rays.

The aunts were more interested in the forthcoming visit of Marion and Richard. While she was helping Aunt Rose with the dishes Elizabeth offered to fetch Uncle Mal's tray from the whare. She longed to be outside in the cool of the evening and she looked forward to seeing Uncle Mal.

As usual he was leaning over the gate smoking his pipe. Elizabeth joined him. "Going for an evening stroll?" he asked.

"Yes, it's so beautiful and peaceful."

Just then the bellbird called, the clear notes ringing through the still air. Uncle Mal removed his pipe and looked down at Elizabeth. "There's something special about that bird," he said quietly.

Back in her room Elizabeth sat by the open window and reviewed the events of the day. The invitation to the Rays had been a complete surprise and Elizabeth did not know whether she was pleased or not. Nevertheless, it was gratifying that Mr. Ray treated her with new respect. Yet, her thoughts kept returning to John Tamati. *Why had he not been at school that day? Was there some new development concerning his wife?* Like a persistent headache these questions throbbed in her mind.

CHAPTER FOURTEEN

Elizabeth woke on Tuesday morning with a strange mixture of dread and anticipation. Then it came to her; this was the day she was invited to the Rays' for dinner. She lay for some moments thinking. As she would not be returning home she must choose clothes that would be smart enough to go out in, yet also be serviceable enough for school. Finally she decided on a navy blue A- line skirt and a white broderie anglaise blouse. She could slip pearl earrings and a matching pearl pendant necklace into her handbag and these would dress up the outfit for the evening.

The decision having been made she was soon ready for school. Aunt Rose appeared in the kitchen just as she was finishing breakfast. "You do look smart this morning, Elizabeth. I take it you won't be coming home this afternoon before you go out for dinner."

"No, I will stay on and do some marking. There is always plenty to keep me busy."

"I just have one word of warning, Elizabeth." Aunt Rose looked serious. "Don't say too much to the headmaster about yourself. I have found that when people suddenly become friendly there is usually something behind it. Be reticent without appearing to be rude, just a word of advice from an old girl." She smiled but there was concern in her clear blue eyes. "You are very open, Elizabeth, but you can't always afford to take people at face value."

"I'll remember what you say, Aunt Rose," said Elizabeth getting up from the table. "Now I must fly." She bent down and kissed her on the cheek.

As she went out to the shed to fetch the cycle she thought over what her aunt had said. *Perhaps there was more behind this dinner invitation than she had realized. Anyway, she would tread warily.*

It was another clear blue morning and even the birds sounded cheerful. As she cycled down the slope from the house Elizabeth enjoyed the sudden rush of speed and the cool air brushing her face. At the school gate Tommy was waiting for her. He rushed forward obviously bursting to tell her something.

"Dad got his job and he starts work today down at the port. He can also get overtime the boss said, so we will have plenty of money coming in now. Mum says perhaps we will be able to buy our own house soon." The words tumbled out without a pause for breath.

"Why, that's wonderful news, Tommy. Tell Mum I'm so glad for you all and I know Aunt Rose will be also." As they went into the building together Tommy was still chattering happily about his dad.

The morning passed uneventfully. The children worked steadily and there was a contented hum in the room that gave Elizabeth a sense of satisfaction. Some days it felt good to be a teacher and she thought she would not swap it for any other job in the world.

At break she went along to the staffroom and the first person she saw was Jeanette puffing away at her cigarette at the opposite side of the table. She pointed to the seat beside her and after Elizabeth had poured herself a mug of tea she went and joined her.

"The big night tonight," said Jeanette with a grin. "I see you're dressed for the occasion. Very smart too, Elizabeth."

Slightly embarrassed, Elizabeth replied. "Thanks, Jeanette. It's hard to know what to wear for school and going out afterwards." The reference to after school reminded her of John Tamati and his non-appearance last night. *Perhaps Jeanette would be the right person to ask as they had both worked for several years in the school.*

Elizabeth tried to keep her voice casual. "I didn't see John Tamati yesterday. Usually he does his training run around the field each evening. Is he sick?"

"Oh, didn't you know? His grandmother died at the weekend and John has gone to the tangi, somewhere on the East Coast in the North Island I believe. He could be away for a week or even longer. You know these wakes; the Maoris make a lot of death." She stubbed her cigarette in the saucer as she warmed to the subject. "The last school I was at, in Tuakau, south of Auckland, we had a lot of Maori children and they were forever out of school for long periods attending tangis. It made it quite hard to teach them."

"But it would be different for Maori teachers surely," said Elizabeth. "They couldn't just miss school like that. It would be so disruptive."

Jeanette raised an eyebrow. "Oh you know our government, Elizabeth. Special exceptions are made for Maoris that would never do for us white people, the pakehas. Just imagine if I took a week off every time a relative died." She paused and said thoughtfully, "All the same, John Tamati isn't your typical Maori; he has hardly had any time off all the time I've known him. I think his grandmother must have been rather special. I seem to remember him telling me once that he was brought up by his grandparents on the East Coast." She wrinkled her forehead as she tried to remember. "Quite an interesting background I seem to recall."

Elizabeth would have liked to ask more but she did not want to appear too interested in John Tamati. She could question him herself when next she saw him. Her heart began to beat faster at the thought. Just then the bell rang and abruptly ended the conversation.

The clock hands seemed to speed up during the day and Elizabeth was surprised when she saw that it was three o'clock. There were three hours at least before she needed to be at the Rays so she decided to fill in time by having a leisurely cup of tea in the staffroom. When she went in David and Mary were sitting together chatting companionably.

"I was just telling Mary about the day I spent at your uncle's place and what he told me about the Dun Mountain railway," David began. "It got me thinking that perhaps the three of us could do the walk up the track following the old route."

"Well, I'm free this weekend," said Mary. "What about you, Elizabeth?"

"I'm not sure. You see my cousin is coming over from Wellington at the weekend and I might be expected to help entertain him."

"Bring him along too. There's the solution," David said triumphantly.

"Not so fast, please," said Elizabeth. "I'll speak to my aunts first."

Elizabeth went back to the classroom thinking about David's suggestion. *It could be the perfect answer to what could be an awkward situation, if she was expected to spend the day with Richard. After all, he was a virtual stranger, as they had only met when they were children. Also, it would be much easier to be in the company of other people, especially bright personalities like Mary and David. Yes, she liked the idea.*

Elizabeth turned to the pile of books on the table and soon was absorbed in marking.

After an hour she stood up and stretched. It was only five o'clock and she felt disinclined to work any longer. She wandered over to the window, and looked out over the empty playing field. A feeling of restless longing came over her. At that moment she would have given anything to see John jogging across the grass towards her, his brown muscled legs moving rhythmically. She missed his face, with its slightly lopsided grin showing the perfect white teeth and the deep brown eyes that glowed as they looked into hers. Elizabeth shook herself. What was she doing daydreaming like this? She sighed and returned to her desk picking up a book to mark. But it was hopeless, she simply could not concentrate, so after she had packed her bag Elizabeth made her way to the women's cloakroom intending to have a wash and repair her make-up.

A mirror over the washstand extended across the wall and sunlight streamed in from a side window. In the harsh light Elizabeth gazed at her reflection critically trying to see herself as a stranger might. It was impossible. All she could see in the mirror was a girl with an oval face, clear skin, regular features and rather large dreamy eyes of an indeterminate colour, neither blue nor green. *One smitten admirer had described her as a Grecian princess, whatever that might mean.* Elizabeth smiled at the memory and her reflection smiled back. She clipped on the small pearl earrings she had brought with her and fastened the necklace round her neck. Then she stood back to admire the effect. Jewellery gave her a certain sophistication she decided and altogether she looked quite suitably dressed for the evening. Glancing at her watch she saw that it was now ten to six, which gave her sufficient time to walk through the school grounds to the Rays' house.

As she left the building and went to the back of the school it all seemed very quiet, the sort of unnatural quiet that descends on a school after the children have gone home. Elizabeth found the Rays' house easily. No 4 was just a few houses on the right as you left the school. On either side of the gate was a high hedge that prevented passers- by from seeing into the garden. The house was set well back and with its covered-in porch was typical of houses built in the twenties.

Elizabeth pushed open the gate and walked up the concrete path between manicured lawns. On either side of the path were standard roses planted at regular intervals. Elizabeth mounted the steps leading to the porch and looked quickly back at the garden. There was not a weed in sight and every shrub and bush had been neatly trimmed. Somehow this is just what she would have expected of the Rays.

She paused in front of the door. As there was an old fashioned knocker and no sign of a bell Elizabeth lifted the knocker firmly and let it drop. The door was opened immediately by Mrs. Ray, but how different she looked. Instead of her usual workaday skirt and blouse she wore a loose-fitting dress made of some filmy material in a rich paisley design which was draped becomingly over her shoulders. *She looks really arty*, thought Elizabeth with surprise.

"Come in, my dear," said Mrs. Ray. "How nice you look. I don't know how you manage to keep so fresh and attractive after a long day at school. Now do come in."

She led Elizabeth along a dimly lit passage and opened a door at the far end. The impression of light and space was almost breathtaking and Elizabeth could see that this was a large conservatory used as a sitting room, with comfortable chairs and settees placed invitingly at intervals. Large pots of trailing plants and brilliant orchids stood against the walls adding a touch of exotic colour to the room. In one corner was a large cage on a stand where a canary threw back its head letting out a full throated stream of sound.

"Now, do sit down and make yourself comfortable," said Mrs. Ray warmly. The room was altogether delightful thought Elizabeth as she sat back on the settee with a sigh of pleasure. "I'm sure you would welcome a drink, Elizabeth. What would you like, a glass of sherry or a cool drink? I can offer your orange, lemonade, coca cola."

"Oh lemonade will do very nicely, thank you," Elizabeth said quickly.

While Mrs. Ray was getting the drinks Elizabeth looked more closely at the room. She noticed an easel in one corner with a picture propped on it, facing inwards. Also against the wall was a stack of pictures with only the backs showing. When Mrs. Ray returned with glasses on a small tray Elizabeth asked, "Are those your paintings, Mrs. Ray?"

"Yes, just a little hobby of mine, I enjoy pottering round with paints."

"I'd love to see them. I notice they are all facing inwards."

"That's because I never think they're good enough to display, but I enjoy working on them all the same."

"What is the one on the easel of?"

"It's an old house I saw the other day in South Street, one of the original Nelson cottages and I had a fancy to paint it."

"Do you like old houses?"

"As a matter of fact I do, especially the early colonial houses that have been left in their original condition, not after they've been modernized." She shuddered.

"You would probably like my aunts' and uncle's place. It is really old, built in 1862 and all original."

"Really, Elizabeth, that sounds fascinating."

Just at that moment Mr. Ray walked in. Like Mrs. Ray he seemed a different person at home. In his khaki shorts and loose Hawaiian shirt he looked relaxed and altogether more approachable. "What's all this about an old house built in 1862?" he said jocularly. "Is that where the tannery pits are? David was telling me about the day he and his scouts were clearing some of them."

A warning bell went off in Elizabeth's mind. *Could this be the reason she had been invited here tonight?*

Mrs. Ray looked at her husband. "That's your period isn't it, Dennis?" Then she turned to Elizabeth, "My husband is doing research into Nelson schools from 1877 upwards so any buildings around that era have an interest for him."

"So you actually live in a house built in 1862, Elizabeth?" said Mr. Ray.

"Yes, it belongs to my two aunts and uncle and I am

boarding with them." Both Mr. and Mrs. Ray looked at her thoughtfully.

Over dinner conversation flowed effortlessly. Mr. Ray had a fund of interesting anecdotes about schools where he had taught during his long career and Mrs. Ray was adept at prompting him when his memory flagged. The meal was served tastefully on a polished table with individual place mats and Mrs. Ray brought in each course without fuss. Elizabeth particularly enjoyed her home made steak and kidney pie. For dessert there was pavlova with boysenberries and cream and Elizabeth thought she had never tasted anything more delicious.

"You do know how pavlova came to be invented, don't you?" Mr. Ray asked Elizabeth.

"Not really."

"Well, it was when the great Russian dancer, Pavlova, came to New Zealand and a chef whipped up a white concoction made mainly from egg whites and sugar and topped it with cream. Very appropriate for a ballet dancer don't you think?"

"Yes, I just wish I could make it. Each time I try, mine sink and go very sticky," said Elizabeth ruefully.

"I'll give you my recipe, Elizabeth. It is very simple and never fails," said Mrs. Ray. "Now would you like to go into the sitting room and I'll serve you coffee there."

Once they were seated in the comfortable chairs sipping coffee Mr. Ray turned to Elizabeth. "I am very interested to hear that you are living in such a historic house. There must be all kinds of relics of the past there:- old photos, journals and suchlike."

Elizabeth noted the shrewd expression in his eyes as he leaned forward slightly. She knew that this was her cue to mention the journals but something restrained her. Those journals were private and they had been given by Uncle Mal to her. She did not want a stranger to the family raking through them, even if it was in the interests of research.

As though he sensed that she was holding something back

162

Mr. Ray persisted. "I have looked through all the records held at the museum and the Nelson Library but it would be fascinating to turn up something quite new."

Elizabeth nodded. "Why are you doing this study, Mr. Ray?"

"It's for a thesis towards my MA degree. I know it seems very late in the day for me but I am enjoying doing the research in a place like Nelson. It was a leader in the field of education in NZ you know. For instance, when Anthony Trollope, the novelist, visited Nelson in 1872 he said that the children were generally well taught and that there was nothing to pay for education. Every householder paid £1 per annum towards the school and for every child between five and fifteen the parents paid five shillings a year, whether the child was at school or not. Trollope remarked that the payments were made as a matter of course."

Mr. Ray continued, "Then there is the Nelson College for Girls. The idea of secondary education for girls before 1900 was still quite new and revolutionary." He chuckled. "One of the guest speakers at the presentation of certificates at the end of the first year actually said that he didn't approve of undue education for women and would be horrified if one of his daughters had earned 'some of these certificates' and that he would 'be sorry to see the grace and charm of women sacrificed to the power of the intellect."

Elizabeth laughed. "I can just imagine how well that comment would have gone down with Miss Kate Edgar and her sister, with their MA degrees." Mr. Ray looked at Elizabeth faintly surprised as though he didn't expect her to have such knowledge.

"I wonder how old Miss Kate Edgar was when she became Principal," said Elizabeth.

"Oh, I can tell you that. She was only twenty-five and her sister, who was appointed Assistant Principal, was even younger. Nobody expected either of them to get married and it came as a complete surprise to the Board when Miss Lilian asked to be released from her contract because she had recently become engaged. One of the Board members had confidently spoken to someone about 'the sheer impossibility of either of the Miss Edgars, but especially the younger, getting married." Both Mrs. Ray and Elizabeth laughed heartily.

"Men still have funny ideas about educated women," remarked Mrs. Ray, "as if marriage is barred to them."

Mr. Ray ignored this comment and carried on. "There were all sorts of teething problems in the early days of the school. The building was not ready for them and they had to use the dining room and upstairs sitting room as schoolrooms at first. But I think the main difficulties were with the staff. You see they all lived in."

"That could create problems," commented Mrs. Ray.

"Yes, apparently there was a clash of personalities between the matron, Miss Bell, and the Principal. Things got to such a pitch that they each sent letters to the Board complaining about the other. Miss Edgar recommended that Miss Bell should be dismissed, but as it happened the matron handed in her resignation and left at the end of a week."

"It must have been very unpleasant living in such an atmosphere," said Elizabeth.

"Particularly as there were only four full-time members of staff including the matron, in the first year," said Mr. Ray, "although there was extra staff for teaching drawing, music and drill."

"I think Miss Edgar must have been a hard person to work under because the music teacher also handed in her resignation and complained of the 'unnecessary and unladylike interference and constant supervision of the Lady Principal."

"What a dreadful woman!" said Mrs. Ray, "I wonder how long she lasted in the job."

"Oh, right up until 1890. She threatened to resign a couple of times and got the Board to agree to her living out and having no responsibility for the boarders. When she did finally resign it was to get married."

"It must have been a brave man to take her on," said Mrs. Ray with a laugh.

"I suppose he had a lot of patience. He was a young clergyman, Rev. Evans."

"Who came after Miss Edgar?" asked Elizabeth curiously.

"A Miss Gibson from Christchurch. The Board didn't make any concessions for her. She had to take a drop in salary and was told she must live in and take responsibility for the general supervision of the boarders. I think the Board's experience with the first principal toughened them up."

"That's very fascinating, Mr. Ray. I can understand why you enjoy delving into old papers if you unearth such interesting material."

"Dennis has always liked looking into dusty old records," said Mrs. Ray looking across at her husband affectionately. She glanced at her watch. "Now, Elizabeth, it's getting late and I see it is dark already. Let us give you a lift home. You can't possibly ride your bicycle through the streets tonight."

Elizabeth protested but the Rays took no notice and insisted on driving her. When they reached the house both Mr. and Mrs. Ray gazed up at it without speaking. Eventually, Mrs. Ray murmured, "How perfect, how absolutely perfect."

"Thank you both for a lovely evening," said Elizabeth, climbing out of the car.

"It's been a pleasure," said Mr. Ray taking her elbow.

Elizabeth stood for a moment as the car backed down the drive, then she walked slowly back to the house. The kitchen light was on but the aunts would have gone to bed some time before. Carefully Elizabeth switched off the lights behind her and climbed the stairs to her room.

Once she was in bed she lay with the blind up, looking down the valley which was clearly discernible in the moonlight. She lay awake for a long time, all kinds of thoughts flitting across her mind. Eventually her body relaxed and she slept.

CHAPTER FIFTEEN

Elizabeth woke next morning to a fine drizzle, the first time it had rained since her arrival in Nelson. She dressed quickly, taking a raincoat out of the wardrobe before hurrying downstairs. She did not know how long the walk to school would take but she allowed for an extra quarter of an hour.

As she was finishing her breakfast Aunt Rose appeared in the kitchen. "I didn't hear you come in last night, Elizabeth, but I didn't think it could be very late. As you know, Gertrude and I go to bed quite early. I hope you had an enjoyable evening;" then noting Elizabeth's hasty movements she added, "Don't stop now. I can see you are in a hurry. Tell me about it this evening."

Elizabeth picked up her satchel and gave her a quick kiss. "I'd better be off. I'm walking this morning."

As she set off down the slope pulling the hood of the raincoat over her head, Elizabeth reflected that she had not walked along this road since her first day in Nelson. That seemed like a lifetime ago and she felt so much older and more mature than the girl she was then.

Once she got into stride she found she was enjoying the walk. The misty drizzle blotted the outlines of the hills and lent a certain mystery to the landscape. Even the harsh colours of the wooden bungalows were softened this morning and

166

Elizabeth could imagine a painter would enjoy capturing the gentle landscape. She thought of Mrs. Ray exclaiming over the house last night. No doubt she would love to be able to paint the old place but somehow Elizabeth could not see Aunt Rose liking the idea. Perhaps this evening she could broach the subject.

It seemed no time at all before Elizabeth was at the school gate. This morning the little gaggle of boys was missing and for once there was no Tommy. Glancing at her watch Elizabeth saw that she was quarter of an hour earlier than usual. As she came to the back of the staffroom she was relieved to see that her bicycle was in its usual place.

It was very quiet and nobody seemed to be around although the entrance door was open. Elizabeth had an urge to tiptoe down the empty corridor as her footsteps sounded so loud. She pushed open her classroom door and went in, feeling a sense of coming home. It was curious but this was now her domain, she could arrange things as she wanted and not even the headmaster would interfere. Elizabeth sat down at her desk and drew her workbook towards her, glancing down at the plan for the day. Then she gazed around the room envisaging the children in their places. Yes, she had settled into the school at last and the daily routines were comfortingly familiar.

At break she looked around for David and Mary. Her heart nearly stopped when she saw John Tamati across the room. He had his back to her so she had time to collect herself by the time David came over to her.

"Well, Elizabeth, Oh, favoured one, do tell all about last night."

"It was really very nice. Mrs. Ray cooked a super meal and well, we talked and the evening went very quickly."

"What about TV? Weren't you going to watch a special programme?"

"Oh, I forgot all about that. I think they must have too, as the subject didn't come up."

"What did you talk about then?" asked David curiously. "It must have been pretty riveting to make you forget about TV."

"Mainly history. Did you know that Mr. Ray is doing research into Nelson schools for his MA degree?"

"That would explain why he was so interested when I was telling him about the tanning pits on your uncle's property. I suppose he thinks there might be some relics of the past lying around there."

"Exactly, but even if there were, I don't think my aunts and uncle would be very keen on parting with them." Elizabeth thought of the journals. Much as she liked David she did not feel free to confide in him. Something warned her against speaking of them to anyone.

"Have you had a chance to talk to your aunts about our suggestion for climbing Dun Mountain on Saturday?"

"Not yet, but I will tonight."

Just then the bell rang and put an end to further talk. As Elizabeth walked back to her room her thoughts reverted to John Tamati and she felt her heart begin to thump. Tonight he was bound to come and speak to her and she felt unprepared to meet him.

As the day progressed Elizabeth became involved with her teaching and she was able to put him to the back of her mind. When the lunch bell rang she decided to stay and have lunch in her room. It was a surprise when Tommy put his head through the door just as she was opening her sandwiches.

"Miss Brookfield, can I come and talk to you, please?"

"Of course, Tommy, you're always welcome."

"Miss Brookfield, I went to Bruce's father's shop last night and there was a lady serving. I asked if Bruce was home and she said he was sick. Then I asked how his mother was and she said Mrs. Bulloch was home from hospital but she was far from well."

"I'm so glad you've told me this, Tommy. I must go and visit them myself. What made you go and ask for Bruce, Tommy?"

"It was Mum. She said Bruce probably has no friends and that I should try to be a friend to him."

Elizabeth felt tears pricking her eyelids. Here was this child, prepared to do what many adults could not bring themselves to do, forgive and forget.

"That was very kind of you, Tommy," she said gently. "I'm sure Bruce would really appreciate having you as a friend." She looked down at the face turned up to hers, with such clear and earnest eyes. "Thank you for telling me this. Now you go and have a run around before the bell rings."

As he scampered off Elizabeth looked after him thoughtfully. She would definitely go to the Bullochs' shop this afternoon, whatever else might happen.

As three o'clock approached Elizabeth began to feel unpleasant flutterings in her chest. She dismissed the children and waited impatiently for them to leave. They seemed in no hurry and one after another came up to talk to her or offer to do a job. Tommy as usual, scrubbed at the blackboard until it was pristine. Elizabeth thanked him and said, "I'm going to call around at Bruce's father's shop tonight to see how he and his mother are getting on. I hope I'll be able to give you a good report tomorrow." Tommy beamed and Elizabeth thought what a different child he was these days.

When he had gone and she was alone at last, Elizabeth took a book from the pile on her desk and began to correct it. Suddenly she felt thirsty and remembering that she had not had her usual cup of tea at lunchtime, she left the room and made her way to the staffroom. Quickly she made a fresh pot of tea and was just starting to pour it when in walked John Tamati. Immediately the heat rose into Elizabeth's cheeks.

"Hello, Elizabeth, I thought I'd join you for a cuppa this afternoon. Is there any tea left in the pot?" He seemed perfectly at ease.

"Yes, I've just made a fresh pot. I'll pour you one." Elizabeth was glad to have something to occupy her hands. She could feel John's eyes on her, aware of her confusion and slightly amused by it.

"Well, aren't you going to ask me where I've been the past few days? I'll bet you thought I was having some Maori days off."

"No, of course I didn't. Jeanette told me you had gone to your grandmother's funeral, somewhere on the East Coast. I'm very sorry, John, it must have been hard for you."

"The hard part was having to join in all the tangi ceremonies. I had forgotten how long and drawn out Maori funerals are. I suppose my Maori side has been swamped by my European side. It all seemed so remote and foreign to me, yet to my Maori relatives it was all very real."

"Haven't you visited your Maori relatives for a while?"

"Not often, since I left the East Coast as a boy of ten."

"Were you living with your grandmother then?"

"Yes, it's a long story. Do you really want to know my history, Elizabeth? I don't want to bore you." His eyes were quizzical.

Elizabeth replied quickly. "Please tell me, John. I know so little about you."

"Well, it begins with my mother and father, of course. My dad was a full Maori from the East Coast, quite well born, related to a chief in fact. When WW2 began he went off to war and was in the Maori Battalion posted to Italy. At the end of the war instead of coming home, he went to England with a mate of his who came from Bristol. That was fairly unusual because most Maoris have a strong feeling for their whanau, or family to you, but his sense of adventure was strong. He stayed at his mate's home and the inevitable happened. He met his mate's sister and they fell in love."

"They decided to marry, against her parents' wishes, and came back to New Zealand. They lived in Auckland and that was where I was born. My dad was a mechanic and had a good job so he did not want to leave the city, but the Maori relatives back home on the East Coast put the hard word on him and said he had a duty to come home and spend time with his parents before they died and to learn from them. Reluctantly he left his job and the house he was buying and took his English wife down to live with his family. It was too much for my mother. She just couldn't get used to Maori ways and she threatened to leave him unless he returned to Auckland. He refused and so she went back to England, leaving me with my father and grandmother."

"How sad!" exclaimed Elizabeth, "It must have been an awful decision to have to make. Did your mother keep in touch with your father after that?"

"Not as far as I know. She got a divorce eventually and I never saw her. My father would never speak of her."

"So you were really brought up by your grandmother then."

"Yes, she taught me all the Maori lore and the names of the ancestors. Best of all, were the wonderful stories she could tell. I think I know every single Maori legend there is. I also learned to speak fluent Maori, which was not much use at school as we got into trouble if we spoke Maori instead of English."

"Did your grandmother speak to you in English?"

"No, her English was very limited, but she did value education and she knew that the way for a Maori child to get on in a European world was to be educated." He laughed. "When she found out I was wagging school to go fishing with some other kids she had me walloped so I never did it again."

"You said you were only with her until you were ten. What happened then?"

"She told my father that he had to take me back to Auckland, get himself a job and a house and send me to a good school. It nearly broke her heart and mine when we left the Coast."

"She must have been a very wise and unselfish woman," said Elizabeth thoughtfully.

"She was a great lady." John gazed past Elizabeth as though looking into the past, "the greatest lady I have known. I just wish I had spent more time with her over recent years and now she's gone." His breath caught in a sob.

Elizabeth put out her hand instinctively and he took it and held it. For a few moments they sat like this and then he released her hand. Looking full into her face he said, "Elizabeth, I didn't mean to burden you with my grief. Forgive me. I shall get over it in time, but please don't withdraw your friendship from me. You mean so much to me, more than you know."

"I won't, John, I promise."

Later, when she thought back to this conversation Elizabeth's conscience reminded her that a promise was a promise and if at any time in the future she wanted to sever her relationship with John Tamati she would be breaking faith with him.

As she cycled out of the school grounds Elizabeth tried to focus on Mrs. Bulloch. Her last sight of the poor woman was when she was being carried to the ambulance, just a bundle tied to a metal frame. Elizabeth had difficulty even recalling her face. When she drew up outside the shop she stood her bicycle on the stand very slowly, trying to postpone the moment for entering the building. What surprised Elizabeth was that everything seemed so normal and even the woman behind the counter had a round cheerful face that was the essence of normality.

"Can I help you dear?" Her voice had a soft Scottish burr.

"I came to ask how Mrs. Bulloch was. You see I'm Bruce's teacher and ..."

"Yes, I know all about you. You're Miss Brookfield and you found my sister when she was near to death." The woman came from behind the counter and stood in front of Elizabeth. "I speak for all the family when I say how deeply grateful we are for your swift action in calling the ambulance."

"I only did what anyone would have done," Elizabeth murmured.

"I'm sure my sister would love to see you. She often mentions you. Do come up to her room."

Elizabeth followed the sturdy figure up the stairs. On the landing Mrs. Bulloch's sister paused for breath before pushing open the door of the room on the right which Elizabeth knew was the bedroom. Elizabeth followed her across to the bed where a little shrunken woman lay. *Surely this could not be Mrs. Bulloch. She looks so old and her face has a ghastly pallor.* Her eyes were closed, but they opened as Elizabeth stood by the bed and she smiled in recognition.

"Hello, Miss Brookfield." Her voice was scarcely above a whisper. "You see, I'm still in the land of the living, thanks to you."

"I'm so glad to see you." Elizabeth faltered. She could not add, "looking well" because that would have been a blatant lie. Instead, she smiled down at the poor wreck of a woman lying there.

"Now you must get yourself well again," she said heartily.

Mrs. Bulloch smiled sadly. "I know I must, for Bruce's sake at least. Did you know I'm going back to Christchurch with my sister as soon as I'm strong enough and Bruce is coming with me? He's not well at the moment either, so my poor sister has a house full of invalids."

"That's no trouble at all, Eileen. I'm glad to be able to look after you," and she smiled down at Mrs. Bulloch tenderly. A tear trickled down the sick woman's cheek.

"Always so kind," she murmured.

"Now you just lie back and think of England and I'll bring you something nice on a tray very soon." Her sister lifted Mrs. Bulloch's head gently, plumping up the pillow behind her. Then she beckoned to Elizabeth to follow her out of the room.

Outside on the landing Elizabeth said softly, "She doesn't look at all well. What does the doctor say about her?"

The woman looked sad. "He says there is nothing medically wrong with her, but she just seems to have lost the will to live. The only thing that keeps her going is her concern for Bruce. She has no interest in her food and has to force herself to eat."

"What is the matter with Bruce?"

"Oh, on top of everything else he went and got chicken pox though he's through the infectious stage now."

"Do you think I could see him? I've had chicken pox anyway."

She led Elizabeth to the next room on the landing and opened the door. It was a large bright room but was in such a muddle that for a moment Elizabeth did not see Bruce for all the toys on the bed. "Hello, Miss Brookfield," he said cheerfully "Look at all my spots. I've got chicken pox so I can't come to school."

"Well, hurry up and get better, Bruce, we're doing a lot of exciting things at the moment and I don't want you to miss out."

"What kind of things?"

Oh dear, why did she have to say that? Elizabeth cast about desperately for something that might sound exciting. "Well, we're making papier-mâché models. It's a bit messy but the children like it."

Bruce was on the point of asking another question but to Elizabeth's relief his aunt cut in at this point. "Now you get this room tidy, Bruce, before your father comes home. I've never seen such a mess in all my born days." She winked at Elizabeth. "Come on, Miss Brookfield, and I'll make you a cup of tea and you can have some of my homemade shortbread."

"Can I have some too, Auntie?" begged Bruce.

"Not until all those toys are put away," she said firmly.

This woman really is a tonic, thought Elizabeth, *just what the family needs, but even with her cheerful solidity what hope is there really for poor Mrs. Bulloch?*

"I'll come again next week," said Elizabeth.

"Please do. I know my sister enjoyed seeing you," said the woman, as she accompanied Elizabeth to the door of the shop. As Elizabeth mounted her bicycle a feeling of deep sadness enveloped her. It would take a miracle to bring Mrs. Bulloch back to health, she was sure.

When she arrived home Aunt Gertrude and Aunt Rose were laying the table for dinner.

"I'm so glad to see you, Elizabeth. I thought we would have to start without you," said Aunt Rose.

"I called in to see how Mrs. Bulloch was."

"And how is she?"

"Not at all well, in fact, she looks dreadful. Her sister is looking after her and she told me that Mrs. Bulloch is not eating. She makes an effort but has no appetite."

"That sounds bad. We will have to think about what we can do for her. In the meantime we must not let our dinner spoil. Gertrude has made us a very tasty cauliflower cheese."

Towards the end of the meal Aunt Gertrude looked across at Elizabeth. "You haven't told us how you got on at your headmaster's place last night."

Elizabeth had to drag her mind back from the events of the afternoon. Last night seemed so very far away now. "It was very pleasant and I discovered that Mr. Ray is doing research into early schooling in Nelson. He is trying to collect as much original material as he can."

"He ought to come and interview Rose. She'd provide him with original material," said Aunt Gertrude mischievously.

"Don't bring him here, Elizabeth, please. I don't like the sound of the man."

"I think you would like Mrs. Ray though, Aunt Rose. She has always been very kind to me. I found out that she paints and is particularly interested in old houses. She had one on her easel, of an early Nelson cottage. I know she would love to paint this house."

"No harm in that, Rose," said Aunt Gertrude.

"I suppose not." Aunt Rose sounded only half convinced. "Anyway, Elizabeth, I am more concerned about Mrs. Bulloch. You were saying before dinner that she was far from well. I have been thinking that the best way we could help her would be to get our Ladies Group to pray for her. We have found praying for the sick has been very effective. In fact, we devote a large part of our time praying for needy people and we have had some amazing results. It sounds as though Mrs. Bulloch's problem is spiritual rather than physical."

"Well, according to her sister the doctor has done all he can for her, but she has just lost the will to live."

"Then this is certainly where prayer can take over from the medical profession. Yes, tomorrow when I go to my meeting I will put forward her name for prayer."

Elizabeth looked at her aunt; *Encased in that frail elderly body was a strong spirit and an unwavering faith. If faith could move mountains then even Mrs. Bulloch might be made well.*

CHAPTER SIXTEEN

The next morning Tommy was waiting as usual at the school gate. He came across to Elizabeth eagerly, "Did you see Bruce last night, Miss Brookfield?"

"Yes, Tommy, he has chicken pox but he is much better now, although he still has the spots."

"Is he coming back to school?"

"Now, that I can't answer; we shall just have to see."

That seemed to satisfy Tommy and he was soon chatting happily beside her. Elizabeth's attention was only half on what he was saying. She was wondering about John and whether she would see him during the day.

At break Mrs. Ray came straight over to Elizabeth. "I have been thinking about that wonderful old house you live in, Elizabeth. I haven't been able to get it out of my mind since I saw it the other night."

"Actually I spoke to my aunts and they seemed quite happy about you painting it." *"Happy" was not exactly an accurate description of Aunt Rose's reactions, but it would have to do.*

"Perhaps I could come up one weekend, either on a Saturday or a Sunday," suggested Mrs. Ray.

"Oh, a Saturday would be fine but I don't think they would like it on a Sunday."

Mrs. Ray's eyebrows shot up. "Why, are they very religious?"

"They are staunch Baptists and don't believe in certain activities taking place on a Sunday."

Mrs. Ray nodded. "I quite understand. Certain members of my family are Baptists and they wouldn't approve of me painting on a Sunday either. I will leave it entirely with you, Elizabeth, to fix a convenient time."

There was a wistful look in her eyes and Elizabeth determined that she would speak to her aunts and make a firm arrangement with them for Mrs. Ray to visit the house. When Mrs. Ray left her to speak to someone else Elizabeth looked all around the room to see if John happened to be there. Even though it was rare for him to come into the staffroom at break Elizabeth still felt a stab of disappointment when he did not appear.

The remainder of the day passed swiftly and as three o'clock approached Elizabeth felt unpleasant flutterings in her stomach. She knew that John would be unlikely to appear until after four o'clock anyway, so once the last child had gone home she took a book off the pile on her desk and determinedly began marking.

An hour went by in this way and then she looked towards the window, but there was no figure in running shorts jogging around the field. Perhaps John was later getting started today. Elizabeth sighed and continued marking. At half past four she stood up and crossed to the window but the field was deserted. She tried to swallow her disappointment and gathered together her books and papers, feeling in the words of Shakespeare that everything was "flat, dull, stale and unprofitable".

Slowly she made her way along the corridor and had nearly reached the entrance when she heard a voice behind her call, "Elizabeth!"

Swinging around, she saw John striding towards her. "Thank goodness, I've caught up with you. I went to your room but you'd gone."

"I looked for you on the field but you weren't there," said Elizabeth smiling.

"No, I'm not training tonight. Look Elizabeth, something unexpected happened last night." Elizabeth's heart lurched. "When I got home my wife was waiting outside in her car. She asked to come in and talk. Of course I couldn't refuse. She said that she had had second thoughts about leaving me and realized she had made a mistake." Elizabeth felt as if someone had thumped her in the chest.

John continued. "Vera said she had been very unhappy ever since she went off. It put me in a spot. As I think you realize, I no longer love my wife. My feeling for her died some time ago. We both seem to pull in different directions."

"So what did you say to her?" asked Elizabeth dully.

"I said she could stay the night but we would have to talk seriously about the future. We sat up for hours but at the end of it we were no further forward. She wants to come back and try to make a go of our marriage."

"And what about you?"

"I can't see us living together as a married couple and quite frankly I am not willing to try. I think you know why, Elizabeth." He gazed deeply into her eyes until Elizabeth could bear it no longer and looked down.

She said quietly, "So if I were not in the picture you might be reconciled to your wife?"

There was a moment's pause. "I suppose that is right, Elizabeth."

Elizabeth struggled with her feelings. At last she said, "If your wife wants to go back to you then you should let her. I do not want to be the one standing in the way."

"I was afraid you would say that," he said sadly.

"I think I should tell you, John, that over the weekend I thought very deeply about our friendship, and where it was leading. I also realized that I was not comfortable with the idea of being involved with someone who was separated or divorced."

John looked hurt. "Elizabeth, I had no idea."

"I suppose it's the way I've been brought up, to think of marriage as a lifetime commitment."

"I have always known you would have high ideals, Elizabeth. Unfortunately, feelings sometimes get in the way of strict principles. If you love somebody outside of marriage can you really continue to live with your wife? It seems like living a lie to me."

"Then perhaps you have to be open with her and tell her how you are feeling."

John said hopelessly, "I tried to explain this last night but it made no difference. She begged me to take her back."

"Then you really have no choice," said Elizabeth quietly.

"Even feeling the way I do about you?"

"Yes." Elizabeth felt a wrenching pain inside her.

"Is that your last word?"

"It has to be. Now I must go." She felt she must leave him or she would weaken, so she left the room quickly. Even then she had an overwhelming urge to turn back and throw herself into his arms, but she fought it. Mounting her bicycle she pedalled furiously until she was clear of the school.

When she arrived back at the house she hoped that she would be able to slip up to her room unobserved but Aunt Rose was in the kitchen and looked up as she came in. "Elizabeth!" she exclaimed, "You're so pale, are you feeling all right?"

"I'm just a bit tired, Aunt Rose. I think I'll go up to my room for a few minutes before tea." Elizabeth hurried from the room to avoid more questions.

In her room she kicked off her shoes and threw herself on the bed where she lay gazing up at the ceiling trying not to think. After ten minutes or so she knew she had to make an effort to pull herself together, so she rinsed her face and combed her hair. Hoping that she looked better than when she came in, Elizabeth went downstairs. Aunt Rose was busy at the stove and had her back to her.

"Is there anything I can do, Aunt Rose?"

"No thanks. You go straight into the dining room. I'll be with you shortly."

Aunt Gertrude was already seated at the table and she smiled at Elizabeth. "Tomorrow night our numbers will have swelled to double," she commented. "Marion and Richard will be with us and so will Mal. It will be quite a party."

Elizabeth dragged her mind from John and tried to concentrate on what her aunt was saying. "What time are they arriving?" she asked.

"They said about three thirty. Apparently the ferry leaves Wellington at nine thirty and the trip takes about three and a half hours to Picton. Then they will take a coach from Picton to Nelson which is about another two hours. I expect Mal will meet them at the coach station," said Aunt Gertrude.

"They should already be here by the time you arrive home, Elizabeth," said Aunt Rose who had joined them at the table. "It will be nice for Richard to have someone his own age here for a change. Have you any plans for the weekend?"

"I thought a walk following the Dun Mountain Railway track might be interesting. Actually, my friends from school, Mary and David, are keen to walk it so I thought the four of us might go together."

"What an excellent idea! I can see that appealing to Richard. He always was an active fellow," said Aunt Rose.

Her aunt's enthusiasm made Elizabeth feel more hopeful. *Perhaps it would not be such a difficult weekend after all. At least it would help keep her mind off John.* Elizabeth offered to go and collect Uncle Mal's tray. It was a relief to be out of doors and as she breathed deeply of the evening air, heavy with the scent of stock and roses and heard the sleepy twitterings of the small birds in the orchard her tired mind was soothed. The sun was setting behind the hills and Uncle Mal was leaning over the gate smoking his pipe.

"The best part of the day," he remarked, removing his pipe and looking down at Elizabeth.

"A good time for quiet contemplation," she said smiling back at him.

For some moments there was silence between them then Uncle Mal said unexpectedly. "How are you getting on with the journals, Elizabeth? Have you managed to read any of them?"

"I've only started the first, when Katey was twelve years old. She was excited about being allowed to take the scholarship exam for entry to a secondary school."

"That's right. She managed to get a place at Nelson Girls' College. She was fortunate that our parents permitted it because times were hard and they could have done with her help at home. Most of the other girls left school after Standard Six. Our Kate was a bright lass though, and she was prepared to work. It's strange how life panned out for her. I think she saw herself at the time as having a university career. Her great heroine was Miss Gibson, the Principal, who had her MA degree. I used to tease Katey and call her a blue-stocking but she was far from that. It is a pity that…" He stopped and drew reflectively on his pipe. Elizabeth wished he would continue but he said no more. The few comments he had made about Katey added to her curiosity about this aunt, whom she was just getting to know, and she determined to continue reading the journal that very evening.

"I'll go in now," she said. "It's been a tiring day."

"Goodnight then, sweet dreams."

As Elizabeth turned the corner of the verandah, suddenly the bellbird called, the notes clear as a bell on the evening air. She smiled and pulled open the door. When she reached her room she plumped up her pillows and leaned back on them, reaching for the journal on the bedside table. Fortunately, she had left a slip of paper between the pages she had been reading and they opened at Tuesday, 2nd February, 1895.

Elizabeth read with growing interest Katey's account of her first day at Nelson Girls' College. She and several other new girls had been ushered into the Principal's sitting room and this was her introduction to Miss Gibson. It is evident that the headmistress made a profound impression on the young girl. She wrote:-

Our Principal's name is Miss Gibson and I was surprised to see that she is quite young. She does not even wear spectacles and her hair is brown and wavy. She has deep blue eyes and when she smiles she is quite beautiful. She asked each of us our names and then she consulted papers in front of her. When she came to me she said, "You have very good examination marks, Katherine. You should do very well here if you work hard." I hardly knew what to say and I think I stammered.

Her observations on Miss Watson, the Assistant Principal, were acute:-

I'm afraid I didn't like her appearance. She has a frown and lines round her mouth. She has a way of looking as if she can see right through a girl and what she sees she does not like. I thought she did not even seem very friendly to Miss Gibson. I was disappointed to hear that she will be taking us for Latin and not Miss Gibson.

Apart from Latin, the other subjects taught in the school were French, physical science and algebra, history and geography, all academic thought Elizabeth. Music and drawing were extras and parents had to pay a fee for these. Katey did not mention whether her father was prepared to undertake the added expense.

By modern standards the school was small, having sixty-four pupils in all. Katey wrote:-

We were taken to the dining room to meet the Matron, Mrs. Mirams. She is quite young but has a commanding

presence. **Apparently she is in charge of the boarders of whom there are only fifteen. The rest of us are day girls, starting from Form 1 and going to Form 6. I suppose that means the oldest girls in the school will be seventeen and eighteen. Really they are young ladies and will have little to do with us younger ones.**

Because of the small numbers several forms were grouped together and Katey was placed in a class that comprised Forms One, Two and Three. It seemed that she enjoyed her first lesson in history and geography because she commented:-

Miss Gribben took us for history for an hour and then geography. I thought she was very interesting when she talked about the Restoration in England because she has been to so many of the places in London connected with Charles 2nd.

Elizabeth noted that history and probably geography were all about the British Isles. New Zealand, being a new country, was evidently not regarded as meriting study. At the end of her first day at the new school Katey was eager to tell the family of her experiences. Their reactions were typical:-

Mother was interested in everything but at supper, of course, father asked lots of questions about what I had learned that day. Rose wanted to know all about the other girls and whether I had made a new friend. Malcolm seemed amused at everything I said. Because he is now in his matriculation year I suppose I must seem very junior to him.

Katey finished her account of this momentous day:-

It has taken me a long time to write this entry but after

today I will keep records brief as prep will take up a lot of my time in the evening.

Elizabeth looked up from the journal on her lap and gazed unseeing through the window, still in Katey's world, where a secondary education was a privilege for girls, and educated women were a rarity. All the time she was reading Elizabeth had been able to push back thoughts of John Tamati, but now the memory of her conversation with him that afternoon came back sentence by sentence and she felt a pain like the twisting of a knife in her stomach.

CHAPTER SEVENTEEN

Friday seemed double the length of any other school day. David and Mary spoke briefly to Elizabeth at morning break and arranged to be at the house the next morning at eleven. Any alteration to the arrangements and they would telephone. At last the bell signalled the end of the day. As usual, Tommy lingered to help Elizabeth with cleaning the blackboard.

"Are you doing anything special at the weekend?" Elizabeth asked.

"My dad is taking us for a picnic to Rabbit Island. He says he will teach me to fish." Tommy's eyes were shining.

"That sounds lovely. You'll tell me all about it on Monday, won't you? Now I must fly. We are having visitors for the weekend."

Elizabeth picked up her satchel and went over to close the window, glancing over at the playing field. There was no sign of John Tamati this afternoon. Although she had not expected to see him she still felt a pang of disappointment. As she cycled home she went over the conversation she had had with him yesterday, recalling every nuance of his voice.

She was surprised to find herself already crossing the bridge over the brook and as she turned the corner she looked up to the old house and once more was struck by its timelessness.

Those old walls had stood for decades while the people within them had grown old and died. Possibly like her, they had suffered heartache and unfulfilled longings yet the house remained with all its secrets. Perhaps one day it would yield those secrets.

She was so busy with her thoughts Elizabeth had quite forgotten that this afternoon Richard and his mother would be arriving and in fact, might already be here. *Yes, there was Uncle Mal's car in the drive.* Elizabeth wheeled her bicycle into the shed and went slowly towards the kitchen. She could hear voices and an occasional laugh coming from the dining room. Feeling suddenly shy, she braced herself to go through the door. The room seemed crowded and Elizabeth had a confused impression of faces all turning in her direction. Instantly, Uncle Mal and Richard stood up. Richard came towards her with his hand outstretched and grasped Elizabeth's hand shaking it warmly. Then he stood back looking at her.

"My, my, I never expected my skinny little cousin with pigtails would grow up so good looking." He had laughing blue eyes and unruly fair hair that refused to sit down, although it was plastered with brylcream.

"And I never expected my naughty cousin would become a respectable lawyer," she rejoined.

"Touché," Martin said and everybody laughed.

Elizabeth turned to his mother. "How are you, Aunt Marion? I hope you had a smooth crossing."

"Oh, we did. The sea was like a millpond and it was just beautiful coming through Queen Charlotte Sound. I felt like a tourist seeing it for the first time." Elizabeth thought how attractive she was, with her blue eyes alive with interest, her short crisp hair and vivid colouring. She leaned forward in her chair and studied Elizabeth.

"I think it must be at least five years since I last saw you, Elizabeth. You were only a girl then and now you are grown up. Do you enjoy teaching here in Nelson?"

"Very much so, it took a little while to get used to, having a class of forty, after twenty-five last year, but now I know the children it is not so bad."

"Do you wave the strap in front of them to cow them into submission, or is your natural charm and personality enough to keep them in order?" Richard said this lightly but there was an appraising look in his eyes that made Elizabeth feel suddenly self-conscious.

"I'm sure Elizabeth's a very good teacher," said Aunt Marion giving Richard a warning look. "Now stop being a tease, Richard, and be sensible for five minutes. Aunt Rose tells me that a programme has been arranged for you tomorrow while I am seeing my friends. That will please you as you always say it's a bore to go visiting with me. Elizabeth will explain what she has planned."

"I have arranged with a couple of teacher friends of mine, to climb the Dun Mountain following the old railway track and wondered if you would like to join us," said Elizabeth forcing herself to meet Richard's eyes. There was something very unsettling about the way he grinned at her.

"What a splendid idea!" he said heartily. "I would be delighted to join the expedition."

Then turning to Uncle Mal and in a tone of voice, quite different from the one he had used to Elizabeth he said, "I am looking forward to seeing the improvements to the property you have made since I was last here."

"Well, let us go at once and leave the ladies to catch up on their news," replied Uncle Mal with alacrity.

"Please excuse us," said Richard making a mock bow in Elizabeth's direction.

The two men went out, talking animatedly. With their going the room suddenly lost life and colour and a short while afterwards Elizabeth excused herself.

"Dinner will be later this evening," said Aunt Rose as Elizabeth was leaving. "We'll be eating at six thirty."

When she was in her room Elizabeth sat on the bed, trying to sort out the kaleidoscope of events that had made up her day. She wandered across to the window and gazed down the valley to the sea. The future seemed as distant as that strip of blue water yet as she looked she saw it sparkling in the sunlight. From somewhere deep inside her came a spurt of hope.

When she went down to the kitchen she was glad to see that Aunt Rose was on her own. "Is there anything I can do?" Elizabeth asked.

"Oh, just butter some bread for me would you, dear. I was wanting to have a word with you about what happened yesterday at the Ladies Meeting."

Elizabeth felt guilty. She had been so taken up with John Tamati she had not given a thought to poor Mrs. Bulloch. "What did happen, Aunt Rose?"

"Well, it was rather strange. We had a visitor from somewhere in the North Island. He has a healing ministry apparently. When he came into the meeting he asked if there was anybody who needed prayer for a friend or someone they knew. I immediately thought of Mrs. Bulloch and when I put my hand up he asked me to come and sit in a chair at the front. Then he asked three of the ladies to come forward and pray with him. They all laid their hands on my shoulder and he prayed briefly for Mrs. Bulloch. Something very curious happened while he was praying. I felt something like an electric current run through my body from my head to my feet. Then when I stood up I felt very light."

Elizabeth could only stare at her aunt. "How amazing! I wonder what it could mean."

"I wonder if Mrs. Bulloch has received a touch from the Lord," said Aunt Rose thoughtfully.

"There is one way to find out. I can ring her sister."

"Would you, Elizabeth? I would love to know."

"I'll ring right away. I've got her number in my address book."

Elizabeth ran upstairs to fetch her book and then went into the parlour to use the phone. Aunt Rose stood at the door listening. Almost immediately a voice answered. Elizabeth recognized the Scottish accent. "It's Elizabeth Brookfield here," she began.

"Oh, Miss Brookfield, I've been longing to speak to you about my sister."

"I hope she's all right."

"More than all right, she's completely well. It's a miracle."

"What happened?"

"It was yesterday, about three o'clock. She was lying in bed and suddenly she sat up. 'Betty,' she said, 'something has just happened to me. I felt a kind of electric shock go right through me and out of my feet. Now I feel perfectly well. I'm getting up.' Then she got out of bed and dressed herself and went out to the kitchen. 'I'm famished,' she said. 'I could eat a horse.' Then we cooked up bacon, eggs and tomato and she ate every bit. Since then I haven't been able to stop her working. She's been right through the house, tidying out drawers and scrubbing everything. She has so much energy I can't keep up with her."

"That's wonderful," said Elizabeth. "Look, I'd like to hand you over to my aunt. I think she can tell you what has happened to your sister."

Aunt Rose took the phone from Elizabeth. "Would you please tell me what you just told my niece," she asked.

There was a long explanation and then Aunt Rose spoke very carefully. "Your sister was prayed for at that very time you mentioned. Three o'clock, wasn't it? I sat in for her and several people laid their hands on me and prayed. I too, felt something like an electric shock go through my body." Elizabeth noticed that there were tears in Aunt Rose's eyes.

"Yes, yes, it is very wonderful," she was saying as the voice at the other end continued. Finally Aunt Rose came off the phone. "We shouldn't really be surprised when God answers

190

prayer, Elizabeth, but I must confess to being moved by such a dramatic answer."

Elizabeth sat down in the nearest chair. Her legs were trembling. She felt overwhelmed by this glimpse of God's power. Her own troubles seemed so paltry somehow. *If God could bring about such a change in Mrs. Bulloch then anything was possible.*

CHAPTER EIGHTEEN

Saturday morning began with a light mist over the hills, but by nine o'clock this had cleared. Elizabeth went down to the kitchen for breakfast and found Richard reading the paper over a cup of tea. Immediately he folded the paper and leaned back smiling at her, his blue eyes crinkling with amusement as his gaze swept over her.

"How is it you manage to look dressy even when you are going tramping in the hills, Elizabeth? Where are your brogues and duffle coat?"

"For that matter where are your tramping boots and waterproof jacket? You look more dressed for the beach," Elizabeth retorted.

"Tit for tat, eh? Well, I like a girl with spirit." Richard grinned irrepressibly. "Look, I've finished my breakfast and read the paper. Here you are, nothing much in the news today." He handed her the paper and stretched lazily. "Now I'll leave you in peace."

He stood up, unfolding his long body and despite herself Elizabeth was aware of his muscular torso. She felt half amused and half irritated with him as he winked at her before leaving the kitchen. She only glanced over the headlines and then made a hasty breakfast. With David and Mary coming at ten she needed time to cut some sandwiches for lunch. She was just finishing when Aunt Rose came into the kitchen.

"Elizabeth, are you going to be able to climb in those sandals?" she asked looking down at them.

"They'll be fine, Aunt Rose, really." *Why was she making so much fuss about her footwear?*

"Well, I think you are going to have a fine day anyway," commented her aunt.

Elizabeth went upstairs to get a satchel which would be useful for carrying lunch and other odd items. Promptly at ten o'clock David's car drew up outside in the drive and he and Mary came to the door. They were both sensibly dressed in jeans and walking shoes. Richard came through to the kitchen a minute later. Elizabeth introduced David and Mary to him and she couldn't help noticing that Richard gave Mary a quick glance then turned to David with a friendly grin. At that moment Elizabeth was unreasonably glad that Mary was plain.

"Have you climbed the Dun Mountain track?" David asked Richard.

"Oh, a number of times, but not recently. It's quite easy but rugged in some places, especially near the top."

"You'll be able to lead the way then," said David. "If every one's ready let's go, shall we?"

He and Richard set off in front, Mary and Elizabeth dropping behind. As they walked along the road, keeping to the grassy edge where there was no footpath, Elizabeth thought how similar the two men were from behind, both slim and much the same height, yet from the front how different: David with his mop of dark curly hair and deep-set brown eyes, Richard with his blonde tousled locks and blue eyes that seemed to be forever dancing, as though he found the world an amusing place.

Mary whispered to Elizabeth. "Your cousin is very good looking."

"I suppose so, I hadn't really noticed," whispered back Elizabeth. "He's an awful tease and can be a bit annoying." Mary looked at her surprised.

193

After they had walked some distance along Brook Street they came to wide track on their left. "This is where the walk begins," said Richard. "It is the incline section of the railway, where the horses would have towed the wagons."

"There don't appear to be any rails or sleepers," remarked David.

"No, they were all uplifted in 1872 when the railway was sold off."

"You seem to know a lot about it, Richard," said Mary, a note of admiration in her voice.

He smiled back at her and Elizabeth felt a twinge of jealousy, which surprised and annoyed her.

"Oh, the Brookfield family are very proud of the Dun Mountain Railway. It shares its birthday with the house and they are never tired of talking about it. You should hear Uncle Mal on the subject."

"Oh, I have," said David. "He got me really interested in the railway and I have been looking forward to walking it ever since."

"From here to Four Corners the cutting is intact, but after that, along to Third House the track has been widened."

"What was Third House?" asked Elizabeth.

"The pub where they stopped and had a drop of beer to help them on their way," Richard winked at her.

"Oh, do be sensible," said Elizabeth laughing.

"Actually, it was a stable for the horses because these were all horse drawn wagons," said Richard seriously. "Anyway, we'd better push on or we'll never get to the top before evening."

The two men chatted companionably as Mary and Elizabeth walked behind them. "Elizabeth," said Mary quietly. "Have you ever thought of a trip to England?"

"You mean a kind of working holiday?"

"Yes, I am planning to go at the end of next year."

"It's something I've always wanted to do," said Elizabeth

wistfully. "Jeanette was telling me about some of her adventures one day in the staffroom and I thought then I'd love to go."

"Well, why not come with me? You will have done two years in the school and have had enough teaching experience to get a job in London."

Elizabeth clutched at the idea. If she had something like a trip overseas to look forward to it would take her mind off John Tamati.

"I think we would get on OK," added Mary.

"I'm sure we would," said Elizabeth, her imagination racing ahead.

"What are you two girls whispering about?" said David turning around to them. "You look as though you're hatching a plot."

"Oh, we've just decided to go to England together," said Mary airily.

Richard swung around and for once he was not smiling. "When are you going - next month, next year?"

"Oh not for a couple of years," replied Mary.

Something like relief crossed his face, Elizabeth noted. *Perhaps he hoped to see more of Mary. Again she felt a stab of jealousy. How silly she was being. She was in love with John and even if Richard were interested in Mary what difference should that make? She was being a dog in the manger.*

By now they seemed to have reached a flat section. "This is the Wairoa Saddle," explained Richard, "and Third House would have been over there." He pointed to a clearing on the right. "After this the going gets tougher," he added, "because there has been a lot of subsidence. Mind where you put your feet."

They all continued walking and silence seemed to have settled on them. Elizabeth found herself thinking about England. *How exciting to visit the Tower of London and watch the changing of the guard at Buckingham Palace. She might even see the Queen.*

They started the climb beyond Third House and it was just as Richard had said, the ground was very uneven. Suddenly

Elizabeth felt her right foot give way and she fell heavily, her ankle turning over. She screamed and tears came unbidden, the pain was so intense. Richard and David ran to her, their faces shocked.

Bending down beside her shoulder Richard said gently, "We'll try to lift you, Elizabeth. Do you think you can stand?"

"I'll try," she said, her face twisting with pain.

"You take her left arm under the shoulder," said Richard to David, "and I'll take the right. One, two, three, lift." Elizabeth bit her lip to stop crying out. Once she was on her feet Richard said to her, "Put your arms around our shoulders, Elizabeth, and we'll take your weight. Now can you put down your left foot and hop?"

"Yes," she said though the movement caused a stab of pain .

"It's a good job we are not even half way," remarked Richard, "and it's all downhill."

"She's only a featherweight too," said David.

Mary took out a handkerchief and dabbed at the tears on Elizabeth's face.

"You are all so kind," murmured Elizabeth and then gasped with pain.

"Just let us take your weight," said Richard. "Don't try to help us."

They went a few yards and stopped.

"Look, why don't you go on ahead to the house and ring for an ambulance?" Richard said to Mary. "That way they may be able to bring a stretcher up the hill. I don't think Elizabeth can put up with more of this. She looks ready to faint."

"Good idea," said Mary. "I'll go as fast as I can."

"Don't you break your ankle too!" yelled David at her retreating back.

"I think the best we can do is let Elizabeth rest," Richard said across to David. "Look there's a good-sized log at the side of the track. Do you think you can sit down, Elizabeth?"

"Yes," she breathed thankfully as they carried her to it.

Once she was sitting down Elizabeth examined her right ankle. It was already looking very puffy and was bulging over her sandal. Richard and David withdrew a couple of feet away and talked together in low tones. Richard came over to her.

"Look, Elizabeth, David and I think we can carry you down the track as far as Brook Street anyway, so we should be there by the time the ambulance arrives."

"Are you sure you can take my weight all that way?"

"Oh, I don't know. With a ten ton Tessie like you we might collapse on the way down," joked David.

"Now you put an arm around each of our necks," said Richard as he and David crouched down beside her. As they stood up simultaneously they made a seat with their hands and lifted her effortlessly.

"You're a mere featherweight," said Richard. "We'll soon have you down to the bottom of the hill."

The two men strode along the track with Elizabeth swinging between them, *for all the world like some kind of Indian princess being carried by native slaves,* she thought. Their shoulders felt warm and strong under her arms and if it hadn't been for the pain in her ankle she would have enjoyed the sensation of being carried by two muscular young men. Neither of them said much but concentrated on moving along as fast as they could, watching the ground for unevenness.

"Not far to go now," said David as they passed a turning in the track. Suddenly there were voices.

"That could be the ambulance men," said Richard and sure enough round the next bend appeared two men carrying a stretcher. David and Richard stopped and waited for them to approach.

"So this is our casualty," said the older one jocularly as the two men placed the stretcher on the ground. "Well, young lady how do you feel?" Without waiting for a reply he addressed David and Richard. "Now you lower the young lady on to the stretcher."

"Just relax, my dear," he said to Elizabeth. "Lie back and let us do all the work. We'll strap you in to make sure you don't fall off." Elizabeth was reminded of Mrs. Bulloch and wondered if she too looked like a trussed chicken. Very gently the older man examined her foot, yet Elizabeth still winced at his touch.

"Mm, looks like more than a sprain to me. Possibly the ankle is broken but we won't know until we've seen the x-ray. Anyway, the quicker we get you to Casualty the better."

The two men lifted the stretcher and set off with David and Richard following behind. Elizabeth felt helpless and rather embarrassed at being the cause of so much trouble but the pain in her foot soon overcame all other feelings and she tried not to cry out when a sudden jolt sent pain shooting through her ankle.

It was a relief when at last they came to the end of the track and she saw in front of them the ambulance pulled up at the side of the road. Deftly the younger man reached up to turn the handle of the back door, which swung open revealing grooves on the floor. The two men lifted the stretcher onto the metal tracks and slid it into the van.

"Are you accompanying the young lady to the hospital?" asked the older man.

"Of course," said Richard as he and David jumped into the back.

The drive to the hospital was smooth but seemed interminable to Elizabeth. As they entered the hospital gates she was relieved that this part of the ordeal was over. The van stopped and the two ambulance men came round to the back and opened the door. David and Richard jumped out and stood awkwardly looking on as the men lifted out the stretcher and placed it on a trolley.

After that it was all confusion to Elizabeth. She was given an injection to relieve the pain and when she tried to remember afterwards the sequence of events everything was a muddle. She remembered her ankle being x-rayed and a serious young doctor squinting at the film, pronouncing that the ankle was fractured in two places. Then she was taken to another room to have it set in plaster. The weight on her leg felt dreadful. Elizabeth lost all sense of time. She wouldn't have known whether she was two or three hours at the hospital. At last, she was taken out to another ambulance and amazingly Richard and David were waiting beside it. They jumped into the back and sat down in the seat next to the stretcher.

"You see, we didn't desert you, Elizabeth," said Richard with his incorrigible grin, "though you've been an age."

"I think we've read every blessed magazine in that waiting room," added David.

"I'm sorry to have been such a nuisance," said Elizabeth tears in her eyes.

"Just make sure you don't make a habit of it," said Richard with a laugh. "Now you've got to face the aunts and my mother. They'll all be clucking around you."

Sure enough, when the ambulance arrived at the house everybody was waiting in the drive. As the two men lifted out the stretcher Aunt Rose came forward to lead them into the house. "We are putting you in Gertrude's room for the time being, Elizabeth. The bed is made up there."

"Oh, poor Aunt Gertrude, where will you sleep?" Elizabeth twisted her neck around to look at her.

"I'm in your room now, Elizabeth, and all of your things have been moved downstairs into mine. Don't worry, I'll enjoy the change," and she came forward to pat Elizabeth's hand.

The two ambulance men waited patiently during this exchange until suddenly Aunt Rose became aware of them. "Oh, I'm sorry to hold you up," she said apologetically. "Please come this way," and she led them round the front of the house and onto the verandah.

As they carried Elizabeth through the open door and into Aunt Gertrude's room it was as though they were entering a shady bower. Carefully the two men lifted Elizabeth from the stretcher on to the bed while Aunt Rose plumped up the pillows behind her head.

"Now I think we'll leave you to have a little rest," said Aunt Rose firmly. "Then in half an hour's time I'll bring you a cup of tea." With that she went out, the ambulance men following her.

Elizabeth was glad to be alone and quiet at last. She lay back on the pillows content to lie in this cool and restful room. Her mind drifted and she dozed for some minutes. Suddenly she heard voices and a soft tap at the door. "Come in," she called. Richard, David and Mary walked in quietly and stood at the end of the bed.

"You're looking much better," remarked Mary, "In fact, quite yourself. It was awful to see you in pain up there on the track."

"If it hadn't been for all of you, it would have been a great deal worse. Thank you, Mary, for summoning the ambulance so promptly and you, Richard and David, for carrying me all the way down the mountain."

"Oh, that was really heavy work," said David grinning.

"Sitting in the casualty waiting room for three hours was the heavy work," said Richard. "I suppose it's a case of, 'They also serve who only sit and wait.'"

"Elizabeth, your aunts have been most kind and given us a lovely afternoon tea," said Mary.

"Yes, scones, jam and cream," said David, "The best I've tasted. By the way, Elizabeth, I will let Mr. Ray know about your broken ankle. I shouldn't think you'll be able to walk for a while, except on crutches," and he nodded at the pair leaning against the wall beside the bed. "So it looks like no school for you for a while," he added.

"Oh, goodness, I hadn't thought of that," said Elizabeth. "I suppose he'll have to get in a reliever."

"Don't you worry about it," said Mary, "Just lie back and rest." She had been watching Elizabeth closely and seen the shadow that passed across her face. "Your class will be fine.

You've got them into a good routine and anybody taking over will find them a piece of cake."

"We'll keep you posted on what goes on. I'll come and plague you every few days," added David grinning. Elizabeth smiled back at him and Mary, grateful for their reassurance.

Richard had been standing by listening. "I think we should let Elizabeth have a bit of peace now," he said quietly. "She's been through rather a lot today."

Elizabeth looked at him surprised. This was a different Richard from the tease she had been accustomed to. He was looking down at her with real concern in his eyes.

"All right, point taken, see you soon, Elizabeth," said David cheerfully.

Mary came over to the bed and took her hand, giving it a warm squeeze. "Don't you worry about anything, Elizabeth, everything will be fine."

As they went out Richard turned round and gave her a broad wink. Once they were gone the room seemed suddenly empty. Elizabeth lay back on the pillows and looked around her. When she had last seen this room it had been full of bric-a-brac. Now that it was clear it was really a lovely room, with its colonial dressing table and beautifully carved wardrobe. The tilted mirror over the dressing table reflected the large rhododendron growing in front of the verandah.

Suddenly through the open window the bellbird called, the notes falling on the still air like a message of hope.

CHAPTER NINETEEN

Elizabeth had a bad night. The weight of the plaster encasing her lower leg and ankle made it difficult to turn and she had to lie on her back most of the night. When morning came she was unrested and her eyes felt sticky. There was a soft knock at the door and Aunt Rose's head appeared around it. "Are you awake, Elizabeth?" she whispered.

"Yes, Aunt Rose," and Elizabeth struggled into a sitting position.

"I've brought you some breakfast." She then came in with a tray, daintily laid with tea things:- a boiled egg, toast in a silver rack, and a small pot of marmalade. Elizabeth had not been hungry but her mouth watered at the sight. Aunt Rose smiled as she laid the tray on the bed.

"I rang your parents yesterday to let them know about your accident and that you were home safe and sound, though with your foot in plaster. I spoke to your mother and father and said that you would write to them. That was all right I hope, dear."

"Oh, yes, thank you for that, Aunt Rose. I will write this afternoon. I do try to write each Sunday and keep them up to date."

Aunt Rose continued. "As you know, Elizabeth, we will all be going to church this morning but we won't be long. Do you think you will be all right on your own?"

202

"Yes, of course, Aunt Rose. I might even have a chance to try out my crutches. Anyway, I have to go to the bathroom using them."

"You be very careful, my dear. It would be dreadful if you slipped and fell. Once you've had your breakfast I'll go with you to the bathroom, just to be on hand."

Elizabeth smiled to herself at the thought of a frail, little old lady trying to pick her up but she thanked her aunt and attacked her breakfast. Aunt Rose stood by and watched with satisfaction as every morsel disappeared. She picked up the tray and waited while Elizabeth struggled to lift her legs over the side of the bed. Elizabeth reached for the crutches before trusting her feet to the floor. Bracing herself she stood up and placed her weight on her left foot. Aunt Rose stood by watching her tensely. Tentatively Elizabeth took a step and then another. "There, I'm getting the hang of it now," she said.

Carefully she made her way along the passage with Aunt Rose following. The step from the passage to the parlour appeared to be an obstacle but Elizabeth managed to swing herself up to the higher level without difficulty. At the bathroom door she said to Aunt Rose, "I think I'll be all right now, thank you."

"Yes, you seem to get along on those crutches as though you've been doing it all your life."

It was with a sense of accomplishment that Elizabeth let herself into the bathroom. It was good to be independent. When she got back to her room she put the crutches beside the bed and swung her legs back on to it. She sat thinking for some time. *Rather than spend the day in bed she ought to dress and try to use the crutches around the house. As Aunt Gertrude had changed rooms with her then her clothes must be in the wardrobe and in the drawers in the dressing table, but where were the journals?* They were nowhere to be seen. Elizabeth felt a momentary panic. *Perhaps Aunt Gertrude had kept them, but no, she would never do that without telling her. Anyway, the room was so tidy Aunt Gertrude had probably swept all her own things from the locker and dressing table and done the same with Elizabeth's upstairs then put everything into drawers. There was only one way to find out.*

Managing the crutches quite easily now, Elizabeth propelled herself across the room to the dressing table and pulled open the top drawer. Handkerchiefs, hair grips, hand lotions, talcum powder and other toiletries were all neatly arranged. In the second drawer were her underclothes and in the third, various tops and cardigans. The journals, with other books and stationary, must be in the locker. Elizabeth tapped her way across the floor and bending down, with difficulty opened the door. Relieved, she saw the journals placed neatly on one side. Lifting them out with her Bible she put them on the locker. Just at that moment she heard footsteps coming down the stairs. It must be nearly time for going to church.

There was a light tap on the door and Aunt Gertrude came into the room. She was wearing a lime green swing coat over a slim navy- blue skirt. *She looks smart enough for the Melbourne races,* thought Elizabeth irreverently.

Her aunt's smile was kind. "You are looking much better, Elizabeth. How are you feeling?"

"Oh, I'm fine, Aunt Gertrude. Thanks for arranging my things so neatly. You are very good, letting me take over your room."

"That's perfectly all right. I just hope you'll be comfortable, dear. I must say I'm enjoying the view from your room down the valley." She glanced around her. "Now when we come home from church I'll get Richard to bring a comfortable chair and a footstool for you so you can sit up." She nodded to Elizabeth and slipped from the room.

A few minutes later the house went very quiet. *They must all have left for church.* Elizabeth once more made her way across the room to the wardrobe. She took out one of her few shop- made dresses, pink crimplene with cap sleeves and a v neck and laid it on the bed. Dressing herself, without putting weight on her broken ankle, was a balancing feat but she managed it. *Now she would go for a walk around the house using the crutches.*

She set off along the passage and swung herself over the step into the parlour. She did the same going down into the kitchen. On her left the door into the dining room was closed. *Could it be locked?* Elizabeth turned the handle. Sure enough it was. Elizabeth stood thinking for some moments. *What was the reason? It couldn't be to keep her out as they would not have imagined her even trying to go in. It must be that they were afraid of burglars, but surely when there was someone in the house that couldn't be a possibility.* Elizabeth gave up the puzzle.

Feeling thirsty she went to the fridge and took out the ginger beer bottle. After she had drunk a glass of the cool sweet liquid she went outside and sat down at the table in the porch. The morning sun was warm without being hot and Elizabeth enjoyed the feel of it against her bare arms. All around her the lazy drone of bees and birdsong filled the air.

Elizabeth sat for some time enjoying the peace and sense of timelessness that seemed to envelope the house. Eventually she stood up and tapped her way along the path that led round the front of the house to the verandah. She was loth to go back into her shady room but sat down on one of the cane chairs, resting her foot on the seat of another and gazed down the grassy bank to the orchard beyond. Here she remained for some time, simply content to sit in the sunshine.

Elizabeth was not aware of the passage of time and it seemed she had only been sitting for a few minutes when she heard the unmistakable chug of the Morris Minor pulling into the drive. She remained where she was and some minutes later Marion's quick step along the passage reached her. The door onto the verandah was opened.

"Oh, there you are Elizabeth. I peeped into your room and

you weren't there so I guessed you would be sitting on the verandah. You are looking much better today."

"I'm feeling much better too and best of all, I find I can get around using the crutches, at least for short distances. How did you find the service?"

"It was good, quite inspirational, though as an Anglican I miss the use of the prayer book."

"Do you and Richard usually attend church on a Sunday?"

"I go regularly but recently Richard has been trying out different denominations. He says he finds the Anglican Church service irrelevant to his everyday life. I suppose everyone has to make their own spiritual journey. What about you, Elizabeth?"

Elizabeth hesitated. "I've always gone with my family to a Baptist church in Auckland but when I came to Nelson I intended to look around at different churches. Now I go with the aunts and Uncle Mal to the Baptist. It seems to please them that we all keep together and so far I've enjoyed the services."

Marion nodded. "I quite understand. I think I would do the same in your place. Anyway, I'd better go inside and see what I can do to help. I'll bring your lunch out here on a tray. Would you like that, Elizabeth?"

"Yes, but soon I hope I'll be able to join you in the dining room."

"Oh, there's plenty of time. Just enjoy being waited on for a few days." With that she disappeared and Elizabeth was once more on her own. A short time later she heard footsteps coming down the passage, a heavier tread this time and Richard appeared carrying a tray.

"Your lunch, Madam," he said flourishing an imaginary napkin. "I hope all is to your liking."

Elizabeth giggled, then entering into the game she said haughtily, "Thank you, James, place it on the table there and I will call you if I need anything further."

Richard did as she bade him, then stood back looking down

206

at her. "You certainly play the part of 'milady' as if to the manner born, Elizabeth."

"I love acting. At college I was in the drama club."

"And had a leading part, I bet."

"Sometimes," she said modestly.

"I'd better skedaddle, but after lunch I'd like to come and sit with you on the verandah. That's if you don't mind."

Elizabeth coloured. "No, I'd like that, Richard. You might be able to answer some of my questions."

"I'll try. See you later then."

When he had gone Elizabeth turned her attention to the tray. The cold chicken and salad looked appetizing and she suddenly felt very hungry. Eating lunch in the open air was enjoyable she decided, even if she were on her own.

Aunt Gertrude was the next to appear, carrying a plate heaped with fruit salad in one hand and a small jug of yellow cream in the other. "I came instead of Richard. He couldn't be trusted not to linger outside talking to you. We all had to wait some time before he appeared for his first course." She said this smiling but her gaze lingered on Elizabeth speculatively.

"My fault, Aunt Gertrude, I kept him talking."

"Hmm," she said picking up Elizabeth's plate, and went back inside.

Quarter of an hour later Richard reappeared, swept all the dishes on to the tray and returned to the kitchen. Minutes later he was back and pulled up one of the cane chairs opposite Elizabeth. "Now what are these questions you wish to put to me?" he asked curiously.

"Well, first of all, Richard, each Sunday morning that I haven't gone to church I've noticed that the door to the dining room is locked, also that there are no photographs anywhere. It all seems strange to me."

"Yes, it is indeed strange and the explanation is even stranger." Richard was gazing thoughtfully at the garden. "You see, Elizabeth, about ten years ago everyone was out of the house. I think they had gone to church and when they returned the dining room was in an uproar. Photographs had been thrown on the floor, yet books and ornaments were still in place and drawers were all open. Naturally, the aunts assumed that thieves had been in the house but there was nothing stolen, not even a large sum of money that was in a wallet in one of the drawers. They tidied everything up and the following Sunday the same thing happened. The room was mayhem." Involuntarily Elizabeth shivered.

"Well, all they could think was that a poltergeist had been at work and so they asked the Baptist minister to come and conduct an exorcism. The poor chap had never been asked to do such a thing before and so he consulted the vicar of the local Anglican Church who agreed to do the exorcism."

"Did that fix it?"

"I believe it did, because they never had a repetition of the problem, but Aunt Gertrude, being a bit of a sceptic, still maintained it could have been someone's idea of a sick joke, so ever afterwards they've kept the dining room door locked, just in case."

"What I find interesting is why there should be a poltergeist in the first place," said Elizabeth, frowning.

"Nobody seems quite sure, but I know a chap who was in the police and he told me they had to investigate a store where boxes kept being stacked up in odd places at night, after the shop was locked. Sometimes chairs were found perched on the stairs at precarious angles. The shop manager was nearly out of his mind. He told my friend that he had been to a séance to try and contact his father and it was after that, the shop had the poltergeist visitation. When the manager left, all the poltergeist activity ceased."

"So it could have been a visitor to the house that caused the upheaval," said Elizabeth thoughtfully.

"Could be, but at any rate after the vicar had done his exorcism there was no further disturbance."

"And what about the photographs?"

'Well, because they were thrown to the ground the aunts decided to keep them in drawers; quite a simple explanation really.

"I have always wanted to see a photograph of the family, especially Aunt Katey."

"My grandma, the beauty of the family from all accounts and clever too. Nobody could understand why she married my grandfather. He was at least fifteen years older than she was and a German, at a time when Germans were unpopular in New Zealand. He actually changed his name by deed pole."

Elizabeth leaned forward eagerly. She longed to find out more about Katey. Suddenly Uncle Mal walked around the corner of the verandah.

"Hello, Elizabeth, hello, Richard. I hope I'm not interrupting. You both seem deep in conversation. I actually came to see you, Elizabeth, since it's now a day after your accident and I haven't spent five minutes alone with you."

Elizabeth smiled brightly at him. "Oh, Richard here has been keeping me entertained with stories about the family."

"I'm afraid I've been monopolizing Elizabeth," said Richard standing up. "It's your turn now, Uncle Mal."

The old man's eyes twinkled. "I'm sure she'd rather talk to a young blood like you than spend time with an old codger."

"No, I'm always glad to see you, Uncle Mal," said Elizabeth stoutly, secretly regretting the time with Richard had been cut short.

Uncle Mal sat down and lit his pipe while Richard went back into the house. The two of them sat companionably in silence for a few moments until Uncle Mal asked, "What actually happened up there on the Dun Mountain, Elizabeth?" She then gave him a graphic account of the walk and how she came to break her ankle, while he listened carefully. She was just describing her experience at the hospital when Aunt Rose appeared with a tea tray.

"I think you are looking tired, Elizabeth. It might be a good idea to go and lie down after you've drunk your tea."

Elizabeth had been aware of tiredness creeping over her and was grateful for the opening to leave Uncle Mal, for although normally she enjoyed his company the effort of talking had sapped her energy. She picked up her crutches and hoisted herself out of the chair. Uncle Mal stood up awkwardly.

"Let me help you, Missy."

"No really, Uncle Mal, I can manage," and Elizabeth swung herself forward to demonstrate. She made her way to her room and was glad to lie down on the bed, feeling suddenly exhausted. As she lay there she turned to look at the journals on the bedside table. She was more eager than ever to read them and hear from Katey herself an account of her strange marriage. Richard seemed to know a lot about his grandmother and Elizabeth wished she had been able to question him further.

Perhaps she would not get a chance now, as he and his mother would be leaving in the morning. She would miss him. At first he had annoyed her with his flippancy and the way he teased her but since the accident his manner towards her had changed. He now treated her more seriously and when he looked at her there was a new expression in his eyes that she could not quite analyze. They still twinkled with mischief but there was something else behind them. She thought again about the locked room and what Richard had told her about the poltergeist and Elizabeth shivered. *She preferred to take Aunt Gertrude's point of view and put down the disturbance to vandals and yet, she could not be sure.*

Determinedly Elizabeth turned her mind to other things. *How strange it would be, not to have to go to school in the morning. Who would take her place and how would the children react to a new teacher? What would John think when he heard about her accident?* At the thought of him Elizabeth's heart began to beat faster. *What would it be like not to see him for several weeks?*

210

*Perhaps it would help get him out of her system, like an alcoholic
being weaned off drink.*

Elizabeth lay back and closed her eyes, trying to banish
from her mind all worrying thoughts. Gradually the peace of
the house seeped into her and she began to feel sleepy.

She was wakened an hour later by the door squeaking.
Opening her eyes she saw Richard awkwardly pushing it open
with his shoulder while holding a tray.

"Oh, you are awake. I've brought your tea as you can see."
As he came across the room to the bed his eyes sparkled
mischievously. "It took a bit of hard talking to get the aunts to
agree to me bringing your tray. They think I will hold them all
up by staying and chatting to you. So I promised on my honour
I'd come straight back, but I will return and fetch the tray and
then we can have a chat. There won't be another opportunity as
we leave before nine tomorrow morning." He grinned down at
Elizabeth. "So, my lady, bon appetit and see you soon."

He placed the tray carefully in front of her, gave a little bow
and left the room. Elizabeth smiled to herself and looked at the
tray. It was laid attractively but she had no appetite, she still felt
full from lunch. She made an effort and managed to eat a couple
of dainty sandwiches and a piece of cake by the time Richard
reappeared.

He eyed the tray, "Not hungry, eh? We can't send that back
to the kitchen. The cook would be offended. I'll help you out,"
and he scooped up a couple of sandwiches. "There, made short
work of those. Now I'll take the tray through and then come
back and have a chat. That is if you want some company."

"Of course, I've still more questions for you, Richard."

He swung up the tray and was gone while Elizabeth adjusted
her pillows and reached into the drawer of the bedside table to
take out a comb and her makeup purse. She didn't want to be
too obviously made up, so after applying her lipstick she
brushed her lips lightly with face powder then flicked the comb
through her hair.

She had just finished when Richard returned. He pulled up the chair beside the bed and looked across at her. "For someone who's supposed to be an invalid you look remarkably well," he commented. "Now fire away, what else do you want to know about this family?"

"It's actually about Aunt Gertrude and Uncle Mal." Elizabeth hesitated. She was not sure how much she should tell Richard about the altercation she had overheard.

Richard frowned and the light went from his eyes. "It's a sad story, that. You see Aunt Gertrude was engaged to an up- and-coming young businessman. He had a grocery store and was doing so well that he was about to open another. He went to Uncle Mal and asked him to invest a large sum of money. As you know, Uncle Mal was a partner in a law firm in Nelson."

"No, I didn't know that."

"I suppose nobody round here ever mentions it. Anyway, Uncle Mal was highly respected and all the Baptist people used his services."

"Was Aunt Gertrude's fiancé a member of the Baptist?"

"Not really. He used to go to services to please her but he wasn't a member. Anyway, to cut a long story short, her fiancé, whose name I forget, gave Uncle Mal this money to invest and he bought shares in a company that promised high returns but went bankrupt. All the money was lost and the fiancé had to sell his business. He broke his engagement and moved out of Nelson."

"Oh, how dreadful for Aunt Gertrude!"

"Yes, I don't think she was ever able to forgive Uncle Mal and of course she never married after that."

"But it was awful for Uncle Mal too. He must have felt bad for ruining the man."

"He did and he tried to compensate him. For several years he paid back every penny he could spare but unfortunately, Nelson being a small place everyone knew about it and people lost faith in the law firm. Uncle Mal and his partner had to sell the business. Uncle Mal was a broken man and became a virtual recluse."

"How simply dreadful!" exclaimed Elizabeth, "Poor Uncle Mal, and all that because he made a mistake over an investment."

"Yes, well, in our line of work you can't afford to make mistakes like that, especially when you're handling other people's money. Still, I think everyone realizes Uncle Mal has done his best to put the matter right, but Aunt Gertrude lost out on marrying the man she loved and that couldn't be rectified."

Richard looked at Elizabeth and smiled. "But all that happened a long time ago and you mustn't let it trouble you. Uncle Mal seems to have got over it now. In fact, I don't think I've ever seen him as cheerful as he is at the moment and even he and Aunt Gertrude are talking to each other." Elizabeth looked out of the window feeling deep sadness for the two lives that had been spoiled.

"Come on, Elizabeth, cheer up. Don't look so tragic. Now before I go there is something I want to ask you." Something in his tone arrested her. She jerked her head around. He was gazing at her, his blue eyes steady. He cleared his throat before speaking. "Look, Elizabeth, I'm not good at making speeches, but now I've got to know you, I'd like to know you better. Would you mind if I wrote to you and even came to see you before long, without mother of course?"

Elizabeth dropped her eyes. Her mind swirled with conflicting emotions.

She stammered, "We are cousins, Richard."

"What difference does that make? We're only second cousins anyway. What about it?" he demanded.

"Well, yes." Elizabeth spoke haltingly. "I would like to get to know you better, Richard." He stood up and looked down at her, a relieved smile lighting up his whole face. She noticed how his curly fringe resisted the brylcream and was flopping over his forehead and that his blue eyes were once more sparkling.

"Now I'd better go, dear coz," he said and seized her hand putting it to his lips. "Goodnight and sweet dreams."

When he had gone Elizabeth lay back against the pillows trying to sort out her feelings. She did like Richard and he was great fun to be with, but beyond that she was not sure. Anyway, she was in love with John and at the thought of him her heart lurched. It was all too soon to make decisions.

CHAPTER TWENTY

Next morning the house was astir very early and Elizabeth woke to the sound of scurrying footsteps above her and on the stairs. Just before they were about to leave Marion and Richard looked in on her. Marion bent down and kissed her swiftly.

"Now don't forget to keep in touch with us and when you are mobile again do pop across to Wellington and stay with us. You are always welcome, Elizabeth."

"And I second that," said Richard, giving her a broad wink.

"Thank you both. I would like to visit you sometime and I promise to write," said Elizabeth, glancing at Richard. "Have a good journey across the water."

Marion looked at her watch and said briskly, "Come on, Richard, we mustn't keep Uncle Mal waiting."

Then they were gone and it seemed to Elizabeth that the house was suddenly empty and lifeless. Slowly she heaved herself from the bed. This morning she had decided she would sit up as much as possible and so she made her way to the wardrobe to look out something comfortable to wear. Aunt Rose appeared in the doorway carrying a tray.

"I see you're up already, Elizabeth. She put the tray down carefully on the bedside table. "Well, they're gone," she said, "Everything now seems a bit flat. With them here it was like home once more, the way it used to be, when there were young people in and out all the time." She gave Elizabeth a shrewd look. "You and Richard seemed to get on well, though I detected a certain frostiness in your manner at first."

"Well, he was a tease and seemed to like making fun of me at first, but then after my fall he was so kind I realized I had misjudged him."

"Oh, yes, he really has a very kind heart. We are very fond of him. Even when he was a naughty small boy he would surprise us by some thoughtful little action." She glanced at her watch. "Now I'll leave you to eat your breakfast and collect the tray shortly." She looked curiously at Elizabeth. "What do you think of doing today? Have you got something to read?"

"Yes, thank you," said Elizabeth thinking of the journals. She would now have an opportunity to read them at leisure and learn more about teaching methods of the past. Then there was Katey. Perhaps the journals would provide a key to her strange marriage.

Sometime later Elizabeth went out to the verandah. She arranged herself comfortably, propping up her right leg on the seat of one of the cane chairs and keeping well back from the sun. It would never do to expose the brittle pages to bright light. She opened the journal at the next entry, dated Thursday, 4th February, 1891.

Today we had our first French lesson with Miss Riche or Mam'selle, as she has asked us to address her. Halfway through the lesson she began to sneeze, a succession of polite little explosions. When she had finished she gasped, "Oh, pardon. It eez the pollen in the air. It always sets me off. And I 'ave come without a handkerchief."

Ellen took one from her pocket. "You can have this, Mam'selle. It's quite clean."

Mam'selle took it from her gratefully and then carried on with the lesson as though nothing had happened. I was impressed by her coolness. Later on she congratulated me

on my good accent and made me read a passage out loud to the class.

When I got home Mother had been baking all morning. She made shortbread, fruit cake, (father's favourite), shrewsbury biscuits and apple cake, which she said was Mrs. Davis's recipe, one she brought out from Dorset. I always enjoy coming home on Tuesdays as it is Mother's baking day and she often tries out a new recipe she has got from a neighbour.

Elizabeth thought for a moment. This entry seemed humdrum, yet it did give a glimpse of a close knit community where neighbours shared freely with each other. Most of them would have been fresh arrivals from England and so retained their English ways. She was amused by the next day's entry:-

Mam'selle waited until we were all sitting down and then she called on Ellen to come to the front. In French she thanked her and with great ceremony presented her with her laundered handkerchief and a little present wrapped and tied with a ribbon. "Merci, Mam'selle," Ellen said hesitatingly and blushed. At recess she showed me her present. It was a little doll dressed like a French sailor. Ellen was delighted with it and said that she was now going to collect dolls and dress them up herself.

When I got home today I told mother all about Mam'selle and the handkerchief but she just sniffed and said, "The French are peculiar. Fancy the woman not having a handkerchief in the first place."

I don't know what she would say about the other teachers. They all seem to have their funny little ways. For instance, Miss Gibson is so clever and can recite reams of Shakespeare and all the major poets but she is quite forgetful. Today she had to leave the class to go and find the register and when she came back without it she said she

could not find it anywhere. That is not the first time she has forgotten it. I still think she is the loveliest lady I have ever seen and when I am grown up I want to be exactly like her. I am determined to train as a teacher in the future.

Elizabeth stopped reading and thought about the academic nature of the subjects studied at the college and the fact that only English history and geography were taught. Suddenly Aunt Rose appeared round the corner of the house.

"I've just had a call from the headmaster of your school, Elizabeth. He sounded very concerned about you and wanted to know how you were. He and Mrs. Ray would like to come and visit you tomorrow after school, between four and five."

Elizabeth was surprised. "That is kind of them." She considered for a moment. "Perhaps he wants some information from me about the class, to pass on the relieving teacher."

"I didn't get that impression, Elizabeth. He seemed genuinely interested in you and asked me quite a few searching questions about your health." Aunt Rose looked at Elizabeth thoughtfully. "Perhaps we have misjudged him Elizabeth."

"I think he changed his opinion about me after the incident with Mrs. Bulloch. He's been quite different since then."

"Anyway, I will be interested to meet both of them tomorrow." Aunt Rose smiled and left the room.

Elizabeth sat back chewing the end of her pen thinking about the Rays. *Perhaps after all, she should mention the journals to Mr. Ray, but whether she wanted to part with them was another matter. She would have to think about that.*

CHAPTER TWENTY-ONE

The next morning Elizabeth dressed carefully. Even though the Rays would not be coming until the afternoon she wanted to be well prepared. Aunt Gertrude came in after breakfast and offered to make the bed. Elizabeth was grateful to her, as it was awkward hopping about on one foot and trying to tuck in bed clothes.

When she had finished Aunt Gertrude looked quizzically at Elizabeth. "So we are going to meet your headmaster and his wife today, Elizabeth. I have the feeling he will want to question us about the past. He probably looks upon us as relics of a bygone era."

"I think he will soon change his mind when he meets you, Aunt Gertrude."

Gertrude was amused, "I'll take that as a compliment, Elizabeth. By the way, those journals you are studying so closely." She bent to look at them. "They wouldn't be Katey's, would they? Did Mal give them to you?"

Elizabeth felt embarrassed. "Actually, he did. He thought that you and Aunt Rose would not be interested."

Gertrude straightened up and shrugged slightly. "He's probably right. I would not want to relive the past. It's all dead and gone as far as I'm concerned." She looked curiously at Elizabeth. "I can't understand why a young girl like you would want to be bothered. At your age I don't think I'd have been interested in old journals."

"It's more than that," said Elizabeth eagerly. "These are first-hand accounts of the education system, especially as it affected girls."

"Oh, I see, you are viewing them as a historian."She raised an eyebrow.

"I suppose so."

"Well, if you come upon anything interesting let me know, won't you."

"Certainly, Aunt Gertrude."

When she had gone Elizabeth turned back to the journal. She had only been reading a few minutes when there was a light tap at the door and both Aunt Rose and Aunt Gertrude appeared.

"We don't want to disturb you, dear,"said Aunt Rose, "but Gertrude and I have something we want to say to you." Their faces were serious and Elizabeth wondered what was coming.

"Gertrude tells me that you have our sister Katey's journals and that Mal gave them to you. We don't mind you reading them and even having them in your keeping, but we would not like you to let them go out of the house and certainly not to lend them to anybody."

Elizabeth had a quick mental picture of Mr. Ray. *Was Aunt Rose telepathic?* At least, now Elizabeth knew what her answer to Mr. Ray had to be if he asked to borrow the journals. Perhaps she could show them to him at least.

Elizabeth said quickly. "No, of course I won't lend them to anybody, but would you mind me showing them to anyone who is interested in history?"

"Just so long as they understand the journals belong here in the house," said Aunt Gertrude firmly."Now to change the subject, would you like to sit with us in the dining room today and prop your foot on a stool? You must find it quite lonely having your meals out here."

"I would love that," replied Elizabeth enthusiastically. "Will Uncle Mal join us?"

"I will certainly ask him," said Aunt Rose.

When the aunts had left the room Elizabeth turned once more to the journal. Most of the entries were short and not of particular importance, although they gave a glimpse into life at the college as seen through the eyes of a junior pupil. The physical education programme seemed quaint. Katey had written:-

Today we had physical training. Miss Gibson herself took us outside and we swung the Indian clubs, over our shoulders and to the side, then bending our knees etc. It was harder than I thought and we all had to keep together. It was quite tiring and at the end I did not want to see another club. Miss Gibson said that club swinging is now quite the fashion in England, and because Miss Edgar introduced it to the college a few years ago we are continuing it. Personally I much prefer lawn tennis and swimming.

Elizabeth smiled. *How different physical education was today in secondary schools, where hockey, basketball and tennis were high on the list of activities. It sounded as though Katey had been quite athletic.* Elizabeth also noticed that there were many gaps in the entries. It seemed that Katey only wrote what seemed to her important. Once she had settled into the routine of school she did not bother to keep a daily record and sometimes there would be a gap of several weeks. One entry caught Elizabeth's eye. It was dated 15th December, 1992:-

Today was the prize giving ceremony for the Boys' and Girls' Colleges which was held jointly at the Provincial Hall. All of our family attended, except for Walter who offered to stay home and look after Gertie. It was interesting to see all the teachers sitting on the platform. Miss Gibson

and Miss Gribben wore their academic gowns and looked very dignified.

Miss Gibson read out the examiners' reports and I was pleased to hear that our third form year had done well in English. She said that Form 3 had read carefully and intelligently Scott's "Lady of the Lake" and "Lay of the Last Minstrel". I suppose that is because we enjoyed them so much. The examiner did mention that, though our composition was good our spelling was weak. I know that is true of me and I will try hard next year to improve.

As far as Latin was concerned Form 3 had done well and our composition and accidence were satisfactory. Comparing the Boys and Girls schools in mathematics the examiner said that the girls were not as accurate as the boys, but their work was neater and showed more care. After the prize giving Mal teased me about this, saying that girls could not think logically and that was why they were no good at mathematics. I pointed out that girls could run circles around boys when it came to neat presentation of their work.

Mr Joynt, the Principal of the Boys' College, made a rather wordy speech and said that he thought the great purpose of education was to teach high moral standards and that this was best attained by having the faith of a Christian which was "the shortest, best, and only way of succeeding." Everybody applauded after he said this and I noticed that father clapped very loudly.

I felt really proud of Miss Gibson when she stood up to speak. She looked very elegant and academic. I was interested in the part of her speech where she spoke about what happened to girls when they left school. She said the old notion that women had nothing to do but look for husbands, had had its day and had led to many unhappy marriages and made many bitter old maids. Up to the present, the chief occupation for educated women had been teaching but now there were other means of a livelihood open to them, such as in the Post and Telegraph Office. She said that before a girl took up teaching she should consider whether it was the right calling for her. There were many teachers who hated teaching and she sincerely pitied the children under their charge. "If girls disliked teaching let them take up some other calling as no life was happier than that of a worker in congenial work." Finally, she said that every girl who struck out a new career was a pioneer and did good work for her sex.

Listening to Miss Gibson I was glad that I actually want to be a teacher because I cannot imagine doing any other kind of work. The idea of working in the Post and Telegraph office has no appeal for me, nor would I want to be doing household work or be in a factory.

After the speeches came the prize giving and I was delighted when my name was called out for coming first in English. When I went forward to receive my certificate I felt very nervous in front of everyone but the man who handed it to me smiled very kindly and said, "Well done, Katherine."

Finally, the matriculation results were read out and Malcolm had passed with Highly Commended. That was a proud moment for our family and I noticed Mother dabbing her eyes with her handkerchief. I thought Mal looked very fine when he went forward to receive his certificate.

At the end of the evening when we went home Mother and Father said it had been one of the proudest moments of their lives, to see two of their children distinguish themselves scholastically. Father added that he hoped we would go on to make a great success of our lives not just in the academic sphere but that we would become outstanding Christians, which was more important than anything else.

Elizabeth came to the end of this entry and thought over

what Miss Gibson had said in her speech about occupations for women. She must have been very far sighted, as even in 1891 she could see that women did not have to get married to find fulfilment. *Her advice to girls, not to take up teaching simply because it seemed the only option open to them, was very sound. How sad to be in a profession like teaching and hate it. Really Miss Gibson's ideas were very modern and if she had been living today she would have been an outspoken Women's Libber.*

While Elizabeth was still pondering Miss Gibson's speech given so many years ago, there was a tap at the door and Uncle Mal's white head appeared around the corner. "Are you coming for lunch, Elizabeth or are you still immersed in those dusty journals."

"Oh, they're not dusty at all, Uncle Mal." Elizabeth looked up her eyes shining. "They're amazingly modern. I'm so excited by what I'm learning, especially about education for girls in the 1890s."

"Yes, ideas have somewhat changed since then."

"I was reading about the prize giving of December 1891 when you gained your matriculation certificate and Katey won first prize in English."

"Well, well, I'd forgotten all about that. After lunch you must show me. Now, we must not keep the ladies waiting."

Elizabeth reached for her crutches and stood up. She hopped towards the door with Uncle Mal following. Even lifting herself over the step into the parlour and down into the kitchen was much easier now. Aunt Rose was at the sink draining the potatoes. Over her shoulder she said: "Go into the dining room and I'll be with you in a minute."

Elizabeth hopped through the door and saw that Aunt Gertrude was at the window gazing out.

Immediately she came to the table and pulled out a chair for Elizabeth and placed a stool in front of her. Aunt Rose bustled into the room with a bowl of steaming potatoes, while Gertrude went out to the kitchen to bring in more dishes.

Once they were all seated Malcolm said a brief grace and began carving meat from the cold joint. It felt like a Sunday to Elizabeth and she had a sudden longing to be back in the hurly-burly of school. Conversation at the table was desultory. The aunts seemed preoccupied and Elizabeth was busy thinking about the journal entry she had just been reading.

"Uncle Mal, after you had passed your matriculation exam did you leave school and go to work immediately?" Elizabeth asked.

He thought for a moment. "No, I stayed home for a few months and helped Father and Walter in the tannery. I think Father hoped I would learn the trade and take over from Walter, as it was clear he was planning to go on the mission field."

Both the aunts watched him closely. "But my heart was not in it and Father soon saw that I was not much use. He agreed that I could enter a law office as a clerk and at least, that way I would be earning my living and being trained in a profession."

"Didn't you have to go to university and take a degree?" enquired Elizabeth.

"Not necessarily. In those days we could study extramurally and pass an examination called the LPE, or Law Professional Examinations which qualified one as a solicitor only. The big advantage was that we could stay in the provinces and not have the expense of attending university."

"So that meant you were able to live at home while you were studying to be a lawyer."

"Yes, as you can imagine, law became a popular profession."

"What would you have to do if you wanted to be a barrister?"

"Well, you only had to practice as a solicitor for five years."

There was a pause and Aunt Rose spoke. "I've made your favourite pudding today, Mal, apple pie. We had such a good crop of apples this year I put some out at the gate for people to help themselves and I see most of the bags have gone. Perhaps when your headmaster and his wife arrive this afternoon, Elizabeth, we could offer them some."

Elizabeth thought Aunt Rose was quite adroit in the way she had turned the conversation from law. She had noticed Aunt Gertrude stiffen as Uncle Mal began to speak.

When the meal was finished Aunt Rose said to Elizabeth, "I think you should go to your room and lie down, dear so that you can be fresh for your visitors."

"I really feel perfectly all right, Aunt Rose."

"No, you must lie down and give that ankle a chance to rest properly. You have been sitting up all morning."

It was pointless to argue so Elizabeth took up her crutches and hopped back to her room. As she entered its cool shadiness she was glad to stretch out on the bed and relax against the pillows. She turned towards the half open window. A slight breeze that hardly stirred the curtains blew gently across her face like a caress. She closed her eyes and within minutes was asleep.

She woke with a start. For a moment she could not think what day it was. Glancing at her bedside clock she saw that it was three o'clock. She must have been asleep for over two hours. It was definitely time to get up and prepare for her visitors. She decided to change from her clothes of the morning and to put on something fresh.

Thinking it would be more pleasant for the Rays to sit on the verandah rather than in her room she went outside and settled herself on one of the cane seats, propping up her foot on another chair. It was not long before a car pulled into the drive and a few minutes later Aunt Rose appeared around the corner of the house, followed by Mr. and Mrs. Ray. They had evidently come straight from school, judging by their clothes.

"Well, Elizabeth, you certainly couldn't have chosen a better place to recuperate," said Mr. Ray gazing around appreciatively. "Are you sure you didn't plan the whole thing?" Everybody laughed, even Aunt Rose.

"Do sit down," she said, "and I'll go and make a cup of tea."

"That sounds lovely," said Mrs. Ray. "Can I help you?"

"No, you sit down and chat to Elizabeth. I expect she wants to catch up on the school news."

"Talking of which, I have quite a bit of mail for you, Elizabeth. You are a very popular young lady," and Mr. Ray produced a large brown envelope stuffed with letters, handing it to Elizabeth. "Every child in your class wanted to write to you, so I've clipped their papers all together," he said. "Quite a few of the staff gave me letters for you as well."

"I'll look at them later on, but please thank everyone and say that I will reply to them. How is the reliever getting on?"

"She's managing very well. She said that she has seldom met such polite and helpful children. She particularly asked me to thank you for your clear and well thought-out work plans. She is finding them very helpful and so far has kept closely to them."

Elizabeth cheeks grew warm. "I'm glad she is happy," she murmured.

Just then Aunt Rose came round the corner carrying a tray piled high with tea things. She unloaded them carefully, placing on the table a large china teapot with matching cups and saucers, then a plateful of fluffy white scones, a bowl of raspberry jam, and a dish of thick yellow cream. Mr. Ray's eyes gleamed. "What a feast!" he exclaimed.

"I haven't ever seen cream that colour in the shops," remarked Mrs. Ray.

"From our own cow," said Aunt Rose.

"You never told us you lived in paradise," said Mrs. Ray laughing. "No wonder you look so bonny, Elizabeth. You're living on the fat of the land."

"We grow pretty well everything and make our own bread," said Aunt Rose modestly. "Now I will leave you to have your afternoon tea and catch up on your news."

When she disappeared Mrs. Ray said, "It's idyllic here, so peaceful. All you can hear is bird song. I suppose we get used to being surrounded by noise:- children's voices, bells etc. How lovely to escape from it all!" and she leaned back in her chair her eyes half closed. "You are a very lucky girl, Elizabeth. Tell me, what are you doing to keep yourself busy, as you can't go far? Have you taken up needlework?"

Elizabeth drew in her breath. *How much was she prepared to tell them?*

"Actually, I am doing what Mr. Ray would call historical research. I have the journals of one of my great-aunts and I am reading them carefully. Her first entries were when she was twelve years old in 1890."

Both Mr. and Mrs. Ray stared at her. "You mean you have the original journal of 1890?" Mr. Ray spoke slowly.

"Yes, once we've had tea I'll show you," said Elizabeth.

After that, it seemed the Rays could not finish their tea and scones quickly enough. Mrs. Ray gathered up the cups and saucers and stacked them on the tray. Elizabeth stood up on her crutches and went indoors to fetch the journal she had been reading. Making sure that there were no crumbs on the table, she placed it carefully in front of Mr. Ray. He reverently turned the first page while Mrs. Ray looked over his shoulder. They read the next few pages and Mr. Ray looked at Elizabeth, his eyes alight.

"This is a wonderful find, Elizabeth. To be able to see how education affected a girl in 1890, especially an intelligent girl like Katey, who in our day would have gone to university and..."

"Become a teacher, as she probably did anyway," interjected Mrs. Ray wryly. "Have things really changed that much for girls?"

"Well, at least she would have had tertiary education," said Mr. Ray. "Elizabeth, I know this may be asking a lot of you, but do you think I could borrow this journal for a short while?"

"Unfortunately, the aunts have said I must not lend it nor let it go out of the house."

Mr. Ray looked as though he had received a blow. "Such a precious document of the times," he murmured to himself. "Now what can we do?"

A sudden thought occurred to Elizabeth. "Look, I have a lot

of time on my hands. What's to stop me from making a copy of the diary entries?"

"What a marvellous idea!" exclaimed Mrs. Ray, "That would solve the problem, wouldn't it dear?" turning to her husband.

"Yes, but it is a long tedious job," he said slowly.

"I wouldn't mind it at all. I find the diary fascinating and I've been reading it slowly trying to take it all in."

"If you were prepared to do that I would pay you for your time," said Mr. Ray.

"I'm already being paid for doing nothing for six weeks, as it is," said Elizabeth with a laugh. "No, I would happily do it."

Aunt Rose came round the corner of the verandah. "You all look very happy," she remarked. "I've just come to take away the tea things."

"That was a delicious afternoon tea," said Mrs. Ray quickly. "I don't know when I've had scones and cream like that. You should serve them in the garden like they do in England. The tourists would come flocking."

"Gertrude and I did consider that once, but decided it would take up too much of our time, and now we are too old." Elizabeth was surprised. *There was a lot she did not know about her aunts.*

Mr. and Mrs. Ray stood up. "We really should be getting along," said Mrs. Ray, "Thank you for your hospitality, Miss Brookfield. Goodbye, Elizabeth, we will keep in touch with you."

Aunt Rose looked at Mrs. Ray. "Oh, before you go, I would like to say to you, my dear, that if ever you wanted to set up your easel here in the garden you are very welcome. Come any time."

"I will certainly take you up on that offer. Thank you so much," replied Mrs. Ray.

She bent down and kissed Elizabeth on the cheek. "Goodbye, my dear. We'll see you before long."

When they had gone it suddenly seemed very quiet. Elizabeth sighed and drew the packet of letters towards her.

229

CHAPTER TWENTY-TWO

Elizabeth's hands were shaking as she drew the envelopes from the packet. The children's letters she put to one side and then studied the handwriting on each of the envelopes. One was written in a bold hand. She opened it and had a stab of disappointment when she saw that it was from David. She put it down unread and opened another. The writing on this was rather untidy and she saw that it was from Jeanette. She laid it down on top of David's and opened the third. This was from the secretary and was on headed notepaper. She placed it with the others. The last one must surely be from John. Hardly breathing she drew it from the envelope.

It said simply:-

Dearest Elizabeth. I am missing you and thinking of you all the time.

All my love,
John.

Elizabeth sat back holding the letter in her trembling hand. Her heart was thudding. *How could it be possible for ten words to have such an effect?* John's image rose before her, and she seemed to see his brown eyes burning into hers. Elizabeth sat still for several moments until the welter of emotion had subsided and she felt calm enough to read the other letters.

David's was brief and breezy. He said that he would pop in some time during the week, possibly Thursday. Jeanette's letter was just the way she talked, entertaining and discursive. The last letter, from the secretary, requested the name of Elizabeth's doctor because she would require a medical certificate and enclosed was a form to be filled in.

After Elizabeth had read these she turned to the children's letters which had been clipped together. Most of them included a drawing with a message beneath it. Some made her smile, but when she came to Tommy's her eyes filled with tears. He had so obviously taken pains over his writing and spelling as there were still traces of rubber on the page where he had made alterations. At the end of the letter he said that he and Bruce were now good friends and would like to come and visit her together.

The letter from Bruce was crumpled and had a dirty thumb mark in the corner but even he had tried to commiserate with Elizabeth:

"It must be orful to brake your ankel, did it hurt much. Me and Tommy want to come and see you soon when you are feling beter, mum is much beter now."

Elizabeth smiled at this composition, misspelt and ungrammatical as it was. She lay back in her chair and thought over the kind messages that had been sent to her from staff and children alike. How strange that only a month or two ago she had not known of the existence of any of them, even John Tamati. She tried to push him out of her mind. He was too disturbing.

Determinedly she reached for the journal. *The best way to deal with unwelcome emotion was to keep busy* she thought. She found a blank exercise book, filled her fountain pen then began to transcribe the diary entries. The work was curiously satisfying. As Elizabeth reread the words written by Katey so long ago, the girl took a hold on her mind and Elizabeth found that she was living through the events of Katey's life, experiencing her hopes and fears. For the next couple of hours Elizabeth worked on and then sat back to give her hand a rest. Idly, she flipped over to the last page in the journal and noted that the final entry was dated 19th December, 1893.

Today is my last day at Nelson Girls College and I have very mixed feelings. I am sorry to leave school because I have been happy here and learned a great deal, yet it is time to move on and leave school days behind me. The next stage of my life is now beginning, when I will take my place in the adult world. I am so thankful that I have been accepted for teacher training in the New Year, although it means leaving home and going to live in Wellington.

I was glad to have an opportunity to thank each of my teachers today and give them a token gift. Miss Gibson was very kind. She wished me well for my future and said that she believed I had a great future ahead of me as a teacher and that she would like to see me back at Nelson College in that capacity. When I thanked her and told her that she had been my inspiration ever since I had arrived at the school at the age of twelve she pressed my hand, murmuring, "Dear Katherine, thank you for that. You've no idea what it means to me." She turned away to hide her tears I think. I do intend to keep in touch with her. Now I am finishing this journal at the end of my school days and when I begin another it will be 1893.

After reading this Elizabeth closed the journal and set it to one side. She thought back over her own life and the people who had influenced her. She could not recall anyone like Miss Gibson and she supposed that an educated woman, who still retained her femininity, would make an impact on an impressionable girl like Katey. Perhaps Miss Gibson herself had experienced rebuffs and rejection. She had stepped outside the norm for her day, by pursuing a career rather than marriage. The knowledge that Katey admired her and in fact, had made her a role model would be a tremendous encouragement. Miss Gibson was indeed an interesting person and Elizabeth found herself thinking about her as she continued to copy the diary entries.

That afternoon she went for a walk around the garden using her crutches and at four o'clock followed Bessie as she ambled across the paddock to the milking shed. There, Elizabeth sat down on an old wooden chair and watched Uncle Mal as he milked the cow, enjoying the rhythmic splish splash as the milk hit the bucket. Neither she nor Uncle Mal spoke much, but there was an easy comradeship between them that did not require words.

"Uncle Mal," she began as he sat with his back to her, leaning into Bessie's flank. "What would you like me to do with the journals once I have finished reading them? Aunt Gertrude and Aunt Rose do not want them to go outside the house."

"I realize that and it poses a problem. I think perhaps you had better return them to me for the time being but I will make sure in my will that they finally come to you. What you do with them in the future is entirely up to you, Missy, though I would advise you against handing them over to a museum. Once they get into the archives they become public property and I think you would agree that they are quite personal. I think my sister Katey would rather you had them than a museum. Although she was academic she had a warm and impulsive nature and was inclined to pour out her feelings on paper."

"I have noticed that," replied Elizabeth quickly. *What revelations awaited her in the adult journal? She could hardly wait to read it.*

The next morning Elizabeth went out to the verandah as usual, taking the second journal with her but leaving behind her pen and notebook. She seated herself comfortably in one of the cane chairs and opened it at page one. The first entry was dated 5th February, 1895.

Today was my first at the Model School. The building was not at all what I expected being built of red brick. It was rather forbidding from the outside and could have been a prison, hospital or what have you. At the entrance was a small office and before entering the building I had to produce my letter of introduction to the Principal. The old man sitting at the desk perused my letter then looked over his glasses and gave me a curt nod. "Take the first door to the right and you will see the Principal's office. Your interview is in ten minutes time."

I did as he had instructed and waited outside the door, looking at my watch every minute or so. Promptly at 10 o'clock I knocked on the door and a voice inside called, "Come in." I expected to see an older man like Mr Hodgeson, our school inspector, so I was surprised when a youngish man with a neatly trimmed black beard stood up from his chair and reached over to shake my hand. He had keen brown eyes and a ready smile and I felt immediately at ease with him.

"So you are Miss Katherine Brookfield," he said. "I have a very warm commendation from your headmistress, Miss Gibson, about you. She says here," and he glanced down at the letter, 'I fully recommend Katherine Brookfield as a suitable candidate for teacher training and I have every confidence in her ability and steadiness of character.'

"Well, after that, I could hardly turn you down, could I Miss Brookfield?" he said breezily, "so welcome to the Model School of Wellington. Would you present yourself tomorrow morning at nine o'clock and be ready to begin class at nine thirty. You will be attached to Miss Brown in Room 6. She takes Standard 4 girls. At this stage you will be

observing her teach and assisting when you are required. Later on, you will be expected to take certain lessons. I look forward to watching your progress."

After this I was free for the rest of the day so I decided to have a look around Wellington before going home to my sister's. I had already spent the weekend with very little to do, except admire the baby and I was ready for a change of scene.

Wednesday, 6th February, 1895

I met Miss Brown today. She wears spectacles and her hair is drawn back severely in a bun. She could be any age between thirty and forty-five. She was polite but not friendly, which I suppose is natural for a senior teacher in her position. She made me feel young and gauche although there was nothing in her manner that one could object to. She invited me to sit at the back of the room at a desk and suggested I take notes while I observed her teach.

There were fifty girls in the class and they sat at double desks. They were well behaved and worked industriously throughout the day. I noticed that Miss Brown had an unerring way of asking the least attentive pupil a searching question and when the girl hesitated or became confused Miss Brown said nothing, but simply looked at her severely and often the poor child broke down. I did not like this and felt embarrassed and uncomfortable but I suppose it is not for me to question an experienced teacher's methods of teaching, but I cannot help comparing Miss Brown with Miss Gibson, who was always encouraging when we struggled to answer a question. I'm afraid I felt rather homesick for Nelson College today but no doubt I will get used to the new regime.

Thursday, 7th February, 1895

Today I made a friend, another of the new student teachers. Her name is Ellen Simmonds. She is an Auckland girl and seems quite sophisticated compared to the other thirty-three. She has beautiful thick fair hair which she arranges in a plait coiled around her head and talks entertainingly. She had us all laughing during the lunch hour with a story about one of the children in her class. Apparently, her supervisor is less strict than Miss Brown and allows the children more latitude.

The Principal, whose name is Augustus Lightfoot, came into the classroom today. He walked around the room looking over the children's shoulders. Finally he came to me and asked me quietly how I was settling in. I noticed that Miss Brown was watching so I kept my answers brief and non-committal. I did have the feeling that Mr. Lightfoot sensed my diffidence. I feel so much more at ease with him than Miss Brown. Oh that he were my supervisor!

Thursday, 14th February, 1895

Life is settling into a routine. I catch the tram each day from my sister's house and arrive at the school by quarter to nine which gives me time to hang up my coat and straighten my hair before going to the classroom. Miss Brown has asked me to take the register so that she can get on with preparation for the day. I enjoy this task as I am becoming familiar with the pupils' names and am able to address them individually. I also have other tasks that keep me busy during the day, such as marking the exercise books. I particularly enjoy reading the compositions and try wherever possible to put some helpful comment after the work.

Tomorrow I am going to take my first lesson, which is history. My subject is the bubonic plague and the great fire of London. It is a topic I am interested in and I will try to make it come to life for the children by drawing a picture of a rat and also the closely packed houses of London.

Friday, 15th February, 1895

My lesson was a disaster. I had prepared it well, so I thought, and explained to the class what life was like in 17th century London. They listened carefully and after my explanation answered my questions intelligently. Then they began asking me questions about the times and I was simply not able to give them satisfactory answers. For some of the questions I had to admit that I simply did not know. The children did not seem concerned about that, especially when I suggested they go away and try to find out the answers themselves, by consulting books in the library. I did notice that the class was much more animated than usual and less restrained.

I did not think I had done too badly but at the end of the day when Miss Brown discussed the lesson with me she was very critical. She said I must never, never admit to lack of knowledge because that would make the children lose respect for me as a teacher. She said that I should be the one to ask the questions not give the children an opportunity to put me in a spot. She criticized my manner with the class and said that I was too friendly and should keep my distance. Oh dear, I seemed to break every rule in the book, but how am I going to model myself on her when it does not seem to be in my nature? When I think back to Miss Gibson and her handling of a class it was all so different.

Wednesday, 20th February, 1895

I took another lesson today; this time it was geography, the coal mining areas in the British Isles and the importance of coal mining to the industrial welfare of Britain. Again I made more mistakes, which were pointed out by Miss Brown. Ironically the children appeared to enjoy the lesson and several came to me at different times and told me little anecdotes about family members who had worked in the mines around Britain. Nevertheless, Miss Brown said that it was a poor lesson and she must be right. Her report will go to Mr. Lightfoot and I feel very ashamed that he will see it, after I came to the college with such a glowing recommendation.

Thursday, 21st February, 1895

Mr. Lightfoot called me into his office today to discuss the report he had received from Miss Brown regarding my progress. He looked at me searchingly for a few moments.

"I find it hard to reconcile this report with the high recommendation I received of you from your school. What is going wrong, Miss Brookfield?"

I must confess that my eyes filled with tears at his kind tone. "I really don't know, Mr. Lightfoot," I began. "I try to model myself on Miss Brown and her methods, but it doesn't seem to work for me. Despite my efforts I seem to do all the wrong things." Then I began to cry in earnest.

Mr. Lightfoot did a surprising thing. He came right out from behind his desk and put his hand on my shoulder. Then he said softly, "Do not cry, Katherine, you have the makings of an excellent teacher. Believe me, you will succeed. These so-called mistakes you are making are very trivial. The important thing is that you are able to

238

interest the pupils and give them a desire to learn. Next week I will come and observe you taking a lesson myself."

I left his office feeling completely different. I now have recovered my self-respect and whatever Miss Brown says, in future I will remember his kind words.

Elizabeth closed the journal thoughtfully. She felt pity for Katey struggling against the discouragement of her associate teacher and wondered how she would fare when she was observed by Mr. Lightfoot. *He did not seem to act like a typical headmaster. What could be his background?*

CHAPTER TWENTY-THREE

It was Saturday morning, a fortnight after the accident. Since the Rays' visit there had been phone calls from David and Mary to enquire about Elizabeth's welfare but neither of them had been able to come to the house. Elizabeth had been so busy with the journals that she had not noticed time passing.

She was having a leisurely breakfast with Aunt Gertrude and Aunt Rose when all of a sudden the phone rang. Aunt Gertrude got up with alacrity.

"Who can that be at this hour?" she exclaimed. A few minutes later she came back to the kitchen. "That was your friend, David," she said smiling. "He would like to know if it is convenient for himself and Mary to pay you a visit this afternoon. He may have a surprise for you as well. I told him that I was sure you would be glad to see them both." She raised an eyebrow. "That is right, isn't it, Elizabeth?"

"Of course," said Elizabeth quickly, secretly regretting she would have to put the journal to one side today. By the time she had finished her Saturday chores, which took twice as long when she was on crutches, there would be no time for reading.

As she busied herself tidying the room Elizabeth looked longingly at the journal as it lay on the bedside table. No, she had to resist the temptation to open its pages and read on. Katey now occupied her thoughts most of the time and Elizabeth wondered what twists of fate lay before her.

Lunch was at twelve thirty and these days Uncle Mal joined them. The atmosphere between himself and Aunt Gertrude was no longer strained and Elizabeth noticed that she made a point of including him in conversations. Uncle Mal was quite relaxed with her and at times jovial. "So your young friend is coming to see you this afternoon," he said to Elizabeth.

"And Mary as well," replied Elizabeth.

"Oh, yes, that pleasant young woman teacher. I have the feeling that she has set her cap at David, but there is not much doing on his part."

"Not while Elizabeth is around," added Aunt Gertrude.

"David and Mary are very good friends," Elizabeth said defensively.

"But that is all," persisted Aunt Gertrude.

"I think we should drop the subject," said Aunt Rose looking warningly at her sister.

"Anyway, it is very nice that they are coming to see Elizabeth. I must see that we put on a good afternoon tea. Do you think they would like a sponge, Elizabeth?"

"I'm sure they would," and Elizabeth's mouth watered at the thought of one of Aunt Rose's light-as-air sponges, topped with thick cream. Aunt Gertrude and Aunt Rose cleared the table and got on with the dishes. They refused to let Elizabeth help in any way.

"You can't dry dishes while you are on crutches," said Aunt Rose firmly. "You go out to the verandah and sit and talk to Mal. He will be glad of your company."

"While he smokes his pipe," added Aunt Gertrude smiling.

So Elizabeth and Uncle Mal sat in companionable silence for some time until he looked up and said, "So what more have you learned about my sister, Katey?"

Elizabeth started. It was uncanny the way he tuned into her

241

thoughts. "Oh, she went to train as a teacher in Wellington and she encountered some difficulties with her associate teacher."

"Did she indeed? She never told us about that. Her letters to the family were always cheerful but did not really tell us a great deal. I always thought there was more going on than she let on. I had the feeling that she passed through something critical because when she returned home she was quite different from the happy- go- lucky girl she had been." He drew on his pipe thoughtfully. "Then of course she fell ill for some time and when she recovered she was thin and pale and no longer the bonny lass she had been."

Elizabeth listened carefully. *So something was going to happen to Katey that would change her life. What could it be?*

Shortly afterwards, Uncle Mal stood up. "Well, I'll be going to have forty winks now. When your guests have spent some time with you let them know that I would be happy to see them. Your friend David is a fine young fellow." Elizabeth watched him walk away, noting his upright back and firm step. He was so different from the shambling old man he had been the day she arrived in Nelson.

At two thirty Elizabeth heard a car chugging up the road and guessed it must be David's old Holden. A few minutes later he and Mary came round the corner of the house and behind them, looking a little sheepish, were Tommy and Bruce.

"What a lovely surprise!" exclaimed Elizabeth, "You've brought Tommy and Bruce with you. How are you, boys? I can't tell you how glad I am to see you, and you and Mary of course," she said looking first at David then Mary. "Now do sit down and tell me all the news of school," she said encouragingly to the two boys who were gazing wide eyed all around them.

Tommy was the first to reply. "We've got a new teacher, Mrs. Fairleigh. She's quite kind but she does not do very exciting things with us, like you did, Miss Brookfield."

"Yes, and she's old and not at all pretty," added Bruce. "When are you coming back, Miss Brookfield? We are all missing you."

"That is very nice of you, Bruce, but I hope you are being helpful to Mrs. Fairleigh."

"Oh, we are, Miss Brookfield, and I still come early to school to help her, like I did for you," added Tommy.

"I'm glad to hear that. Now why don't you take Bruce to see Uncle Mal, Tommy? I expect he will like to show you around his shed where he milks the cow."

"Come on, Tommy," said Bruce impatiently, "Let's go."

"Before you disappear, tell me, Bruce, how your mother is."

"Oh, she's fine. My aunty has gone back to Christchurch now. She said there was nothing she could do at our place because Mum is such a ball of energy. I've got a letter she said to give you," and he pulled a crumpled envelope out of his pocket and handed it to Elizabeth.

"Ok, lads, I think you can go now and leave Miss Brookfield to us." David winked broadly at Elizabeth as the two boys jumped out of their seats and ran down the verandah steps.

"They've been at me all week, asking to come and see you," said David, "so I thought it would be a good idea to bring them today. Anyway, how are you, Elizabeth? I must say you are looking very rested. Being laid up for a few weeks can't be a bad thing."

"You break your ankle and see how you like it," retorted Elizabeth.

"It would drive him mad," said Mary. "He can't sit still for longer than five minutes."

"Now, now, girls, be fair. There's only one of me against two of you."

Elizabeth relaxed and enjoyed the banter. After an hour or so Aunt Rose appeared with a tray and David's eyes lit up when he saw the sponge, generously topped with cream and decorated with strawberries.

"I suppose the boys are with Mal," said Aunt Rose. "Send them to the kitchen when they appear. I've made something special for them."

A short time later Tommy and Bruce came running round

the corner of the house. "Uncle Mal sent us to have our afternoon tea," panted Bruce, his face glistening with perspiration.

"Go round to the kitchen and see what Aunt Rose has for you," said Elizabeth.

When they were out of sight Mary turned to Elizabeth casually. "Oh I nearly forgot to tell you the big news. John Tamati is leaving."

Elizabeth felt her stomach drop away. She was sure all the colour had drained from her face but Mary appeared not to notice and went on blithely. "I think he's moving up north but he hasn't said more than that." Elizabeth did not trust herself to ask any questions for fear that she would betray herself, so she merely nodded in a casual fashion though inwardly her mind was whirling. The subject of John Tamati was soon exhausted and David and Mary moved on to other topics. Elizabeth tried to concentrate on what they were saying but she could only make mechanical replies.

At last David said, "I think we should be going. Elizabeth is looking tired. As soon as those boys appear we'll make tracks." Just at that moment Tommy and Bruce came round the corner of the house. "Come on you two. We have to be off. Miss Brookfield needs some peace and quiet. Say your goodbyes."

Tommy and Bruce came up to Elizabeth's chair and stood looking solemnly at her. "Please get better soon, Miss Brookfield, and come back and teach us. It's not the same without you," said Tommy.

"Yes please do," echoed Bruce.

Elizabeth felt her throat catch and she blinked rapidly, "Thank you for coming to see me, boys. You've no idea what it means to me. Keep working hard at school and tell the other children I look forward to seeing them all again, when I can walk." She looked up at David and Mary who were standing ready to go. "Thank you both for your visit and do come again."

"Oh we will, never fear," returned David.

Then they were gone and once more Elizabeth was alone.

She tried to grapple with the thought of John Tamati leaving. *Maybe he would be gone by the time she returned to school. How empty it would all seem.* She felt as if an icy hand were clutching her heart.

As she sat huddled in her misery suddenly there rang out the clear call of the bellbird. Almost simultaneously Aunt Rose appeared in the doorway. She had two letters in her hand. "Sorry, Elizabeth, these came for you this morning and I forgot to give them to you," and she handed them to Elizabeth. "Dinner will be ready in half an hour," she added and disappeared.

Elizabeth turned over the letters wonderingly. One was from Wellington. That was bound to be from Richard but the other had a local postmark. She slit it open and immediately knew before looking at the signature that it was from John. The words danced before her eyes and it took some moments for her to settle down to read it.

My Dearest,

Before you receive this you have probably heard that I am leaving the school and moving right away from Nelson. I feel I owe you an explanation, dear Elizabeth. When my wife pleaded to come back and live with me I did not know the real reason. She finally told me that she was pregnant and that it had been confirmed by her doctor. We have been married for five years but she had never been able to conceive so this came as a complete surprise. I feel I cannot leave her at this time so I have decided to stay with her. I do not feel I could continue to see you every day and be strong enough to carry it through so I made the decision to move from the school and right out of the area. I have accepted a position in Napier and will be moving in a month's time. That means I will probably not see you when you return to school, so this has to be goodbye. I want you

to know that you will always be in my heart dear, dear Elizabeth.

With all my love,

John.

The letter fell from Elizabeth's hand on to the table and she sat motionless gazing at a leaf on the ground. *So it was all over. The decision had been taken out of her hands. John Tamati was gone for good. She would probably never see him again.* Strangely she felt nothing. Then gradually a new sensation began to steal over her; as though a burden were rolling from her shoulders. She felt suddenly light and buoyant. *Was it possible that joy and pain were opposite sides of the one coin?*

Her eye glanced down at the other letter lying on the table. Idly she lifted it and slit it open. The writing was almost indecipherable but Elizabeth managed to read the scrawl. It was a breezy letter full of amusing items which made Elizabeth smile. Then right at the end Richard had added, "I find myself thinking of you constantly, Elizabeth, All my love, Richard."

Elizabeth stood with the letter in her hand thinking. *How odd that this letter had arrived in the same post as the one from John.* Suddenly she remembered the grubby envelope that Bruce had pressed into her hand. She had slipped it into the back of the journal. Elizabeth opened it and took out the letter. The handwriting was neat and carefully formed.

Dear Miss Brookfield,

I just want to convey to you my thanks for all you have done for me and my family. Because of you I am alive today. I understand that your aunt had special prayers made for me and I would like her to know that since then I have regained my interest in life and seem to have more energy

246

than ever before. My marriage has been transformed and I feel I love my husband more than even when we first married. We are so happy now and I know Bruce is a more secure child.

May God bless you, Miss Brookfield, and reward you with great happiness.

Yours sincerely,

Eileen Bulloch

Elizabeth reread the letter and sat thinking for a long time. *It was more than coincidence that these three letters had arrived the same day.*

CHAPTER TWENTY-FOUR

The next day was Sunday and as usual, Uncle Mal and the aunts set off for church leaving Elizabeth at liberty to do what she wanted. She decided to use her crutches and go for a walk in the garden. There was something very soothing about being totally alone and free to wander at will. She sat on the seat under the apple tree and gazed around her enjoying the mingled scents of stock and roses. A line of a hymn came to her as she looked at a vivid scarlet rose climbing over an archway across the path:- "I come to the garden alone while the dew is still on the roses..."

This particular morning Elizabeth felt more at peace than she had for many weeks. Since reading the three letters yesterday all tension had ebbed out of her. She felt that she could trust God to take care of her and that He was in control of every circumstance. Slowly, Elizabeth made her way back to the house, pausing every now and again to enjoy the flowers that grew alongside the path. Even the sound of the birds was joyous this morning, like a hymn of praise.

When she got back to her room Elizabeth picked up the journal and went out to the verandah. She settled herself comfortably into one of the cane chairs and began to read. She noted that there were frequent gaps between the entries, as Katey only recorded what was significant to her.

Friday, 15th March, 1895.

Mr. Lightfoot came to observe my lesson today. I had prepared it well and was not in the least nervous. He sat at the back of the room taking notes unobtrusively. I was hardly aware of him there. Before I had finished he slipped from the room. Miss Brown took over from me and made no comment about the lesson. The day proceeded as usual and it was only half an hour before the end of the day that a child came to the door with a note for me. It was from Mr. Lightfoot and simply asked me to come to his office at the end of school.

I duly presented myself at his door and knocked timidly. "Come in," he called and when I opened the door he came forward and shook my hand.

"Katherine, I just wanted to say how impressed I was by your lesson this morning. You had the children interested and your handling of the subject was confident and masterly. I have given you an A on all counts. I know that you have the makings of an excellent teacher and I want you to know that I have total confidence in you." Then he paused and looked a little embarrassed. "Now I wish to speak to you not as your principal but as a man. I wonder if you would care to accompany me next Sunday afternoon to an organ recital at St Mary's Catholic Church in Hill Street. A friend of mine is playing and I would dearly love to have your company. What do you say, Katherine?"

Well, I was overcome. All I could say was, "Yes, Mr. Lightfoot, I would be very happy to accompany you."

He looked relieved. "Then that is settled. I will call for you at two o'clock at your lodgings. You had better give me your address." I wrote it on a piece of paper and then I excused myself and left his room. My thoughts were in a whirl. I had never suspected that he looked upon me as anything but one of his student teachers but now it seemed he had a personal interest in me.

Saturday, 16th March, 1895

When I told Alice of the invitation from Mr. Lightfoot she looked dubious. "It seems a bit odd, Katey, that the principal of a teacher training institute would want to keep company with one of the students. I just hope that his intentions are honourable towards you." I felt shocked at such a suspicion.

"If you knew what a kind man he was you would not even think such a thing," I said to her. I felt I had to defend Mr. Lightfoot. "At any rate you will be able to judge what kind of a man he is when you meet him on Sunday," I said.

Sunday, 17th March, 1895

It is evening and at last I have a chance to record the varied impressions of the day. Mr. Lightfoot duly arrived for me very punctually and spent a few minutes speaking to Alice. I could see that he had made a favourable impression on her, especially when he admired the baby. He arrived in a cab and it was waiting to take us to St Mary's. As we bowled through the streets he pointed out all the new buildings that had been erected in Wellington over the past four or five years. He seemed to know a lot about architecture and remarked on this style or that.

When we arrived at St Mary's I was impressed by its size and grandeur. Inside it was beautiful but austere and I felt a little uncomfortable with all the statues to the saints and the Virgin Mary. Everything is so bare in a Baptist chapel. What impressed me most was the organ with its immense pipes rising to the ceiling. The sound reverberated thrillingly around the building as the organist played a concerto by Bach. I have never heard such beautiful music.

At the end I wished we could sit through it all again. Two hours had seemed like five minutes.

Mr. Lightfoot asked if I would like to take tea, which was provided in an annex behind the church. We sat at a table and had a pot of tea and a piece of cake. Naturally, we discussed the music but when there was a pause in the conversation he asked me about myself and my family. That led to my asking about his background. He told me that he had arrived in the colony only seven years ago, that his family was still in England.

It seems that his father expected him to go into the army like his older brother. Instead he had gone to Oxford University but after a year he had lost interest in academic studies and wanted to travel abroad. He had heard about New Zealand and was drawn to the idea of living in a young country where great advances were being made in all fields. He was particularly interested in education and so he decided to take a degree at Canterbury University.

One thing led to another and finally he told me that he is an 'Honourable' but he prefers not to use the title in New Zealand. His family is what is classed as 'landed gentry' and they own a large estate on the outskirts of Bath. As he spoke I felt there was an even greater chasm between us. Our two backgrounds are so completely different. He must have guessed what I was thinking as he took my hand in his and said, "This is New Zealand, Katey, where all men are on an equal footing. It's not family background that matters but what you are able to achieve on your own. That is why I came to New Zealand. You are fortunate to have been born to early settlers who have this independent outlook and I can see that it is bred in you."

After that I relaxed and lost my awe of him. We chatted for some time when suddenly he looked at his watch and said he must return me home or my sister would wonder what had become of me. He said with a wink, "She might even think I have run off with you." We managed to get into one of the cabs waiting outside and arrived home just after six o'clock. Mr. Lightfoot helped me from the carriage and escorted me to the front door and after a brief word with Alice returned to the cab. Once he was gone Alice was full of questions. When I told her that Mr. Lightfoot was an Honourable her attitude towards him underwent a subtle change. It is strange how people even in NZ are impressed by a title.

Monday, 18th March, 1895

I said nothing to the other students about my outing with Mr. Lightfoot. In fact, I have decided to keep my own counsel and not confide in anyone, not even Ellen, who has become a good friend. I can only trust the pages of this journal for they will never be read by anyone apart from myself. At least, in this journal I can record my feelings and impressions quite openly. When I saw Mr. Lightfoot in the corridor today he nodded at me in a friendly yet impersonal way, using the same manner towards me that he would to any of the student teachers.

Friday, 22nd March, 1895

Mr. Lightfoot stopped me in the corridor after school just as I was going to the cloakroom. He asked me to step into his office for a few minutes. As soon as the door was closed he said, "Thank goodness, Katey, I am able to speak to you. It has been torture this week keeping up the pretence that you are just another student." I was amazed at his tone which was quite impassioned. "Ever since Sunday I have found myself thinking about you." He paused and looked at me a little embarrassed. "You may find this strange but I must speak to you. Do sit down," and he drew up a chair for me and another for himself so that he was sitting facing me.

"What I have not told you is that your headmistress, Beatrice Gibson, wrote to me about you at some length." I must have looked surprised because he continued, "Yes, you see we knew one another rather well. We both attended the University of Canterbury in Christchurch. Beatrice was the belle of the university. There was no other girl who could hold a candle to her. I think all the male students were a bit in love with her. I certainly was. For three years we were friends, actually closer than friends. I wanted to marry her but Beatrice was active in the women's franchise movement and attended rallies, signed petitions etc. to get women the vote. She seemed to look upon marriage as another restriction for women and she would not agree. For a couple to live together was acceptable to her, but marriage was out of the question. When we came to the end of our university life Beatrice went off to take up a teaching position in Christchurch and later on became Principal of Nelson Girls College. When you came here, Katey, it was as though you were Beatrice all over again; you are so like her, not only in looks but even in mannerisms. I have the feeling that you modelled yourself on her. Is that right?" He looked at me searchingly.

"Well, yes," I said. "I admired her tremendously, from the very first day I started at the school, and because she was a teacher I wanted to become one, like her."

"I thought as much," he said thoughtfully. "Beatrice has that effect on people. She has a certain magnetism that draws people to her. You have it too, Katey, and that is why I want to continue seeing you." He looked at me anxiously. "How do you feel about that? I know I am older than you. I am thirty to your seventeen, but surely age does not matter.

Would you like to continue our relationship?" I felt very confused and could only look down. "Do not give me an answer right away, Katey," he said quickly. "Think about it over the weekend and I will await your answer."

Shortly after that I left the room and went home, thinking of nothing else but the question he had put to me.

Saturday, 30th March, 1895

Today I spent with Mr. Lightfoot. He has told me to call him Augustus when we are outside of school, but I find it difficult. We walked all around Wellington city and he pointed out to me the new buildings and explained their architecture. Usually I take no notice of buildings and certainly know nothing of architectural terms, but after today I will be much more observant. Augustus makes everything so interesting and he has a fund of amusing anecdotes that keep me laughing. I do so enjoy his company.

Saturday, 6th April, 1895

Alice suggested I invite Augustus for dinner. I wondered how he would respond to this invitation but he accepted gladly. The evening passed off remarkably well. Fortunately the baby was in bed so Alice was able to give her whole attention to the conversation at the table. Between herself and the cook we had a delicious meal and Augustus remarked on the excellency of the food. The fish course, which was scallops done in a light batter, was really the highlight of the meal, although the leg of lamb was very tender too. Augustus seemed quite at home amongst us and the conversation flowed easily. Afterwards both Alice and her husband remarked that he was a "charming man."

Saturday, 13th April, 1895

Augustus took me out to dinner at the most exclusive hotel in Wellington. The décor and table settings were impressive. The waiter who served our table was very deferential to Augustus and I had the feeling that he dines here frequently and is known to the staff. Although Augustus says very little about his background I think he may be enormously wealthy, because he dismisses money matters quite airily. I do not know what this meal cost but it would have been expensive. Augustus ordered a bottle of vintage wine and wanted me to have a glass. When I refused and said that I was teetotal he raised his eyebrows but did not try to force me. I could see that he was quite a connoisseur because he studied the wine list carefully and questioned the waiter on the vintage.

Augustus kept me entertained once more by his anecdotes. I asked him about his reasons for becoming a teacher. He said that he has always had an interest in education and is concerned that all children, whatever their backgrounds, should have the opportunity to receive a first rate education so that they can make their way in the world. He deplores the public school system in England that gives children from wealthy backgrounds such an advantage over the working classes. This was his chief reason for coming to New Zealand, where there is more equality of opportunity.

I have the notion that he may have ambitions to enter parliament so that he can influence policy. He said that the 1890s in New Zealand had seen great progress in many fields. The passing of the Women's Suffrage Bill was a great step forward, so women in New Zealand now have the vote. He mentioned in passing Miss Gibson's involvement in the women's movement. Apparently New Zealand is the only country in the British Empire where women have the right to vote. Then there is the old age pension which will be a good thing for all people irrespective of their financial situation. Augustus was very enthusiastic about all aspects of New Zealand life and said that he wishes Great Britain was more progressive.

At the end of the evening he ordered a cab and took me home. At the door he took both my hands in his and said, "Katey, since you came into my life I have been a very happy man. You have no idea how you have restored my interest in life." I pondered on these words as they seemed to conceal a great depth of meaning. I wonder if he was referring to his attachment to Miss Gibson and his loss of her. I find myself being a little jealous of their relationship and I wonder if I am only a substitute for her. I never thought I could have negative feelings regarding Miss Gibson and I am surprised at myself.

Thursday, 18th April, 1895

I am still feeling numb. After school today Augustus called me into his office. He was looking very serious. "Katey," he said, "I am afraid I have bad news. My father has been taken very ill. My mother writes that he may not have long to live and that he wants to see me. I have made a booking on the earliest ship to leave Wellington. The ship leaves tomorrow at 2pm."

I tried to express my sympathy about his father but inside myself I felt cold. Augustus took my hand in his and said, "Katey, I don't know how long I will be away from New Zealand because there will be a lot of matters to attend to and there is my mother; she will need my support as she and my father have always been close. The worst aspect of leaving New Zealand is that I will be parting from you and you have become very dear to me, almost as dear as life itself. I will continue to keep in touch with you by letter, but as you know there is sometimes a three month gap between sending a letter and receiving an answer."

He then looked at me very solemnly. "Katey, you are young and you have all your life ahead of you. You are also very attractive and you may have many offers of marriage. I was going to propose to you very soon but now that I am leaving New Zealand I could not bind you to any promises. It would not be fair so, Katey, I want you to remember me but consider yourself free."

At that I broke down and sobbed. I felt as though my heart were breaking. He came and put his arms around me and held me close. I could feel his warmth and strength as he pressed me to him. Then he kissed me, on my mouth and my forehead, murmuring all the time. "Katey, I love you, my dearest."Finally he held me at arm's length and said, "This has to be goodbye, Katey. I hope before God that we shall meet again."

I tried to get a grip on myself and though my eyes were brimming with tears I said, "May God bless you, Augustus, and give you a safe voyage home. I will be thinking of you constantly."

Then somehow I found myself outside and walking towards the tram. I remember nothing of the journey home as I was crying all the time. When the tram drew up at the stop before ours I got off to walk the rest of the way home. I did not want Alice to see my swollen eyes. As it was, when I got home she was out and so I was able to go to my room and cry in earnest. Then I washed and by the time Alice returned I was looking fairly normal. She did not ask me any questions and I told her nothing about Augustus' imminent departure."

Elizabeth stopped reading at this point. She had been so caught up in Katey's account that she felt moved to tears. *It* seemed unbearably painful that just when Katey had discovered love she was going to have it snatched from her. It seemed fairly obvious that Augustus would never be able to return to New Zealand. How would she cope?

Frustratingly this was the last entry in the journal. What had happened to Katey after that? There was one person who might be able to tell her. Elizabeth went to find Uncle Mal.

CHAPTER TWENTY-FIVE

Elizabeth went around to the whare. The door was open and there was a smell of pipe smoke in the air. Uncle Mal had seen her and came to the door. "Hello, Elizabeth I heard the tapping of your crutches and deduced that you were coming to see me? What can I do for you, Missy?"

"Oh, I just wondered if we could have a little chat."

"By that I imagine you want to ask me some questions. Why don't we sit on the veranda? That is more comfortable than the whare." Once they were seated Uncle Mal lit his pipe and looked at Elizabeth shrewdly. "Now fire away, Missy."

Elizabeth took a deep breath. "It's about Katey. You said that when she returned to Nelson she was unwell. What was wrong with her?"

"Well, she had been at the Model School in Wellington only a few months, staying at our sister Alice's home. She became weak, went off her food and then contracted pneumonia. The climate in Wellington is quite different from Nelson. She very nearly died but fortunately she pulled through and Mother and Father insisted that she come home to Nelson to recuperate.

"And after that?"

"She never returned to Wellington. It appears she had no desire to finish her teacher training there."

"Did she give up teaching altogether?" said Elizabeth surprised.

"No, sometime later she went as an assistant at her old school in Hardy Street. She passed her exams and became a fully qualified teacher. And a very good one," he added.

"When did she marry?"

"I think she was about twenty-three. We were all very surprised because the man did not seem her type at all. For a start he was older than she was, about thirty- eight and a German, although he had an English name."

"Did Katey ever confide in you why she chose to marry him?"

"I do remember her saying once that Mr. Stephens was a very godly man and she admired his dedication. He was planning to go to China as a missionary."

"Perhaps that was why she married him."

"Possibly, at any rate soon after their marriage they both went to China as missionaries and that was the last I saw of her. Oh dear, that revives sad memories."

He took out his handkerchief and blew his nose loudly. Elizabeth hardly dared to put further questions to him and for some time there was silence. But it was Uncle Mal who continued. "Katey died out there you know, of some tropical fever. She was never strong after the illness in Wellington. But she did leave a child, a boy, Charlie, who is Richard's father. He was the favourite nephew of both my sisters. They spoiled him dreadfully when he came to stay with us. He was a great lad," and he chuckled reminiscently, "as mischievous as they make them, but full of life. Young Richard is just like him."

He looked at Elizabeth, his eyes twinkling under their bushy brows. "Now does that answer all your questions, Missy? I seem to think that you read something in those journals that sparked all this off."

Elizabeth hesitated. *How much should she tell him?* "I was interested because the diary entries came to a sudden halt and I wondered what had caused that."

"Well, now you know. All the same I can't understand how such a healthy girl as Katey succumbed to the Wellington climate so easily."

Elizabeth kept quiet. At this late stage it was probably better to keep Katey's love affair concealed. *After all, hadn't she chosen to confide only in her diary thinking it would never be read.* At that moment Elizabeth determined that Katey's secret would remain safe with her. *She would never tell another soul.*

Uncle Mal looked at his watch. "I'd best get along and attend to Bessie. She'll be coming down to be milked soon. I'll see you at tea time, Missy."

"Oh, goodbye, Uncle Mal, and thank you."

When he had gone Elizabeth sat back in her chair and thought. *So, Katey had fallen into a 'decline' as the Victorian novelists would call it, once Augustus had left New Zealand, and so it had been easy for her to contract pneumonia. Perhaps she even wanted to die. Anyway, when she recovered she had no desire to return to the Normal School.*

Elizabeth frowned as she thought over the facts as Uncle Mal had presented them. Katey had to make some sense of her life so she dedicated herself to teaching, then when she met a man who had an even higher sense of dedication she decided to accept him and leave her old life behind her.

Elizabeth thought of her own situation. *What was she now going to do, to fill this dreadful void left by John Tamati? It was too much to think about at this moment.* She closed her eyes and fell asleep.

Suddenly she woke. A voice was calling her, a man's voice, "Miss Brookfield. It is you, isn't it?"

Elizabeth looked up into a kind face. There was something familiar about the eyes. Confused she said, "Who are you? I haven't been called Miss Brookfield for years."

"I'm Tommy White. You probably don't remember me but I was a pupil of yours back in the 1960s."

"Tommy! Of course I remember you. I've just been reliving the past. I must have fallen into a doze here and dreamed I was back in 1962. Anyway, what a coincidence that you should be here today!"

"The reason I'm here is that my wife and I are considering buying the old house. Oh, this is my wife, Gail." The woman standing quietly beside him stepped forward to shake Elizabeth's hand. She was small and delicately made, rather on the lines of Mrs. White, Tommy's mother, though her hair was brown and her eyes, as she smiled at Elizabeth, were brown nearly black.

"I've heard so much about you and the time that Tommy visited the house here when the aunts and Uncle Mal were so kind to him. You were his favourite teacher of all time," she said laughing.

"He was my favourite pupil of all time," Elizabeth responded. "How is your mother, Tommy?"

"She's well, getting older of course, but she still lives in the house she and Dad bought in Nelson. Dad died a few years ago," he added.

"And what about Bruce? Are you still in touch with him?"

"Yes, he has a car business in Christchurch and whenever we go there we stay with him and his wife. But what about you?" he asked curiously. "I called you Miss Brookfield just now, but you said it had been a long time since you were called that."

"Oh, I married. My name is now Elizabeth Stephens. My husband Richard died a few months ago. We married at the end of 1962. I was going to have a trip to England with Mary Fletcher, one of the teachers at the school, but I married Richard instead. Mary didn't go to England either. She married David Welch a few months later. You may remember him."

"Oh yes, he took Bruce and myself to visit you at the old house when your leg was in plaster." Tommy grinned. "I hoped he would marry you. You were much prettier than Miss Fletcher."

"I wonder what has happened to them both. We lost touch after Richard and I moved to Auckland. Anyway, when I saw on the internet that the old house was for sale I came down to look at it. I had a sudden whim to come back and live here, but of course the house is too big for a woman on her own. It is much more suitable for a family."

"Yes, I've always longed to live here. The house represented something very special to me. My happiest times were connected with your family. Do you remember Mr. and Mrs. Ray?"

"I should think so," said Elizabeth. "I suppose they have been dead for many a long day." A thought occurred to her. "That picture, the one in the parlour. Of course, it was the one Mrs. Ray painted the time my leg was in plaster. She must have presented it to the aunts and Uncle Mal. Oh dear, it was such a long time ago and yet it seems like yesterday." Elizabeth suddenly felt very tired.

Tommy noticed her grow pale. "Look, we've finished viewing the house. We will make an offer on Monday. But now I'd like you to come to our place and have a cup of tea. Then we can take you back to where you're staying."

He put out an arm to help Elizabeth and as she stood up there came clearly through the stillness of the garden the clear ringing notes of the bellbird. Elizabeth listened. Nothing was changed after all. While the bellbird sang this would always be a place of peace untouched by time.

THE END

CPSIA information can be obtained at www.ICGtesting.com
Printed in the USA
LVOW040011021111

253064LV00002B/7/P